MOONSTROKE II
Alien Territory

MOONSTROKE II
Alien Territory

Blaine C. Readler

MOONSTROKE II, Alien Territory

Visit us at: http://www.readler.com

E-mail: blaine@readler.com

ISBN: 978-0-9992296-0-6

Printed in the United States of America

To Ken Weidele a second time, because a friend who calls you his Big Toe deserves a second go-around.

ACKNOWLEDGEMENTS

Thanks to Michael Carlson and MTB for their proofs.

Another grateful nod to Michael Ilacqua for the cover design:
http://cyber-theorist.com
Check out his new book:
http://thephantomparadigm.com

Walking with a friend in the dark is better than walking alone in the light.

——Helen Keller

Chapter 1

"I don't think I can do it, Daddy," Katlin said.

Sitting in the holding area, waiting for her turn to walk in front of the cameras, she felt weary, tired and old beyond her seventeen years.

"Of course you can, Peaches," Arthur Cummings said.

She glared at him, but he was grinning. She smiled and shook her head. "You're doing that on purpose."

"What?" he asked, feigning innocence.

"You know. You only call me that now when you want to poke at me."

Peaches had been his pet name for her all the twelve years they'd been stranded on the Moon.

"Why would I poke at you?" he asked, but his grin gave away his play-acting.

"You're trying to distract me."

He shrugged. "Is it working?"

She leaned towards him and wrapped her arm around his neck. "What would I ever do without you, Daddy?" she whispered into his ear.

"Grow up, probably," he said.

She let go of his neck and gave him a playful push. "Do you think I'm becoming a twip?"

"I didn't say that. On the other hand, it wouldn't hurt to make some friends, you know."

Twip was the term she'd made up to describe the other university freshmen in her classes. On the far-side moon base, isolated from both Earth by distance, and the other teens by an artificial class structure, she had spent hours imagining what life on Earth must be like. Fueled by the few movies on the base and the plethora of books she'd read, her imagination had been filled with friends she could talk to, laugh and debate with. Instead, she found her classmates … shallow. Yes, immature, even. They didn't laugh, they giggled. They didn't debate, they jabbered. It wasn't that they didn't welcome her, it was that she avoided them.

"I'll make friends," she said. "Just as soon as I find some."

He was giving her his reprimand brow. "You're not a twip, but maybe a snob?"

She looked at him. *Is he right?* she thought. *Am I a snob?* She shook her head forcefully. "I'm not going to compromise myself just to have friends. Besides, they wouldn't really be friends in that case."

His grin returned, and he nodded. "You're right, as usual. Peaches."

She sighed. She didn't want to be right, she just wanted real friends, like she had started to have before leaving the Moon so suddenly.

She knew that her father was struggling under the weight of the Earth as well. It was as if the crushing gravity had drained them of life, accelerated their biological clocks. It had been an arduous first month. She couldn't even walk when they'd arrived three months before. She had struggled to even breathe. She'd known that Earth gravity was six times that of her childhood home, but no amount of knowledge could have prepared her for the physical assault of experience. It was like a lead blanket had been thrown over her, and then barrels of sand on top of that. Her calves had grown grotesquely thick with the grueling daily grind of exercise, but still thinner than the other girls.

The return to Earth had been even harder for her father. Far more difficult. He'd grown older before her eyes as he recovered from his wound. His hair, graying at the sides, had turned practically white. When the med genie had recommended that he return to

Earth for treatment after being shot by Mad-Meyer, the electronic logic hadn't taken into account Earth's deep gravity well. The genies only consider what their algorithms have been designed to include.

Her father was watching her, waiting. "You'll do just fine out there," he said, gesturing towards the door that would take her to the lit stage facing a packed studio.

"I'm going to flop around."

He shook his head, not understanding.

"A fish out of water," she explained. It was one of the few English expressions that she understood first hand. On the Moon, she'd spent hours watching the swarming animals in their tanks, animals that would later become part of her meals.

"Just be yourself. Tell the truth, and look at the hosts. Ignore the audience—pretend they're not even there."

"That's easy to say. There's more people out there than the entire population of Daedalus Base."

He lifted his shoulders. "Don't fixate on that."

Just then, the muffled roar of applause could be heard, the crowd reacting to the first guest.

The door burst open, and the applause was suddenly crisp and present—something impossible to ignore. It was Ian Baxter, and he immediately shut the door behind him, stuffing the audience back into their muffled distance.

Baxter, handsome and topped by hair that was way too youthful, was her stepfather, a relationship that tore at her heart. He was also a lawyer for United Products, the company that had established the far-side Moon base, and which still claimed ownership. Katlin had returned to Earth expecting to find a mother ready to wrap her arms around both her and her father, but instead stood waiting next to an imposter father.

She couldn't blame her mother—after all, everyone had assumed that the entire base was wiped out in the massive solar flare, and twelve years is a long time. But Katlin blamed her anyway. Not for herself, but for her father, whose heart was broken into a thousand pieces. Katlin still had a father and mother, but her dad had lost the wife he'd waited so long to see again.

Her father's face went dark. "You can't talk to me, you know."

"I'm not here to talk to you," Baxter said. He flipped his thumb at Katlin.

She wanted to bite it off. She knew that in other circumstances she would have found him no more offensive than the insincere corporate lawyers she'd seen in the old movies. As it was, she loathed him. She didn't let on, not even to her father. There was too much at stake. United Products was one of the largest companies on Earth—worth more than many countries. They were dangling a sword over her father's head, and she had to tread carefully.

Besides, she had a plan.

Baxter looked expectantly at her father, who snorted, and stood up. "Knock 'em dead," he said to her, kissed her forehead, and left.

Baxter sat down next her, and poked at his pad a moment.

"Are you here as a lawyer, or my stepfather?" she asked.

Watch it, she reminded herself. She hadn't meant it to sound so snarky.

He either didn't catch the tone, or chose to ignore it. "U-P hasn't brought litigation against *you*," he said, looking up. "I'm here just as your dad with a little advice before you go on."

Katlin gritted her teeth, restraining from retorting that she had just one dad.

"They may ask you why Cummings won't talk to the press," he said.

Cummings. Not "your father." That would be admitting he wasn't the bona fide thing. She was used to it, though. For twelve years, he was "Cummings" by the only other adults in her life—the two scientists Louden and Julius, and Mad-Meyer. The nexgens—thirty-seven orphans—called him Zeedo, a word that had evolved from "CTO," Chief Technical Officer.

"Dad told me to just tell the truth," she said.

"Of course," Baxter said. He made a teepee with the tips of his fingers. "There's many ways of telling the truth, though."

"You don't want me to say that he's under a gag order?"

"I'm not telling you what to say. I'm just suggesting that you might want to be careful out there. You can't take words back."

Katlin considered. It was a balancing act, fishing for information without making it obvious. "U-P wants my father to say that he never considered the base abandoned, don't they?"

The subtle twitch of an eyebrow was answer enough. "He told you that?"

"Of course not. He would never violate an agreement." She looked him in the eye. *Here goes.* "Besides, he'd risk losing twelve years of back pay, right?"

Bingo! Again that tiny bounce of eyebrow.

"He didn't tell me that, either," she added. "It's obvious, with what's at stake."

Baxter looked at her mildly, an expression she imagined lawyers were taught in classes. "And what do you think is at stake?"

She shrugged, emphasizing the obviousness. "Daedalus Base. Billions of dollars of platinum."

"Really?" he said casually. He was fishing as well.

It didn't matter. She was repeating speculation that was all over the media. "Yes," she said, suppressing a sarcastic tone. "U-P has lost all rights to the base."

"Really?" he repeated, managing to sound genuinely surprised, perhaps part of the same college class. He pretended to be thoughtful a moment. "I imagine the risks go in both directions."

She watched the eyebrow. "For example, maybe indicting my father on grounds that he abandoned his post by coming back to Earth now."

Veracity twitched his eyebrow, but he quickly wrinkled his brow in faux confusion. "He's a scientist, a civilian. This wasn't a military venture."

Katlin shrugged again. It was no secret, everybody was talking about it. "U-P is threatening to invoke some arcane ruling from the nineteenth century—something about implied national interests when private companies take federal funding to establish ... what was it called? 'Footprints in new lands?'"

She knew every word of the 1836 court ruling. The fishing is over, though, once you throw in the whole bucket of bait.

He looked at her blandly. No twitch, no hint of response.

The game suddenly frustrated her. The Moon had been so simple. Everybody knew their role, and the only struggles were simple survival. "Do you think that maybe U-P worries about litigation *against* them? I mean, us—my father, me, everybody else still on the moon—bringing suit for abandonment by *them*?"

The bland features turned to stone, and she realized that she'd crossed a line. She pretended a sigh. "That's silly, of course. Everybody knows that U-P isn't at fault."

A wave of panic washed over her. *What the crimps did I just say?* She glanced around, reassuring herself that there were no witnesses.

Baxter was watching her curiously. "Is this something you've been thinking about? Bringing litigation against the company?"

"No! Of course not!" she exclaimed back-peddling madly. "It's just … an obvious possibility."

He nodded slowly, waiting for her to pull the noose tighter around her own neck.

She clamped her mouth shut. He waited. It was a standoff.

The door flew open, and her handler motioned frantically for her. She thought of him that way—her handler. It was his job to get her ready and onto the stage at the right moment.

She stood up, and remembered *the plan*. She leaned over and gave him a quick peck on his forehead, suppressing a grimace. "Thanks for stopping by."

She had intended to call him "dad," but her mouth wouldn't form the word.

"Break a leg," Baxter said as she was about to walk through the door. "Oh, by the way, the stipend's working out okay?"

She nodded and walked out. It was a final jab, a reminder that U-P was paying her college tuition and providing a monthly allowance.

"This is going to be so much fun," her handler exuded as he led her towards the intermittent bursts of applause.

She wondered if he'd attended the same law school acting classes.

They stopped just out of sight of the audience. Kristen could see the stage area now. Casey Jappeno sat on a small sofa angled so that she was partially facing both the audience and the guest sofa.

The live-streaming talk show was the most watched in its class—purportedly ten million viewers, although from what Katlin had seen around campus, a lot of "viewers" paid only sporadic attention as they went about their day. *Everybody* streamed *something* all the time. Some portion of those ten million just happened to have the show programmed into their view schedule.

Casey glanced their way, and Katlin's handler nodded. The attractive host stood and bid the popular movie star farewell, and the audience burst into sustained applause as he strode off, waving all the way. Katlin knew the star was popular, because the handler had told her. Still standing, Casey waited for the clapping to subside, and then explained that they had a special treat, a surprise guest. The show was fortunate to have, for the first time on live streaming, the young woman who had returned from the Moon after twelve years of dark isolation. Casey held out her hand in welcome, and Katlin's handler practically pushed her on-stage. High heels had come back into vogue while Katlin was on the Moon, and she cursed her feet as she tried her best to appear dignified as she walked to meet her smiling host. She wasn't sure which had been more difficult—learning to walk in six-fold gravity, or balancing on these ridiculous stilts.

Dignified or not, the crowd exploded with raucous applause. One, three, and then the entire audience was on their feet cheering. *They must think I flew back by myself*, she thought. *Maybe they're cheering that I haven't tripped.*

Casey leaned in to give her a hug, which took her by surprise—she'd forgotten that on Earth everybody hugged. Katlin hadn't mastered the technique, and ended up wrapping her arms around the woman, as though they were lovers. "Okay," Casey whispered in her ear. "Sit down now." Sitting in heavy gravity was its own adventure, and Katlin essentially fell back onto the cushions.

She was mortified. The interview hadn't even begun, and she'd already made a complete fool of herself. If anything, the audience was cheering even louder. *Are they laughing at me?* she thought. No, they seemed genuinely ecstatic that she sat there looking at them.

Earth wasn't anything like the old movies.

Casey rolled her eyes humorously at Katlin and held out her hand, palm down, a gesture for the audience to cool it. The clapping subsided, and the crowd took their seats. "I think they like you," Casey said. "Maybe I should be jealous."

Katlin looked at her. Was it a question? She didn't know if she was expected to comment. She'd watched a few late night talk shows, and guessed that she was supposed to come back with something funny. "No—freaks are always popular."

7

Freaks? she thought, moaning silently to herself. Hesitant laughter trickled down from the audience.

Casey smiled wryly and tilted her head a little to the side, a gesture of gentle commiseration. "It can feel that way sometimes, can't it? I know what you mean."

She'd saved the situation, turned it from a clumsy stumble to a shared struggle, a first step into what promised to be a worthwhile and intimate conversation. This was her job, and she was good at it.

"First," Casey said, "I want to thank you so much for coming. I have to say, it is a true honor."

At this, the audience erupted again with wild applause, forcing her to wait a moment for the din to settle. Casey had made it sound as though Katlin had chosen her show above all the rest, a vote for the best of the best. There had indeed been dozens—maybe hundreds—of offers that her U-P representative had turned away. The reality was that U-P had finally relented because Casey's show had offered a sum that, had she turned it down, would have raised eyebrows. This one appearance would go a long way towards paying her keep for the first year at college. Katlin had assumed that U-P had been watching out for her, keeping the media hounds at bay, but now she wasn't sure.

"I imagine it was difficult adjusting," Casey said when the clapping petered out.

'Difficult' would be a euphemism, Katlin thought. She might not have come if she'd known what was in store. "It wasn't so bad. I did have to learn to walk."

"You couldn't *walk?*"

"I couldn't even stand up. Imagine if you suddenly weighed eight hundred pounds."

"Oh, honey, that's how I feel every morning," Casey said to audience laughter. "I was thinking more of the … social aspect. How do you find Earth boys?"

Is this what you want to talk about? she thought. *I find Earth boys silly and immature.* "Oh, Earth boys are fine. I'm still trying to just fit in."

"No boyfriend yet, I guess. You must have had boyfriends on the Moon. I understand that the Moon base was essentially all kids your own age."

You're paying me a huge pile of money for pillow talk? We'll see about that. "The Blast—what you call the Great Flare—killed all the mining workers, leaving just four adults to raise thirty-seven small children, plus me. For twelve years Daedalus Base was operated like a military installation, with the children taking up the mining tasks of their deceased parents as they became old enough. This was done as much to maintain structure and purpose for the maturing children as to continue the platinum extraction. Inevitably, though, it established a class system, with the adults—and me—at the top, and the nexgens, as they called themselves, at the bottom."

Casey watched her with just enough concern to show she was interested. "Surely it wasn't as bad as that sounds?"

"I've been accepted into college because I had a full education based on the extensive base library. The nexgens were given an elementary education, and then taught what they needed to operate the base. They didn't even know who first walked on the Moon."

The host's concern had turned genuine—not for the nexgens, but for her show.

I've blown it already, Katlin thought. This audience didn't want to hear uncomfortable truths. "But you're right," she said. "It sounds worse than it was. It wasn't that bad."

At least not for me.

Casey sat back and propped an elbow on the sofa armrest, a visible transition of tone. "So, what do you like most about Earth?"

"Everything's new."

"I think my ten-year-old daughter would point to her closet and disagree."

At that, the audience burst into laughter.

"I guess it's relative," Katlin said. "I wore three jumpsuits for four years until I outgrew them, and then four of my father's for the next eight years. That left him with just three jumpsuits."

"My! Not a lot of accessorizing opportunities—but, why did you wear your father's clothes? Surely there must have been women's outfits from the, um, previous workers?"

Do you really want to know? "Colors."

"I don't understand. Your father's colors provided better compliments—?"

"The workers' jumpsuits were burnt sienna, and the

managers'—and scientists'—were blue. I was not a worker. Besides, other than color, all the suits were the same, there were no women or men's suits."

Casey nodded and gave Katlin a look that might have been commiseration, or equally, a warning. "I imagine you had to come up to speed on today's fashions."

Katlin shrugged. She didn't know how to talk about fashion. It was like being asked to talk about the rituals performed by priests in the Catholic Church—she'd seen them performed in movies, but could only guess about the meanings. "It's not just clothes that are new."

"Of course. Cars? Movies?"

"Doors."

"Doors?"

"And lamps, and clocks—we'd been abandoned for twelve years, but virtually everything on the base is twenty years old. Things were—*are*—breaking down."

Casey was wearing that look of mixed concern and interest. She glanced at the audience. "Surely abandoned is extreme."

"Yes, it is. Fortunately, the base was designed to be nearly self-sufficient, and thanks to the diligent efforts of three scientists, and later, the contributions of the nexgens in maintaining—"

"No, honey, I mean that the term 'abandoned' seems … harsh."

Katlin blinked. *Is it possible she doesn't understand what happened?* "After the Blast—the Great Flare—we were completely, one hundred percent, on our own. There were no attempts to help us, to even find out if we were alive."

Casey glanced again at the audience. "Honey, it was all we could do to keep ourselves alive—you've heard, I'm sure, that nearly a million people in America alone died from exposure and starvation the first year."

"I've heard numbers closer to one hundred thousand."

Casey paused. "Katlin, honey, the point is that our nation was deeply crippled. Your base on the Moon was a lot better off than we were."

"Except that thirty-seven nexgens lost their parents."

Her host looked at her hard, reprimanding. "We all suffered."

Why are we arguing? Katlin wondered. This was supposed to be a feel-good talk show, take people away from their troubles. "But you recovered. You have new cars and clothes."

Casey looked at her with a little half-smile, one you might give a child complaining that they never get to have any fun. "You continued to mine the platinum," she said.

"Not me. Remember, I was in the upper class."

"I mean the base overall. You—the whole base—continued to perform the tasks you were established to do. You continued to fulfill your purpose. Quite successfully, I understand."

What the hell? What was she trying to do? There it was yet again—that glance at the audience. Who was she looking at …? Baxter! He sat there in the second row, watching carefully.

It now made sense why U-P had agreed to the interview. Casey Jappeno had sold out. This was a public deposition. She was trying to get Katlin to admit things that supported U-P's case. "As I already said, the platinum mining was predominantly a means to provide the nexgens some structure."

That damn glance!

"You indicated that structure for the—nexgens?—was only part of the reason."

"Fine. It was, I would say, ninety-six percent of the reason. Without the need to provide structure for the nexgens—the abandoned nexgens—we would not have done any platinum mining whatsoever."

Katlin could feel that her face was red. She didn't know if she actually believed what she'd said—Mad-Meyer, after all, would have pressed for continued mining. She was talking on the record to the lawyers who would be pouring over the show's transcript.

The audience fell dead quiet. They knew they were witnessing something unusual.

Casey glanced at Baxter, and then at her lap. Katlin saw that she was holding a small pad. *They're going to drag me across the coals if I let them*, she thought. "U-P hasn't even attempted to relieve the base," Katlin said.

Casey glanced at Baxter, and again at her pad. This was off script.

"If it weren't for Captain Namazi," Katlin continued, "the Moon base would still be abandoned to history."

The show's host made no pretense of hiding the pad now. She poked at it, looking for her cue.

Captain Namazi was an officer in the nascent space fleet of Greater Persia, what used to be Iran, Iraq, and Syria. It was he who had discovered the abandoned base, and brought her and her wounded father back to Earth. He had made several subsequent supply trips to the base, returning to Earth with platinum in trade.

Katlin felt settled just thinking about him. She'd admitted to herself that he was a large part of the reason she'd left the Moon.

Casey looked up at her. She was all confidence, a professional at sitting in that chair. "Julius was one of the scientists on the base, is that right?"

They don't want to talk about Namazi. Fine. "Daedalus Base would still be given up for lost if Greater Persia hadn't invested heavily in developing space transport in order to trade with the Chinese Moon base—"

"Katlin, honey, we were talking about Julius—a scientist stationed on the base, right?"

You *were talking about him.* "It's your show. Yes, Julius was the engineer. He basically kept the base functioning. He could barely keep up with essential equipment that was breaking down. He had to perform triage, so there were a lot of conveniences we take for granted here on Earth that we'd lost along the way—"

"He sounds like a genius."

"Well, sure. I guess. He was very competent at maintaining—"

"In fact, his doctoral thesis had been in noise-embedded signal processing, isn't that right?"

"I honestly don't know. I was six years old when I arrived—"

"I'm told that his thesis had a lot of application with communication technologies."

"Really, I can't comment on that—"

"I'm told that with just a little tweaking, your communication equipment could have been modified to link with the Chinese satellite in orbit around the Moon. You could have contacted Earth."

"What are you talking about? We had no idea that the Chinese satellite was operational. Everything—*everything*—had been destroyed by the Blast—"

"In fact, isn't it true that Daedalus Base failed to contact Earth when they could have, so U-P didn't abandon the colony, it was effectively hiding—"

"This isn't a discussion," Katlin said suddenly. She hadn't intended to say that, but was glad she did.

"What do you mean?"

"We can make this easier if you just tell me what you want me to say."

Casey's face went hard. This wasn't good for the reputation of the show. Whatever payoff she'd gotten from U-P, Casey would protect her show above all. She put the pad aside. "I'm sorry, Katlin. Tell me, what would you like to talk about?"

This caught her by surprise. She should have been ready. "Um, maybe your audience would like to know what life was like on the Moon."

"Good idea, honey."

The look in the woman's eyes betrayed the familiar tone. The popularity of her show wasn't based on tame descriptions of everyday life on the Moon.

"Well, let's see," Katlin started. "First of all, I guess it's important to understand that day and night are each two weeks long—"

"There's no police authority there, is there?"

"Why, no. It's just a small base, and the nexgens inherited a worker union that included disciplinary actions—"

"So, Meyer's death was never actually investigated, was it?"

Katlin stared at her. She couldn't breathe. The nightmares had started after she'd returned to Earth, after all the excitement and scramble to get Namazi's crippled shuttle back into orbit—with her along—had time to settle. She'd relived the moment in her dreams dozens of times, where she lifted the makeshift weapon to her shoulder, carefully aimed, and killed Mad-Meyer, who had already murdered one of the nexgens and was aiming to murder Van, the nexgens' leader. It was justified manslaughter. She knew it. Everybody said it.

Just not an actual government authority.

In her dreams, Mad-Meyer turns and looks at her through his helmet faceplate. They stare at each other for a second before she pulls the trigger, and he flies away. The reality was different, but this was her new reality.

"Katlin?" Casey said.

She jerked. Casey was watching her carefully, like a cat might when cornering a mouse. Katlin looked off to the wings, but the lights made it impossible to see her father. "That's right," she said. "The production manager's death was never investigated." Casey's gaze bore into her, drilling to find juice for the show. "However …"

"However what?" Casey asked, so patient, yet imperious.

Everybody knows it was justified. Except that the story was just hearsay for everybody except Van. "Nothing." Any attempt to defend herself would only sound pathetic. *Just tell the truth,* her father had told her. But truth only has value when people choose to listen.

A flashing light, out of view of the cameras and audience, signaled a commercial break, and, in a daze, Katlin accepted the handshake and thanks from Casey, and allowed herself to be led off the stage by her handler.

Her father was waiting, and, looking into his face, she wondered why he was so angry with her. His gaze wasn't following her, however, and he grabbed a fist full of the handler's shirt and pulled the shocked man close so that he was peering straight into his eyes. He held the terrified man's gaze a moment, and then pushed him roughly away. "Come on," he said to Katlin as he wrapped an arm around her shoulders, "let's get the hell out of here."

She had never seen her father lay a hand on anybody, and she walked along in wonder.

"I'm so sorry, Katlin," he said. "We were snookered."

"No," she said, feeling strength returning now that she had her father with her, "I'm the one who's sorry. I warned you that I was going to flop, though."

He shook his head. "No, you did the best you possibly could. They had you trapped. I miscalculated. U-P is taking this a lot more seriously than I'd imagined."

They walked out of the studio, past impassive guards, and onto an elevator.

"U-P has blocked the coms from the Moon," he said when the doors closed.

She blinked. "How can they block them? They're not there *to* block them. And in any case, how do you block a transmission with a satellite—?"

"I don't mean physically. They've somehow convinced the Chinese to shut down communications with Daedalus Base."

The base had been piggy-backing off the Chinese satellite in synchronous orbit on the far side of the Moon, the one that Casey had talked about. Namazi had placed a ring of Greater Persian communication satellites in low orbit, but the old equipment at the base wasn't able to link with these.

"We can't talk to them?" she asked.

"That's right. Once again they're isolated."

Katlin suddenly felt as though she needed to sit down. It was all too much. Talking to Van—and Tyna and Burl—was a lifeline in a way, for her as much as them. Daedalus Base still felt like home, and Earth an exotic land that she wasn't yet sure she liked.

"Namazi can bring them new com equipment on his next trip," she said. It would be weeks away, but at least it was something to look forward to—getting back online using the Greater Persian satellites.

He sighed.

"What now?" she asked.

He looked at her and shook his head. "Greater Persia has registered a petition with the UN for recognition of the base's independence. The Lunar Commission has agreed to consider the case."

Katlin's eyes popped. "That's wonderful!"

This was exactly why U-P was fighting any indication that they had abandoned the base—it could be used as grounds to find that the base was a colony now deserving independence.

Her father nodded. He wasn't happy, though. "The president was expecting this. He immediately broke all diplomatic ties with Greater Persia, and Congress is debating sanctions tomorrow."

Katlin felt dizzy. "Even if Namazi sets up communications with his satellites, the US won't allow us to link in, will they?"

His answer was another sigh.

Chapter 2

Van winked off his radio com link, grabbed Tyna's head, and mashed his helmet against hers. "We have to ask Namazi for a temporary repair kit! Who knows when we can get a custom seal made!" he yelled loud enough that the sound carried into her air space. This was the method the nexgens used to converse when they didn't want others on the com link to hear.

They were inspecting the outer door of the personnel airlock, the small one used to cycle two or three people at a time. The hanger lock was huge in comparison, and sacrificed too much residual air to be used other than when they deployed the salvaged Chinese rover. A micro-meteorite had gouged the edge of the personnel lock door, and deformed the inner seal enough that air leaked when the lock was pressurized.

Her reply came through thin and distant. "Deik's going to make you give up the new hanger compressor!"

Van knew this. Cost wasn't a factor, as the nexgens had mined enough platinum to buy Namazi's entire space ship—a whole fleet of ships. Volume and weight were the defining limits to each of Namazi's loads from Earth. There was more than enough capacity on Namazi's ship for both the repair kit and hanger compressor, but Deik insisted on including "personal essentials" each trip. This was a euphemism for luxury items—essentially toys.

So Van had to choose. Either way they were going to lose air, but they used the personnel lock a lot more than the hanger. Even with a fully functional hanger air pump, it wasn't possible to evacuate all the air. Until he could convince Deik to have Namazi ferry up oxygen extraction equipment, they'd have to limit the rover use to emergencies. It was a shame. Burl had put so much work into refurbishing the Chinese vehicle.

He winked on his com link. "Van here. We're cycling back through."

A burst of uncontrolled static made him wince. The suit's radio was definitely on its last leg. New suits were on the essentials list, but it would be months before they trickled to the top. Maybe a failed suit and a dead nexgen would change Deik's perspective. The newly elected base leader was just a reflection of the majority of nexgens, of course. That's why they'd voted for him over Van.

Burl's voice came on the link. "You two have had enough alone time?"

It was silliness, since Tyna had moved into Van's twenty-five square meter apartment a month ago. But silliness was Burl's standard fare.

"It wasn't alone time we needed," Tyna replied, "just time away from you."

"I understand," Burl said. "Like most men, Van occasionally needs to escape the sense of inferiority."

"Burl, you're seventeen years old. You have a ways to go before you're a man."

"Tyna, are you the mouthpiece for Van's jealousy?"

"Don't encourage him," Van said. "He'll just wear you down."

"I accept your surrender," Burl said.

Two years younger than Van, Burl could outdistance him in mental tussles. This was one reason Van liked him as a friend. What fun is someone duller than you?

Deik, on the other hand, was nearly Van's age, yet Van found him tiresome in his bluster and need to dominate every conversation. The tables had turned in the election, however. As the head of the worker's union, Van had represented authority under Mad-Meyer and Arthur Cummings. Now he bent to Deik's popular will.

When the lock genie turned the indicator green, Van removed his helmet. Sure enough, the unmistakable whistle of escaping air marked the meteorite's impact point. To someone living with a finite amount of oxygen, it was a terrifying sound. He removed his glove, and ran his fingers along the outer door seal, but could detect no rush of air. This at least was a relief. They wouldn't be trapped inside the base waiting out the weeks it would take to repair the seal.

Of course, since the primary reason for going out onto the airless surface was platinum mining, Van would welcome the small amounts of lost air. Lost air wasn't his biggest problem.

The inner door opened to reveal Burl waiting for them. He made a little gesture towards the small gathering behind him where Deik stood talking to Namazi. The Greater Persian captain nodded when he saw Van and Tyna. Normally glowing with gracious smiles, Namazi had been subdued this visit, his black, close-cropped beard seeming to mimic his dark mood. "I'm glad you're here, Van," he said. "I'll be leaving soon to catch the next transport orbit."

Namazi used a shuttle craft when landing on the Moon. The larger transport ship never ventured beyond the orbits of Earth and Moon, and the quarter million miles between.

Van smiled. "The feeling's mutual—we're always glad when you're here."

Namazi's sober face slipped the slightest grin. "For the treasures I bring, no doubt?"

"Luxury goods, along with the occasional incidental life-saving items," Van said, throwing a glance at Deik, who stood looking sour. The base leader would have much preferred that Van and Tyna stayed outside.

"Oh, you would do just fine on your own," Namazi said. "You managed admirably for twelve years.

"Maybe we were lucky. We'll need a repair kit for the lock seal. That would have been a catastrophe before you found us."

"I say what he brings on the next trip," Deik said.

Van glanced at Tyna, who rolled her eyes. "Fine," Van said. "Who needs air? It's probably overrated."

"I didn't say we won't ask for it. You just have to go through me, is all."

Van shrugged. He didn't say anything, depriving Deik the satisfaction.

"Well, Deik," Namazi finally said, "shall I put a repair kit on the list?"

The base president scowled, glaring at Van. "It's Deik," he said, correcting Namazi's pronunciation. "It rhymes with stick."

Namazi raised one eyebrow. "Or dick?"

"Yes," Deik snapped. "What are you smiling at?" he asked Tyna.

"Is that a new rule?" she said. "It's now illegal to smile at Deik's name?" she said, emphasizing the pronunciation.

Deik's face was red.

"I'll add the repair kit." Namazi said, breaking the tension.

"But the hanger compressor—" Deik started.

"Comes off the list," Van cut in, finishing the sentence.

Van stepped back. He sensed that Deik was about to throw a punch.

Namazi glanced at his pad. "Time is ticking away, and there's something I need to discuss before I leave."

That was the second time Van heard him use the phrase. He wanted to ask how time could "tick" away, but it would have to wait until the next visit.

Namazi glanced at the nexgens crowding the corridor, faces watching silently, the full span of teenage years. A visit by Namazi was a high point in their lives. The otherworld alien was as novel as oceans of water, water enough for an animal larger than the rover. "Can we talk in private a minute?" he asked.

Deik shrugged. "We can step into the lock storage."

This was essentially a large closet where the space suits used to be stored during the two-week-long days when they self-banished themselves inside—before they overcame their fear of another solar flare. Namazi glanced inside, and pointed. "In there?" he asked skeptically.

He was from Earth, where livable space was measured in acres. To the nexgens, the closet was just another room. Squeezing together was their existence.

"If you don't want them to hear," Deik said, gesturing at the crowd, "I can chase them away—"

"You can ask them to leave, you mean," Tyna said. "You don't own the base."

"They'll leave if I tell them," he said to Namazi.

"No. That's not necessary. This little room will be fine."

Deik followed him inside, and Namazi's head re-appeared. "Van. Could you join us?"

From inside, Deik said, "We don't need him."

Namazi glanced at him, and then looked again inquiringly at Van. They had a special relationship. Defying Mad-Meyer's orders, Van had been the first member of Daedalus Base to meet Namazi when he'd arrived three months before, ending their twelve-year isolation, and then Namazi had returned to aid Van when Mad-Meyer went berserk on a murderous rampage.

Deik glared at him when he stepped inside. "You're just going to listen, understand?"

Van looked him in the eye, neither nodding agreement, nor objecting. Unlike Tyna, Van had grown tired of reminding Deik just what limited powers the elected president wielded. Now he just ignored his peer's unwarranted demands.

Namazi swung the door shut and said, "I want you to know that Greater Persia has submitted a formal motion in the UN to recognize Daedalus Base as an independent colony. This is a first step. If affirmed, it does not yet grant you complete nation sovereignty—United Products would still have claim to initial investments, for example. Our UN representative is suggesting that U-P be entitled to the platinum mined during the first four years following the Great Flare. The reasoning is that this can be assumed to represent the point of abandonment—they should have made some attempt to contact you by then."

"Oh, no," Deik said. "They don't get one dime."

Namazi looked pained but resigned at the response.

"Let's maybe take the long view," Van said. What he wanted to say was "Don't be a damned fool," but Deik was the president, and had final negotiating power. "We can't do a thing without someone championing our cause on Earth. We can't afford to be stubborn, or Persia may give up on us. In any case, there was hardly any platinum mined the first years." To Namazi, he said, "We were still quite young, and adjusting to the deaths of all our parents. I didn't start mining until I was twelve—five years after the Blast."

Deik was staring at him. "You're supposed to just listen."

Van stared back.

"You'll have some time to think about it," Namazi said. "You will obviously have to be involved in the final negotiations." He glanced around, peering at the ceiling and corners. "We have a more pressing issue, though. There are no—" he twirled his finger in a circle—"recording devices?"

"No," Deik said. "Do you want Van to go get a recorder?"

"No! What I'm about to talk about cannot be recorded—not even written down. Nobody can know that I've given you this advice." He looked uncomfortable, not used to such subterfuge. "To make a case for your independence, you will have to appear to be a mature, autonomous, fully-functional colony."

"We are!" Deik, said. "We had elections."

Namazi took a breath. "Yes. That is a start. A very small step. U-P is denying that you have any legal grounds, despite the US Congress's own earlier proclamation that abandonment constitutes a primary trigger for colony independence."

"That's when they shot themselves in the foot trying to get China's colony declared independent," Van said.

"Exactly. But U-P maintains that even if there were legal grounds, it is unreasonable to imagine that a bona fide autonomous colony could be administered by teenagers."

"Some of us question it as well," Van said. He didn't look at Deik, but he sensed the angry glare.

"I have faith in you," Namazi said. "This is your home, and you have been maintaining it all your lives. And I've seen you in action under stress." He looked at Van, who felt his cheeks grow warm. "But now you must prove that you can not only manage the base, but yourselves as well."

"Why all the secrecy?" Deik asked.

Namazi's face turned dark again. "U-P is spreading the idea that Greater Persia has its own sights on Daedalus. Evidence that I am helping you would bolster U-P's claim, and also undermine the premise that you are able to self-rule."

"But, you are helping us," Van said quietly.

Namazi visibly winced and his shoulders drooped.

"Anyway," Deik said, "we don't need your help. We're doing just fine."

Van and Namazi stared at him. "How much platinum have we mined in the last three months?" Van asked.

"What's that got to do with anything? We have enough platinum to last us for years—our whole lifetimes!"

"I'm not so sure of that," Van said. He was thinking about the ever-more expensive luxuries they were asking Namazi to bring, and the myriad of failing expensive equipment that they depended on to keep their home functioning on an airless, sterile world.

"Regardless," Namazi said. "Deik, I believe that it will be important to demonstrate that you are actively mining. A truly independent colony embraces a means for long-term self-sufficiency. Earth will expect you to join the global economy. They want to see examples of trade goods. You have just one thing to offer. You must be able to demonstrate that you can participate in ongoing trade production. It doesn't matter how much you have stocked up, the point is that you are operating as a trade-producing partner."

Deik rolled his eyes. He hated being lectured.

Namazi gave him a hard look and pressed on. "I know that this may be difficult to hear, but you must understand how important it is. Right now, Earth views you as a bunch of kids sitting on a pile of candy."

Deik scowled and shrugged.

"And you'll need to draw up a constitution."

"We have that already!" Deik said.

"I mean a real one. What you have is a framework for managing a mining base, and you borrowed most of that from Meyer. You need to define how you're going to legislate, and judicate, and set parameters for an executive branch. I'm assuming that you'll have a democracy, but that's up to you. You need to decide if you want a bicameral congress, or a parliamentary system—"

Namazi stopped. Deik was staring at the ceiling. Van wanted to punch him.

"We're talking about the future of your home," Namazi said quietly. "I strongly suggest you dig into your library and research systems of government. Worst case, you could simply model it on the United States Constitution."

Namazi waited, but Deik continued studying the plumbing above them. The captain looked at Van, who gave a little nod. Namazi turned a tiny smile and nodded in return.

"I must be going!" Namazi said, looking at his watch.

Outside the little room, Tyna and Burl waited, eyebrows raised in anticipation. Behind them, filling the hallway, were the rest of the nexgens, arrayed by age.

"Can we tell them about … uh, Greater Persia's … you know?" Van asked.

Namazi nodded. "It will be all over the news by now."

"Throw us a crumb!" Burl called, imitating a French Revolutionary peasant while balancing on one leg and waving the cane he'd fashioned, which served as his other leg.

Van looked across the expectant crowd. "Greater Persia has made a motion in the UN to have the base declared an independent colony," he said loud enough for everyone to hear.

The crowd stood silent for a moment, and then broke into cheers. Van held up his hand for silence. "Don't get too excited. It hasn't been accepted yet, and it's just a first step—"

Van spun around when his hand was yanked down. Deik was glaring at him. "I make the announcements," he growled.

Van stared at him, and then nodded. "Be my guest."

Deik scanned the crowd. "Yes!" He glanced at Namazi, as though looking for a cue. "We'll soon all be … free!"

The nexgens were silent, a little perplexed. They thought they'd won their freedom when Mad-Meyer was killed.

"Hurray for Greater Persia!" Deik called.

The nexgens applauded. This they understood, since to them, Greater Persia meant Namazi himself.

Deik glanced at Namazi again, but the captain looked on soberly, offering no suggestions. He seemed to be deep in thought.

Burl and Tyna stood nearby, and Tyna said, "Maybe we should ask to become a colony of Greater Persia instead of the USA."

"Yeah. Then we'll all be … free!" Burl said, mocking Deik.

"Be careful of what you wish," Namazi said quietly.

"What do you mean?" Van asked.

Namazi didn't answer, instead glancing again at his watch. "Maybe someone should go and tell Louden—ah! Finally."

At the far end of the hallway, the younger nexgens were squeezing aside to make way for the rotund scientist, suited up and ready, carrying his travel bag. The older nexgens—the ones who'd had the most interaction the last few months—patted him on the back as he passed.

Van turned to comment, and saw that Tyna's eyes were wet. Everybody loved the stout man. Along with Cummings and Julius, he'd been one of the three scientists alive after the Blast. The nexgens had always liked his easy-going manner, but they'd grown to adore him the last few months. He'd become their surrogate father as he taught them how to use and care for the lab equipment. He gazed across the crowded hallway, and wiped the slick spacesuit of his arm across his eyes, which simply smeared his tears. Namazi had not mentioned the hundred pounds of platinum being left behind, supplanted by Louden's extra girth.

When Louden reached them, Burl lifted the stump of his amputated leg. "Want to say farewell to your best work?" he asked, and Tyna backhanded him across the chest, sending him toppling sideways into Louden's arms.

The scientist placed his hand on the edge of the stump. "May this be the most difficult task I ever have to face," he declared solemnly.

"Difficult?" Burl said, pulling himself upright. "One takes a saw in hand and hacks away. Maybe you should have sharpened it first."

Tyna rolled her eyes and pretended to strangle him.

Under the med-genie's expert eye, Louden had amputated Burl's leg after Mad-Meyer shot him, exposing the limb to a period of vacuum. The large man hadn't eaten for an entire day afterwards, attesting more than words just how arduous it had been.

Tyna took Louden's hand in hers. "We're going to miss you."

"No more than I will you," he said.

"You don't have to go, you know. If you stay, we'll pamper you like a king—"

"No!" Namazi said. The unusually harsh tone drew all eyes. "It's important that all the original adults leave," he added more softly. Julius had left weeks ago, essentially as soon as Namazi opened a berth.

"Otherwise U-P might claim that he represents an unbroken continuity of management," Van offered.

Namazi looked at him. "Good point, Van."

Van was simply finishing Namazi's thought, but the look the captain gave him was a cue. He wasn't supposed to be helping them in their bid for independence.

"Come, Louden, we must go," Namazi said.

"Indeed—before Baxter finds a way to lock the doors."

Baxter was the U-P representative that Daedalus Base had chosen as their contact. The company had included him in the initial list of candidates, presumably thinking that, as Katlin's stepfather, he might gain preferential treatment. They were correct, at least to the extent that Van was able to convince Deik to choose him. Baxter had been pressuring Louden to stay, offering a number of reasons and monetary incentives. The one reason he never spoke of was the very one for which Namazi was insisting he now leave.

They watched as Louden clumsily donned his helmet. This would be the first time in over fifteen years that he'd be going outside. He seemed nervous, and Tyna reached over to help him. "Tell Katlin we said hello," she said to Namazi over her shoulder.

"I haven't seen her since she returned to Earth," he said.

Tyna blinked. "I'm sorry … I mean—"

"It's not from a lack of desire," he said. The solemn demeanor turned harder. "It's difficult to travel between the United States and Greater Persia."

From their tiny isolated home on the Moon, they imagined the Earth as one big park and city. Van was constantly reminding himself just how far apart the nations were from each other, both in distance and culture.

"You would see her more if she'd stayed here," Tyna said, seeming surprised at the realization.

"Yes," Namazi said. "That's true. She's where she belongs, however," he added with a sigh.

"She belongs where she'll be happy," Tyna said. "Is it where she *wants* to be?"

Namazi shrugged. "You saw how excited she was to return."

"That was three months ago. A lot can happen in the meantime."

Like she can't see Namazi, Van thought.

"It is beyond my control, in any case—come, Louden, into the vacuum we go."

The light above the lock had turned green, indicating that it was pressurized, and Namazi pulled open the door, and stepped inside. Louden followed, but got caught in the narrow opening. For one panicked moment, Van thought he wouldn't fit, but Tyna gave him a push, and he popped through. Tyna swung the door closed, and that was it. Namazi and Louden were gone.

On previous visits, all the nexgens would go outside to watch Namazi's sleek antimatter shuttle launch back into orbit, but the leaking seal prevented all but essential transits now. The nexgens remained crowded together, jamming the corridor, as though waiting for something. Whispered conversations filled the space, imbuing a sense of drama. It was as though the defective seal had spread to threaten the inner sanctum.

The whispering wasn't the air leaking away, however, but the security. Louden's departure marked the first time in their lives that no adult walked the halls of their home carved from the living rock of the Moon, no adult to remind them what needed to be done, to assure them through reprimand and censure that however much they grumbled and balked, a higher power was watching over the world, intervening before catastrophic missteps led to disaster.

For the first time in their lives they were alone.

"Say something," Van whispered to Deik.

"Like what?" he whispered back, glancing at the thirty-five pairs of eyes watching him.

Van took him by the elbow and turned them away. "They're scared. Just reassure them."

"They're not scared."

"Then, what are they waiting for?"

"I don't know. I'll tell them to leave."

"You're the base leader."

"So what?"

"So, lead."

Deik glanced again at the crowd. "There's nothing to say."

Van held his rival's gaze. The thin beard Deik wore so proudly now seemed pathetic, a premature reach for manhood. *He's scared as well*, Van thought.

Van turned back to the citizens of Daedalus Base. Deik may have been voted president, but he was still the union leader. He had no actual role now, since Mad-Meyer's death had eliminated his negotiating position. The nexgens still looked up to him, though. If he hadn't been so pragmatic running up to the election, if he had promised goodies for all, he might be president instead of Deik.

He scanned the group. "You've been running the base ever since you could pick up a screwdriver. Whatever knowledge you lacked about the operation was purposefully kept from you. But now that we have access to the library, we don't need Louden, or Julius, or … Meyer. We've been self-sufficient from the beginning, and now with Earth com links, and Namazi's regular shipments, there's nothing that can harm us."

The faces followed him silently. They wanted to believe.

"Except maybe an overabundance of vacuum," Burl said, and then yelped as Tyna elbowed him in the stomach.

Van had been waiting for one of the nexgens to bring it up—Burl had simply pushed the issue to the front of the line. "The lock seal repair kit is on the way," Van assured. "The air loss until then will be miniscule."

"It's replacing the hanger compressor's spot in the shipment," Deik said, stepping up. "The chocolate and game consoles are still included."

Van threw Deik a puzzled glance. They were trying to reassure their people about safety. Was he purposefully undercutting Van?

But then Van looked back at the crowd. They were nodding in satisfaction. Goodies were more reassuring than hard reality.

He never have a chance at the presidency.

The lock beeped behind him, and he turned to see the green light lit. He nudged Burl. "You were going to make sure the lock genie kept the chamber evacuated when idle."

His friend frowned. "I did. She's an idiot."

"She's software."

"She can still go insane. She decided to stop talking years ago, and never explained why."

The lock door popped open, and Linda, a fourteen-year-old nexgen came through. That explained it. She'd gone to check on the hydraulics reservoirs at the mining platform a quarter mile away, and must have cycled back through the lock as Namazi and Louden came through.

Before Katlin killed Mad-Meyer—before the entire controlled routine of the base came crashing down, freeing the nexgens of virtual servitude—the mining operation would always begin in earnest as soon as the sun set for the long, two-week lunar night. Nobody went outside during the lunar day, not after the Blast—at least, not until Namazi's arrival broke the shackles of a routine based on irrational fear.

Platinum mining had ceased altogether after that. There was irony in this, Van knew. Just when production could have doubled—no need to break for two weeks of daylight—the force behind it had died a just death. Without Meyer's threats of misdemeanor points, the motivation for mining the precious metal had evaporated. Charged with enough misdemeanor points, a nexgen would be temporarily deprived of mythical "archiving"— the storing of one's consciousness, one's soul, for future restoration in the event of death. Archiving had been a lie fabricated by the adults as a means for keeping the nexgens in line, for Meyer to make sure that he carried through with what he'd been sent to the Moon to do—mine platinum.

Linda removed her helmet and scanned the assembly until she found Van. She waved to him, and he followed her into the lock storage room. Linda had a crush on him—Tyna had told him, not with jealousy, but humor. Linda glanced outside to make sure nobody had followed. "Van, I have bad news," she whispered.

"One of the hydraulics tanks is leaking?"

The vacuum didn't harm the fluid, but once it mixed with the lunar soil, it was ruined.

She shook her head. "That would only affect the mining."

Her frightened eyes stared at him.

"Linda, what's the problem?" *What could be worse than a leaking lock seal?*

"Van, the feed was disconnected."

"The solar feed?"

She nodded glumly.

"That's not possible …"

It was possible. He'd sent a sweep crew out at lunar pre-dawn two weeks ago. This was part of base routine. The acre of solar panels that provided the base power sat next to the mining platform, which threw up dust. There was no Moon breeze, but the dust was negatively charged, and migrated to coat every surface, including the panels. The sweep crew cleaned away the dust with a positively charged mesh. There wasn't really any dust to clean, since there'd been no mining, but it was one of the few duties that Deik agreed to let him continue as union leader, and Van was taking any opportunity to divert the nexgens from their newfound games and movies.

Van put his hand to his head. "They forgot to reconnect the feed," he said.

"Looks like it," Linda said. "It was Maya's turn to run the checklist. She's been … distracted."

With the influx of romance video books. Van knew. The sweep crew disconnected the feed during sweeps to prevent shock from back-voltage, and the checklist was supposed to ensure that everything was back to operational condition.

"We're in trouble, aren't we?" Linda whispered even softer, as though keeping the bad news from the walls.

Van nodded. He couldn't lie. The original design of the base provided for a three-hundred percent margin, meaning that the bank of batteries could supply the base for eight weeks—four times a normal two-week charge cycle. After nearly twenty years, however, the tired batteries now barely held four weeks' worth. Not only had they not been charging the batteries the last two weeks, but they'd actually been drawing from them. The decades-old storage was nearly exhausted.

And the sun was setting in less than twenty-four hours.

"Did you reconnect the feed?" Van asked.

"Of course," Linda replied.

"Okay. We'll get one day's worth of charge—"

"Not even," Linda said, "since the sun's at a low angle."

Van sighed. "Right. If we shut down all non-critical equipment ... oh, crimps, it's no use. There's no way that even one full day of charge is going to get us through two weeks—"

He heard someone calling his name. He stepped out into the corridor, and Jira, Burl's understudy at the com shack, saw him and pushed her way through the crowd. "The link's down!" she called when she was still only halfway there.

"What are you talking about?" Van asked. He wasn't even trying to hide his irritation.

"The com link! It's *down!*"

"You probably lost focus with the satellite," Burl said. "You can let it auto adjust the dish position. I showed you how—"

"No!" Jira said, finally reaching them. "The carrier signal is still there. It's not the physical link. There's still a message coming through. It's just repeating that Earth-side is refusing to accept the connection."

"Crimps, oh, crimps!" Van muttered as he sprang for his suit. He *had* to catch Namazi.

He froze. They all felt it through their feet, the distinctive rumble of the Moon shaking as super-heated water slammed it at over fifty-thousand feet per second.

Captain Namazi was heading for orbit.

Chapter 3

Katlin sighed, picked up the pad, and stared at the words. It was the third time she was attacking *Pride and Prejudice*. She didn't get it. Why people would be drawn to the novel was completely beyond her. The world it depicted was so unfathomable, it might as well have been a fantasy, where there would at least be dragons, or wizards, or magic rings—anything to provide a reason to stay awake. Her literature professor insisted that this was one of the greatest novels—if not *the* greatest—ever put to paper. It was supposed to be infused with humor, but Katlin found only befuddled nonsense.

This was why her father was so determined that she get a proper education, something beyond the vast store of knowledge of the base library. Katlin was far ahead of her freshmen classmates in math and science. Her father had made sure that she absorbed the rudiments and ever advancing sequences, until she was able to converse intelligently with him and Louden about quantum mechanics. When it came to the humanities, though—literature, philosophy, and history—she'd been pretty much on her own. He had insisted that she spend time on the subjects, but he'd let her pick her material, probably because he didn't feel particularly knowledgeable himself.

It was humbling. She'd felt smug when she found that her peers knew nothing about partial differential equations. They had only the vaguest idea who John Irving was—one of her favorite classics authors. They all shared familiarity, however, with a whole host of literature that they'd read in high school. She only knew that Mark Twain had written a book about a slave and a runaway boy, and that William Shakespeare wrote plays that included a lot of tights and swords. Talking with them made her feel just as the nexgens must have with her.

"What goes around, comes around," as she heard people say.

She'd finally had to admit that picking her own material limited her total scope of education. Either that, or the standard fare of assigned high school literature wasn't necessarily the best offerings of humanity, but formed a shared cultural base within which the future citizens could find common ground.

Either way, if she wanted a degree, she'd have to somehow plow through Jane Austin's commentary on English society at the time of the founding of the United States.

She turned when there was a knock on the door. Beau stuck his head in. "Hey, Kat—you busy?"

"Very," she said, tossing the pad on her bed. "Please come in and stop me."

Beau was her best friend at the college. Actually, he was her only friend. He was attracted to her in a romantic way—he had as much as admitted it. She didn't return his romantic affection, and guilt sometimes visited her at night as she lay awake in bed. She wasn't leading him on—that would mean pretending to be open to the possibility. She consoled herself with this, and made sure he understood how much she valued his friendship at least. She would be unbearably lonely without him.

Her father called him her "Faux Beau."

She had tried to fit in with her classmates. She did okay one-on-one, but that circumstance was rare in a dormitory, essentially a commune, where privacy was found only when you pulled the covers over your head. When in groups, her classmates seemed to be speaking a different language. She understood the words, but the sentences often had only vague meanings. It was as though she was a visitor in a foreign country, which, of course, she was.

"So, here it is," Beau said, pulling his pad from his pocket and giving it a couple of pokes.

"No," Katlin said. "Please, no."

"Oh, come on. It wasn't so bad." He held it up so that she could see herself on stage with Casey Jappeno. "In the last twenty-four hours, your slice of the show had over twenty-five million hits—three times as many as the rest of the show. You're a celebrity, kid."

"That, you plebian, is exactly what I don't want."

"Why'd you do the show, then?"

She sighed. "We needed the money. I didn't expect it to be a booby-trap."

He sat on her bed and picked up her pad. He looked at her. "You like this stuff?" he asked, concerned.

"I hate it. It's on the assigned list."

"There's been probably a dozen movies made of it, you know."

"That would be cheating."

He shrugged.

"Do you suggest the zombie version," she asked, "or the one where an alien poses as an English vicar?"

"They're not all screwball versions."

"I guess the point I'm making is that they're all interpretations. I've heard that the prof includes specific details on the test just to catch the cheaters."

He shrugged again. "You could drop out and do the talk show circuit. Then you could host your own show—*Mornings with the Moon-girl*."

"You know that I hate you, don't you?"

The media had called her that for the first few weeks.

"You only think you do because you're rebelling inwardly about the truth," he said.

There it was—the invitation wrapped in humor. As she had done before, she ignored it. "You never had to read it?" she asked.

Beau was a senior, and had finished English Lit 101.

"Each instructor creates their own assignment list. I hacked them and picked the class with the list I liked the best—or, rather, the one I dreaded the least."

"You're kidding."

"No. Why would I pick the one I dreaded?"

"I mean, you're kidding about hacking their lists—you're obviously not kidding."

Beau was in the software engineering program, a veritable genius with artificial intelligence, including encoding and security measures, at least according to him.

"I didn't get caught."

"This time."

"Even if I did, I'd just delete the evidence later. No evidence, no charges."

"You're dangerous. You know that?"

"That's my career goal."

"To battle the Org?"

He looked at her a moment, and got up to close the door. "It's not a joke," he said quietly. He looked genuinely worried.

"I'm sorry," Katlin said. "I'll be more careful. But you have to admit, it sounds a little bizarre."

He had taken her into his confidence and described a secret federation of corporations that held true power, pulling the strings of government puppets. They called themselves simply the Organization—Org for short. They colluded, carving out markets to avoid competition, while working together to beat down serious rivals in any market, including both consumer and military development.

"It's all true." He studied her. "Kat, you could get us both killed. They're so protective of their secret that simply knowing the key players is a death certificate."

"You mentioned that. You see how it makes for a convenient excuse, don't you?"

He rolled his eyes. "Yeah, I know. Anybody who might have known about them is conveniently dead—the classic backdrop for a whacko conspiracy theory."

She nodded slowly, thoughtfully. "Couldn't have said it better myself."

He stared at her with furrowed brow. "Kat, you're the only person I've told. I trusted you."

Katlin's heart sank. She'd hurt him. "Beau, I'm sorry. You're right. It doesn't matter whether I believe it all or not. I promised to keep it secret, and I am going to take that very seriously."

She returned his gaze, reiterating with her eyes what her words had said.

He nodded, and smiled, but then his brow furrowed again. "Kat, you know why I flew back to Colorado last month?"

"You went to your uncle's funeral. He was your favorite uncle." She was glad to show she'd been paying attention.

He nodded.

She shrugged. "So what?"

He looked at her.

"No!" she said.

He nodded again.

"You're telling me that—" she let her voice drop to a whisper, "they killed him?"

His furrowed brow rose in confirmation.

"Oh, come on! You said he'd died in a car accident."

"That could have been technically true."

"You're saying they caused the accident?"

One eyebrow went up. "His car went off the road in Utah, and plunged a hundred feet into a canyon."

"Okay … that doesn't prove a lot, other than that it might be an easy way to fake a death."

He shook his head. "He hadn't told anybody that he was going to Utah. He had no business there. The gas tank exploded. My uncle was burned beyond recognition, other than dental identification."

She put her hand on his. "Oh, Beau, that's horrible. I'm … sorry."

"Still not to the point," he said, being careful to keep his hand under hers. "The police investigation found evidence of gasoline splashed around the car."

She looked at him. "If the gas tank exploded, there wouldn't be any residual fuel."

He smiled sardonically and nodded.

"They added gas later?"

He lifted his shoulders. "They had to make sure he was … burnt completely."

She shook her head. She didn't understand.

"They were destroying evidence of torture."

She stared at him. "You know this?"

"Let's say that I'm very confident."

She shook her head again. "The police would have come to the same conclusion about the spilled gasoline. There would have been a criminal investigation."

"Nope."

"Why?"

"The report was changed. References to the residual gasoline were removed."

"How do you know?"

He just looked at her knowingly.

"You're a genius with encryption and security," she said, emphasizing "genius" just enough to make it a little sarcastic.

"I hacked the Utah Highway Patrol. It was pretty trivial."

Katlin sat back, absorbing it all. "Crimps!" she whispered.

"Crimps?" Beau said, smiling.

She waved it off. "It's something we said on the base. Beau, you have to tell somebody—the FBI?"

He looked concerned.

"I know, I know," she said. "That would just get *you* killed next. Why, for God's sake, would anybody be torturing your uncle?"

"Not anybody—the Org. He was an old-school journalist. He went after sources."

"He was investigating them?"

"Yes. It all started with Ritkens—the senator from Arkansas. My uncle was looking into allegations of kickback. That turned out to be a dead-end, but Ritkens recruited him to join his own investigation of unaccounted spending by the military. That in turn led my uncle to the Org, the very existence of which Ritkens was skeptical."

"But, why would they torture your uncle? Are they sadistic as well as hungry for world domination?"

He gave her a look.

"Sorry," she said. "I shouldn't joke about it."

"They were convinced that he had an accomplice, somebody who had inside access to their records."

"Did he tell them?"

"No."

"Actually, that was a dumb question. How would you know? How *do* you know?"

"Indirect evidence. Remember, I have a talent for poking into places that are meant to be poke-free."

She glanced at the clock. "Oh! I have to go!" she said, jumping up. "Can we pick this up when I get back?"

"Where are you going?" he said, getting up to give her room.

"Meeting my stepfather for lunch."

"I thought you don't care for him."

"I don't. It's not a social engagement."

"It's business?"

"He thinks it's social. He seemed a little surprised that I agreed to meet him."

"So, why are you going?"

"Do you know who my stepfather is?" she asked, putting on her jacket.

"You told me—he's a lawyer."

"But, who he's representing?"

Beau shrugged.

"U-P."

Her friend's eyes went wide. "Kat! They belong to the Org!"

She patted his shoulder. "I promise not to get in any black limousines," she said, and turned to go.

"Kat," he said, taking her elbow.

She turned.

"Kat … just be careful."

She smiled and gave him a hug before running out the door.

His arms were reluctant to let her go.

∞

Baxter was already at the table when the Maître d' showed her to her seat. He rose to greet her, and she was surprised to find another man getting to his feet as well. Her stepfather introduced him as Mr. Teirel, and Katlin had the sense that he wasn't happy to have him there. "He's a representative from U-P," Baxter explained.

Katlin gave the interloper a quick glance—balding, a little pudgy, expressionless eyes—just what she'd expect from a corporate drone. "I thought this was going to be a social lunch," she said, sitting down.

"It is," Baxter said, taking his seat as well. "Mr. Teirel and I had a morning meeting, and I invited him along," he explained, while carefully folding his napkin across his lap, thus avoiding her eyes. "He's in from Washington," Baxter said, finally looking at her, as if this explained why he would naturally be included.

You're lying through your teeth, Katlin thought, surprised. There were plenty enough reasons why she didn't like her stepfather, but dishonesty hadn't been one of them. He at least looked uncomfortable about it.

"What do you do with U-P?" she asked Teirel.

"Consultant," he replied.

That was all. He sat looking at her as though she was something inanimate and slightly interesting.

The guy gave her the creeps.

Well, if he wasn't interested in conversing, fine—it meant that she was free to ignore him. "You set me up," she said to Baxter.

He blinked and re-folded his napkin. "You're talking about the *Casey-J Show?*"

"Of course. Are there other ways you've set me up that I don't know about?"

Baxter glanced at Teirel. She was putting him on the spot. Good. "I thought you wanted a social lunch?" he said.

"We can't be social until this is addressed. Why did you do it?"

He took a breath. "Casey asked me to help with some background. When she interviews, she needs material to draw questions from. I simply related facts about the base and its history."

He looked at her innocently. Reading his tone and face, one would conclude that she was blowing things out of proportion. He wasn't lying, he was a master at bending perception. He was a lawyer.

"She was building a case for U-P," Katlin said. "She was reading *your* questions from her pad."

Baxter seemed troubled, concerned for her with these gross exaggerations. "Katlin, honey, everybody on Earth uses their pads to keep notes."

She could have slapped him for the obvious patronization, a veiled insult. "Please don't call me 'honey.' We're not related."

He raised an eyebrow at this, but abstained from commenting on the obvious contradiction.

"Don't play innocent," she said. "You coached her on how to establish points for U-P's case against Daedalus Base—Julius's failure to figure out the com link, and Meyer's …"

"Killing?"

She felt her cheeks grow warm. "I was going to say death."

"U-P has no case in the US court system against Daedalus Base," he said. "How can they bring a case against their own property?"

"You know what I mean. Daedalus has declared independence."

"Workers on an offshore oil rig can declare independence—that doesn't mean they're suddenly a sovereign entity."

"That's not the same thing."

He shrugged.

"What about the petition in the UN for Daedalus's independence?"

He waved it off. "Persia's just politicking, attempting to counter sanctions."

"That were imposed *because* of their stand on the base."

"Those were introduced to supplement existing sanctions. The US is doing its own politicking."

She looked at him, gauging his sincerity. *Is this true?* she thought. Was Greater Persia just using the base as a pawn in the international high-stakes game?

Time to mine for some gold. She watched his face. "I tried to call the base this morning, but couldn't get through—something about unavailable service."

Baxter threw Teirel a quick glance. "Now who's playing innocent?" he asked her.

Her warm cheeks turned hot.

"You know quite well that U-P has blocked communications," he said.

"How can they get away with it?" she said, pleading when she wanted to sound strong. "It must be … illegal!"

He shook his head slowly. "It's their base. They can decide who communicates with them."

"But, but … even *I* can't get through!"

His face softened, and he reached out to put his hand on hers, but she pulled it away. "You'll get through again soon. The company has to put a halt to the pirating."

She glanced from him to Teirel, but the man's face could have been soaked in Botox. "What are you talking about? Has someone attacked the base?"

"I think you know who."

She stared at him. "You mean Namazi? He's no pirate! He's simply trading—there's so much they need, and if it weren't for him, who knows—?"

"He has no permission. He's essentially a privateer for Greater Persia. They're exploiting an American company's holdings."

He was watching her, waiting for a moment. "I can carry a message to them for you."

"They let *you* communicate?"

He smiled. "Better. Tomorrow I leave for the Moon."

She blinked. It was like saying that he was off to visit the Wizard of Oz. The only ships that plied the space between the Earth and Moon were the Chinese transports, and Namazi. Nobody just "leaves for the Moon."

"Julius is coming along," Baxter said. "He's returning from his vacation on Earth."

Katlin's mind was spinning, and she willed it to focus on one subject at a time. "Julius hated it there. He couldn't wait to return to Earth."

Baxter lifted his hands. He threw Teirel another glance.

"You coerced him somehow," she concluded. "There's obviously some legal point about having a person on site who's employed by U-P."

Baxter just looked at her. The rule of lawyers is to avoid saying anything unless required.

"The fact that he was part of the original staff before the base was abandoned must be part of it," she added.

Her stepfather didn't answer, neither denying nor confirming.

"How are you getting there?" she asked. He had to talk eventually.

"We're catching a ride on the Chinese transport. We've rented a ground shuttle to get to Daedalus."

"Who's 'we'?"

"I think you know who 'we' are."

"U-P," she said. "Why?"

"Why are we going? As I said, Julius is simply returning from some R-and-R. I'll be meeting with the children."

Always the lawyer. Words matter. "So," she said, "you're only meeting with the youngest nexgens? I wouldn't call them that to their face. You may be sorry."

"I can't help the situation. The fact is that they are all children."

"Van's nineteen. Tyna and Deik are eighteen."

"A few are on the threshold of adulthood. But, speaking of those three, I've heard that Van is something of a leader."

"They've elected Deik as their president. You must know that."

Baxter smiled at the thought of children electing a president. The desire to slap him was almost overwhelming. "I heard something about that," he said. "But, this Van, what's he like? I mean, is he a hard-nose?"

"Not at all. Van *should* be their president. He was the union leader—still is, I guess. He has a rare balance of patience and discipline ..."

"What?" Baxter said.

She realized what was happening. "You're fishing. You just want to pick my brain about them. You're going to the Moon for a specific purpose, and you want me to help you. That's the only reason you invited me to lunch." She stood up, pushing her chair back with a rattle. "Baxter, you can go to hell," she said throwing her napkin on the table.

The restaurant had gone silent. She'd gotten loud. For the first time, Teirel's stone face seemed to crack a tiny amount. On impulse, she pressed the advantage. "It's all part of the organization, isn't it?"

Baxter's eyes opened with alarm, while Teirel's narrowed with sudden interest.

She was going to say "Org," but as the words spilled out, she recalled Beau's entreaty. "U-P's legal strategy, I mean," she said, knowing it sounded about as truthful as Baxter's explanation for Teirel's presence.

She stormed off, looking back once to see both men following her departure with laser attention.

∞

Back at the dorm, she tossed her bag on the floor, flopped down on her bed, and stared at the ceiling. She hated Baxter. Was it because the man had torn out her father's heart? Or that he had revealed himself to be an adversary of everything and everybody she considered her home? She realized that this was how she viewed Daedalus Base. If it weren't for her father on Earth, she'd consider stowing away on the Chinese transport, which was a ridiculous idea, but provided solace as fantasy fulfillment.

Maybe she hated Earth as well. She'd have to think about that.

She closed her eyes. Enough thinking for awhile. Time to let her frazzled mind settle.

"Hey, Kat," came Beau's voice.

He'd stuck his head through the doorway.

"Hey, Beau," Katlin said, sitting up and rubbing her eyes.

"You want me to come back later?" he asked.

There was something in his voice. She knew him enough to sense apprehension. "No, come in. What's up?"

Her friend sat down in the only chair. Something was clearly on his mind. He never sat in a chair when there was room on the floor. "How'd it go?" he asked, clasping his hands together.

"Terrible. It was about as social as a rape—sorry, that was brutal imagery."

"Effective. What happened?"

"He was just fishing. Get this—he's going to the Moon tomorrow."

"You're joking."

"This is what he claims."

"Why?"

"He's accompanying Julius—"

"One of the three original adults? The engineering scientist."

"One of four adults."

"Right. Of course."

Beau was studying his hands.

"Don't worry. After the *Casey-J* show and Baxter's innuendoes, you can't possibly hurt me about that."

That was a lie, she thought.

"Baxter's a lawyer," Beau said suggestively.

"Yeah. He's obviously going as a lawyer. It has to be immensely expensive to send him—U-P must believe it will be worth it. He was picking my brain about the older nexgens."

Beau thought about this. "Maybe U-P wants to make a deal with them. Maybe they want five or six years worth of platinum instead of the four that Greater Persia is suggesting."

Katlin bounced her shoulders. "I have no idea. They must have put some serious pressure on Julius to go back, though. That much I'm sure of."

Beau was studying his fingernails again.

"Hey, what's bothering you?" she asked.

He looked up at her, and his eyes were deep wells she couldn't fathom. "Remember how I have a talent for poking into places that are supposed to be poke-free?"

"Of course. You hacked the university records—and the Utah Highway Patrol!"

"Those were child's play. In both cases, they don't have a lot to hide, so they don't burn resources protecting their stuff."

He looked at her.

"What?" she said. She frowned. "Were you poking some place that caught you?"

He shook his head. "I almost wish I had. My uncle might still be alive."

It took her a second to understand. "Oh—my—God! Your uncle's accomplice—it was *you*!"

He nodded slowly.

"Oh crimps!"

He gave a little grin. "Indeed."

"Beau—you must feel terrible! No! I mean, it wasn't your fault. How could you know—"

"It's okay. I live with this every day. There's nothing I can do." His brow furrowed. "Actually, I guess there is …"

"Like bring justice to the Org?"

He smiled wanly. "And while I'm at it, maybe I can stop the next great solar flare."

She looked at him sitting there, slumped and miserable. She wanted to give him a hug. She didn't. That would just complicate things. "In any case," she said, "you have to lie low. They may already suspect you."

He sighed. "Speaking of lying low—or not—while you were at lunch, I poked around to see what I could find out about your loving stepfather."

Katlin rolled her eyes.

"He's a lawyer!" Beau protested. "All's fair!"

"No. It's the fact that you were *poking*. Stop it!"

"Yeah. You're probably right. Anyway, I found something that would make huge news if it were ever leaked."

"His pants caught on fire?"

He smiled. "You wish. No, he's getting messages about a pirate who's been captured."

Katlin felt her stomach clench. "A pirate?"

"You know him, in fact. That Persian pilot who brought you back from the Moon." He threw her a glance. "You talked a lot about him. He just returned from his latest run. Our covert operations guys got him as he was changing planes in Turkey. They're bringing him back to the states on a military jet. What's interesting is why your stepfather was getting this juicy news. It implies pretty strongly that the Org is somehow involved—Kat, are you okay?"

She let it all go. "Oh, I wish I'd never left the Moon," she said crying. "Earth is terrible!" She wiped the tears with her hands.

Beau reached out and wrapped his arms around her.

Oh, what the hell, she thought, and put her arms around him.

Sometimes a hug is worth the trouble it may cause later.

Chapter 4

The corridor outside the movie theatre entrance was jammed with nexgens—mostly the younger ones—craning their necks to see through the doorway. The theatre wasn't intended to hold the entire base, since at the time it was designed, everybody carried their own personal entertainment devices. Mad-Meyer had locked these away after the Blast, but the devices were now back into the hands of their owners' children. This was the first time since the Arrival three months before that the entire base was together. They would normally use the hanger area for base-wide meetings, but that was now occupied by the salvaged Chinese rover.

Van turned on his heel, rounded the corner, and headed for the side door that let into the back of the theatre. Nexgens were packed against the doorway there as well, but they let him through when they saw who it was.

Inside, Deik stood on the small dais, and was just beginning. "It's going to be an inconvenience," he said in a firm voice, "no question about that." The theatre was too small to require a PA system, but with so many nexgens spilling into the hallways, he had to speak with volume. "Van's been checking the battery banks' remaining capacity against our usage, and I'm sure we'll work it out."

Van squeezed in until he was next to Burl and Tyna, behind Deik.

Deik scanned the crowd. He frowned, as though deciding. "We made a mistake. We let our guard down." He glanced at Maya, who covered her face with her hands. "But it was a mistake. We'll try harder in the future, and, well, we'll watch out for each other—check on things to make sure they're done right. But the thing to remember is that we're all in this together."

He took a breath, relieved to be past an uncomfortable task.

"Commendably insightful," Van whispered.

"Tyna coached him on what to say," Burl whispered back. "Anything change in the last five minutes?"

Van didn't respond. It was a dig. He had been checking the battery capacity every half-hour or so, and Burl thought that he was obsessing. He probably was, but it was their lives on the line, for crimps sake.

"Once we come up with a plan, we'll let you know," Deik was saying. "Uh, yes, Linda?"

The fourteen-year-old had her hand in the air. "Maybe Van has something to add," she said, and then dropped her hand and glanced around bashfully.

"I told you, he's checking on the battery banks—"

Several nexgens were pointing, and Deik looked behind him. When he saw Van, he scowled. "You got anything?" he asked quietly.

Van shrugged. He had a lot to say, but he didn't think they were ready for it.

"Let's hear from Van!" someone yelled. Others joined in.

Deik thought about it, and when the young ones began hooting in unison, he nodded and stepped off the dais. "Keep it short," he said quietly to Van.

"Don't worry," Van replied. "They'll be dragging me off when they hear what I have to say."

He stepped up and looked out across the expectant faces. He couldn't remember a time when he'd ever had their complete attention. Before the Arrival, he had stood before them in the hanger each four-week cycle to chair the union meeting, but the only time anybody paid attention was when they had a gripe—they couldn't bring it up directly with Meyer, of course.

"I'm going to give it to you straight," he started.

He paused. That was exactly why they'd voted for Deik. *To hell with it*, he thought. *We're past worrying about politics.* "It's clear that we're going to fall far short of the two-week night. In fact, if we don't take action, the batteries will be exhausted sometime late tomorrow."

The theatre was dead silent, other than the gentle, ever-present whoosh of circulating air—a whoosh that was about to stop for the first time in decades.

A voice called out from among the young ones in the back. "What does that mean? I mean, what happens when the batteries are … exhausted?"

Angry whispers of reprimand filled the rear area. "No!" Van called out. "It's the right question. When the batteries die, everything in the base dies with them."

The faces of the older nexgens wore concern, but many of younger were terrified.

"I'm talking about electrical equipment," Van hastily added. "Nobody's going to die. It's just going to be dark, and … well, it will get cold."

"How cold?" someone asked.

"Not too bad."

"How bad is not too bad?"

Van glanced at his friends. "Burl has been going through Louden's early survey records. The bedrock surrounding us is minus thirty-five degrees—Fahrenheit."

Brows scrunched in thought. "Damn!" somebody said. "That's freezing."

Van sighed. "Exactly sixty-seven degrees below freezing."

The room broke out in frantic chatter. Van raised his hand. "Hold on! It will take time for the air inside the base to get that cold."

"How much time?"

"We don't know—days. But even if it does get that cold, we won't die. I've been reading stories about early Antarctic explorers. They were sleeping in tents when it was colder than that, and there was snow and wind."

"Some of them froze to death, of course," Burl said behind him.

Van threw him an angry glance, but his friend returned his stare with unperturbed equanimity—it was often hard to tell when he was poking fun.

"That's true," Van said, "but that was after they'd pulled their sleds through deep snow for twelve hours against the wind and snow. They died of exhaustion and hunger as much as cold."

"But they did freeze to death," came the voice from the crowd.

"Look," Van said, exasperated, "nobody's going to freeze to death. Forget that. We have clothes and blankets."

Nobody mentioned the pressurized suits they wore when outside. They used them on a daily basis—or at least, they did before the Arrival—and they knew that a full charge lasted barely more than an eight-hour shift. The suits were useless after that.

From the back came a voice of a younger nexgen. "People used to burn wood for heat. Can't we burn things?"

Van glanced again at Burl. "No," he said to the crowd. "Burning stuff makes smoke—like when you put something in the microwave too long. The air filtration will be off. So the smoke will just ... stay around."

"Besides," Burl said, "we don't have wood. Plastic burns, but produces fumes you don't want in your lungs. Also, burning consumes oxy."

The theatre again went dead silent.

"The oxygen regenerator will be off!" the voice in the audience said, as though realizing it for the first time. "Crimps!"

"We've already thought about that," Van said. "Burl has gone through the library to find how much oxy a person uses, and he's been doing some calculations. There's plenty of oxy to hold us over for two weeks."

"Of course," Burl added, "there's the CO_2 buildup."

Van ignored him, and the crowd seemed willing to as well. None of them would understand that danger. "We don't want the batteries to go completely dead, though," Van went on quickly before anybody began probing the subject. "We don't know what will happen to the genies if they're powered down. That hasn't happened since the base was established. Therefore, we have to cut our power usage immediately so that there's enough to keep the genies alive."

One of the nexgens pointed at the LED strips on the ceiling. "Do the lights go off?"

Each apartment included light controls, but nobody had ever seen the lights go off in the common areas.

"We're working on that. The main electrical control is pretty complicated. Like I said, we need to figure how to turn everything off except the power to the genies."

"We should charge all the flashlights before you cut the power," the nexgen said.

"Good point. You should all do that right away." Van turned and gave Burl a warning look. There was no way the old batteries in the flashlights were going to last the whole two weeks, but there was no use worrying everybody about that yet. "No showers, of course," Van said, "and also, you won't be able to flush your toilets."

Howls of protest filled the space.

"Whoa!" Van called, holding up his hands. "Come on! You're not going to die without a shower. It takes power to pressurize the water system."

"We *have* to flush the toilets," a voice called. "Otherwise, we'll *want* to die!"

Van held both hands out in exasperation. "Come on, guys! Priorities! You need to charge your flashlights and get all your clothes and blankets together. And, food—Trevor, right after the meeting, go to the cafeteria kitchen and divide all the non-perishables into thirty-six piles. Everybody gets one pile. Divide up the perishables from refrigeration—that goes first, of course."

"What about the toilets?" somebody else called. "I think that's a priority! You can't eat if you're sick!"

Tyna stepped up next to Van. "Can I?" she asked, and he gladly stepped aside. "Buckets!" she called out.

Everybody stared at her.

"I've been reading stories about the eighteenth century. People didn't have flush toilets then. They just … did their business in holes in the ground—"

"Are you joking?" came a voice. "They just crapped into a hole in the ground?"

"Well, they made little buildings, with seats over the holes. It was perfectly normal at the time. They were called out-houses."

"What did they do when the hole filled up?"

"I don't know. They were pretty big holes. They probably covered them and started a new hole."

"So, you want to break up the floors and blast holes in the rock? That doesn't sound like a real solution."

"You didn't let me finish. In the cities, and in winter, people would use buckets—the rich people had special buckets, with lids. The point is that you can do your business in a container and then cover it. Also, I read that they'd put some ammonia inside to help with the smell, but I think that might mess up the recycler system later."

"What containers?"

"I'm thinking the plastic storage containers from the kitchen, since they have lids—"

She was interrupted by groans and protests.

Van stepped forward again. "Guys! Priorities! Remember? We can open up the recycler's main chamber and empty our containers directly in. We'll figure it out—but not now! Time is *wasting!*"

"Hey!" shouted a voice. "What about our pads? If you can keep the genies alive, we should be able to keep our pads charged."

Van drew his finger across his throat. "Why?" he said. "So you can continue to play games all day long? No. Definitely not."

Again, groans and boos.

Tyna took his elbow and pulled him aside. "Are you sure?" she asked quietly. "They're going to be awfully bored, and, you know, boredom and depression are highly correlated."

Van looked at her. "Where'd you get that?"

She shrugged. "I read. You know that."

"Historical novels."

"So? The people that write them are knowledgeable about all kinds of things."

"She's right," Burl cut in. "Besides, the pads don't take much power. Maybe you could just limit the usage to a fixed amount each day."

Van scowled and nodded. He would take the pads away altogether if it was up to him.

He noticed that Deik had been standing next to them. The base president jumped up onto the dais. "We've talked it over!" he called. "You can charge the pads!"

The room erupted in cheers.

"How about just four hours of use a day?" Van said.

Deik, looked from him to the crowd. "In the interest of conserving," he said, "we'll limit the pads to just eight hours a day. I'll set up group games. The whole base can play. It'll be great!"

Hoots of agreement.

Deik stepped down, grinning. "How's that for morale boosting?" he said.

A natural born leader, Van thought. *Give them whatever they want, and they'll follow you anywhere—until you kill them.*

Van stepped back up onto the dais. "Okay! Trevor, off to the kitchen. Everybody else, gather your blankets and charge your flashlights. Now go!"

As the nexgens dispersed, Burl motioned for Van and Tyna to follow him. They went to a corner, and Burl waited until the area was clear. "There's a piece you haven't thought about." he said quietly.

"And you resisted throwing it in my face in front of the whole base? You're slipping."

Burl's deadpan stare was unambiguous this time.

"Sorry," Van said. "You're really serious."

"People can live in the dark for two weeks—with pads—but plants can't."

"Oh crimps!" Van said. "The Farm!"

He had forgotten about that. The hydroponics section—the "Farm"—where they grew all their food, consumed a quarter of the solar energy collected each two-week day cycle.

"I've been going through the early logs," Burl said. "It took a couple of years at the beginning to get the Farm stable. They had to haul most their food up from Earth for awhile. We'll be able to bring most of it back, but it could take that long again before we're producing enough to feed the whole base."

Van nodded, rubbing his chin. "The Farm's so important, it has its own pressure lock."

"That's used to keep the CO2 partial pressure elevated, but, yeah, it's about the most important function on the Moon."

"It's not life-or-death," Tyna reminded. "We have enough food to last at least two weeks, and Namazi will be back by then."

Van shook his head. "If we let the Farm die, Namazi will be bringing nothing but food for months. Maybe nobody will die, but we won't be able to call ourselves an independent, self-sufficient colony."

Silence.

"Would it be so bad to go back?" Tyna said. "I mean, let Earth take responsibility for us?"

"You mean, U-P," Van said. "The ones who cut our communications."

Tyna sighed. "No. You're right. Nothing's worth that."

Van massaged his face with both hands, rubbing away the dozens of secondary concerns. "Okay," he said, "here's what we do. We cut the power, just as we talked about—only the genies are left alive. We also leave power to the library. We have to dig in and find a solution. The hydroponics should be okay for at least a day in the dark. We have to find a way out, that's all there is to it."

"Um," Tyna said, "isn't that Deik's call?"

"Sure," Van said. "He can agree, and if he doesn't, we'll do it anyway."

"He was elected," she reminded.

"Yes. And when it comes to directing the younger nexgens who elected him, he can do whatever he likes."

"That's not the way a democracy works."

"History is full of coup d'états."

"Van!"

"Sorry, Tyna, but we don't have time for this. Let's take it one step at a time."

As they walked away, Burl said, "The recycler chamber's lid is heavy."

"So?" Van said.

"You're going to have to leave it off."

"So?"

"So, the air filtration system will be down."

Van stopped and looked at him. "I see."

"We may want to save a few blankets to hang over the entrance."

"You think that will help?"

"No. But it will show you at least tried."

Van sighed and walked on.

∞

Burl went off to continue studying the power controls, and Van and Tyna headed for the com shack. Inside the small room they found Jira standing over Mai Dung, the Vietnamese refugee whom they'd saved from the stranded Chinese rover. She served as their Chinese translator.

"Where's Tuan?" Van asked.

Mai Dung's English was still quite sparse, so her six-year-old son, Tuan, helped her with the translations.

"Off playing with the other kids," Jira said. "We won't need him unless we actually connect with somebody. So far, no luck. Either the Chinese aren't monitoring our link to Earth through their satellite, or they are, and are choosing to ignore us."

"I wouldn't be surprised if they are snubbing us. They still claim that we stole their rover." He glanced at Mai Dung. Jira saw him and nodded. She understood. It wasn't just the rover—the Chinese base also wanted Mai Dung to return for criminal prosecution. Her Chinese husband had indeed stolen the rover in order to escape with his family. He was about to be arrested and probably executed. His crime was stealing food to save his son from starving to death. He'd paid the price with his life, giving up his share of the dwindling rover oxygen to spare his wife and son. Mai Dung had been thin as a toothbrush when they'd retrieved her from the rover. She'd gained ten pounds since then, and now looked almost healthy. Tuan's scurvy had cleared up completely.

"Well, keep at it as long as the power holds," Van said. "Take care."

Mai Dung looked up at him. "Take-care!"

He smiled. It was a phrase they'd picked up watching the flood of videos since the Arrival, and one the Vietnamese woman had picked up early.

Van and Tyna set out for the power control station to see how Burl was making out, and when Deik called out from behind them, Van stopped and took a breath before turning.

"Hey," Deik said, coming up to them, "I have an idea."

"How odd," Tyna said.

Deik gave her a quick glance, as though not sure what she meant. "We can tell Namazi to bring an antimatter generator," he said, bouncing his eyebrows suggestively.

Van looked at Tyna, who shrugged. "What would be the purpose?" he asked.

Deik held out his hands, and threw a wide-eyed look at Tyna, pretending to be shocked at his ignorance. "Power? Remember?"

"I know what it's for, I mean how does that help us now? We have no way of contacting Namazi, and even if we did, by the time he could acquire one and return, it will be daylight again. Besides, you don't even know if he could get one. It's not like they're sold on the open market. Also, what happens when we've used up the initial supply of antimatter? You don't just bring along more in a bottle. You don't know if it's even possible to transport the stuff, other than in its original operational system. It requires a powerful and sophisticated magnetic field to contain it. One tiny slip, and BOOM!"

Deik rolled his eyes. "I know all that," he said, although Van had the impression that some of it was news. "I just think it would be a great backup."

"You like it because it's about the most expensive piece of machinery in existence. You love owning a toy that nobody else has."

Tyna gave him an elbow in the side and Van nudged her back. He was tired of patronizing the buffoon.

Deik's eyes narrowed. "It would be a guard against future mistakes."

"There's not going to *be* any more mistakes," Van said, getting hot now. "Who knows what the next one would be? Forgetting to charge an oxy-pack before heading away from the base? If Linda hadn't caught this one, we could have all died! We still might! This isn't like the Earth we see in videos. There's no *room* for mistakes on the Moon."

This was a perspective he'd only developed since the Arrival, reading about Earth, and the early attempts to set up lunar bases.

Deik lifted his shoulders. "Mistakes happen."

"Yeah!" Van shouted. "When the nexgens spend all their time playing games!"

Tyna was looking at him in alarm. Van could feel anger rising from places that had been festering for weeks.

Deik took a step back at the fury. "Hey! Take it easy. We invested twelve years of hard labor. We deserve a break."

"It wasn't the labor that was the problem," Van said. The idea had only now blossomed in his head. "We had it easy compared to coal miners on Earth. We worked six-hour shifts on the platform. Earth miners spent twelve hours a day underground. They went months without seeing the sun."

"We *never* saw the sun before the Arrival."

"That's not the point! The point is that we used to work each and every day without making stupid mistakes—"

Van stopped. *What's the use?* he thought. *Deik's never going to get it.*

The base president was eyeing him. "Are you defending Meyer?"

"No! Of course not!" Deik watched him with one eyebrow cocked. "I don't have time for this," Van said, striding away. "I have to check with Burl."

He heard Tyna's footsteps running to catch up. "Hey," she said. "You okay?"

"We're racing against the clock to shut down the base in time to save our lives, and I have to waste time with an idiot. Other than that, everything's just fine."

She didn't say anything.

"Sorry," he said, putting his arm around her shoulder. She laid her head against his neck, and her hair tickled his ear. It was a tickle that made it all worthwhile.

"You said that it wasn't the labor that was the problem," she said. "What was it?"

"I thought it was obvious," he said.

"Not to Deik. You mean the library, don't you?"

"Yeah. If I'd had to choose between working every day on the platform and banishment from the library, I'd be the first one suited up and standing at the lock."

"I wonder what the rest would choose?"

"Ha! Where did they get the games to load onto their pads?"

"That's an irony, isn't it? They'd have to choose the library so they could get their games, but then they'd be working all the time."

"All the time?"

"Effectively. They'd only have six or seven hours a day to play."

He looked at her.

"That was sarcasm," she said.

"Don't scare me like that," he said, pushing her away.

She pushed him back, and they ran off.

∞

Van was surprised to find the power control room deserted. "Now, where in crimps did Burl go?" he said.

"Maybe to the bathroom," Tyna said just outside the door. There wasn't room for both of them. "One last relief before resorting to a bucket."

From somewhere behind the panels came Burl's voice. "That's a luxury I am sacrificing for the sake of the hive."

That was a term none of them would have used before the Arrival and opening of the library. There were no bees on the Moon.

"How's it going?" Van asked, peering between the panels to find him.

His friend stood on his one leg, reaching into a slot. He paused and glanced at Van. "My stump is itching like crazy, and I really need a shower that I'm not going to get. Thanks for asking."

"Burl?"

"Oh!" he said with mock surprise, "You mean my efforts to save you and the rest of the undeserving hoard from destruction? The Farm circuit was easily isolated, but the genie circuits have to each be isolated live in turn."

"Uh, what does that mean?"

"It means that I have to handle contacts that are hot with 220 Volts," he said, turning his attention back to where his arm disappeared into the slot. "If I'm not careful—"

A loud snap accompanied a bright flash, which continued to float in front of Van's eyes. It was the after-vision, illuminated in the now-dark room. "Burl!" Van called. "Burl! Are you okay?"

"Crimps," came the calm reply.

"What happened?"

"Fate has intervened," his friend replied from somewhere in the pitch blackness.

"Burl, for once can you just answer me?"

Van heard him sigh, and then the rustling as he got back up on his one foot. "That was the main breaker."

"The main breaker …"

"That's 'main' as in the breaker for the entire base."

"Uh, oh. You're saying that the genies have all gone dead?"

"I didn't say that."

"Oh, good."

"But that's what it means."

Chapter 5

"You're not taking Beau's warnings seriously, are you Daddy?" Katlin said.

Her father was driving the rental car, and Beau was busy in the back seat with his gear. The amber glow from the car's display softened her father's weathered face and seemed to wash away the worry that had etched it even deeper since returning to Earth.

"No I don't—no offense, Beau," he said over his shoulder.

The college senior grunted his affirmation.

"The idea that the government—"

"The CIA," Beau corrected.

"That the government," her father continued, "would execute a foreign national is just not tenable."

"Then, why did you agree to come?" Katlin asked.

He glanced at her. "I owe a lot to Namazi. The whole base does. I want to do whatever I can."

"But yet you don't think he's in danger."

It was like their times on Daedalus. She would needle him, and he'd patiently accommodate her.

"I said I don't believe that his life is in danger."

"Daddy, I don't understand."

He glanced at her again, as though gauging what to say. "Honey, there's a belief as old as mankind that people can be induced to cooperate using … unconventional incentives."

"Daddy, I'm not a child. You're talking about torture."

He sighed. "There's various sorts of inducements—extortion, blackmail, reward—"

"But it's torture that you're worried about."

He nodded slowly as he watched the road glide beneath the splashes of light thrown by the headlights.

"I still don't get it, Daddy. You say that you're sure they won't let us see him, that they won't even acknowledge his presence. Why did you come all the way from Virginia?"

He smiled. "To convince them in no uncertain terms that we know he's here—because we trust Beau's cyber talents."

The accomplished hacker grunted.

Katlin furrowed her brows.

"Look, honey," her father said, "I—we—hold a certain amount of celebrity status. They know we can easily get the media's attention. Showing up in the middle of the night demanding to see him has shock factor. It's going to make them think twice before applying ... shall we say, visible pressure."

"Visible pressure—a euphemism for disfiguring scars." She glanced back at Beau, but she couldn't make out his face in the dark. She'd made a promise, but she had to know. *As long as I don't use the word*, she thought.

"Why do you think the government would go to such trouble to grab him?" she asked.

Her father took a moment to answer. "U-P has friends in Washington, I guess. It's hard to imagine a company that large that wouldn't."

She saw Beau's head look up in the dark, but he bent right back to whatever task he'd set for himself.

"For U-P to arrange for Baxter to fly off to the Moon," he continued, "and to get Julius to go along, for God's sake, well, they're obviously very serious. Namazi's a thorn in their sides, and the US government clearly doesn't care about damaging relationships with Greater Persia."

He'd stopped short of including the participation of a larger entity—the supposed Org. She had promised, so she let it go.

"Here we go," her father said, turning off the highway.

"What's up?" Beau asked.

"We're there."

"We're *there?* Already?"

"Not soon enough for me. It was a five-hour flight to El Paso, followed by a two-hour drive. I want to have my futile argument with the Holloman Air Force Base commander, and then find the nearest motel to crash."

Extending away to the west, hidden in the darkness, lay the vast expanse of the White Sands Missile Range, where Robert Goddard perfected the operating principles of liquid-fueled rocketry, which Von Braun then expanded into the WWII German V2 rocket. After the war, Von Braun accompanied a handful of his V2s and engineers to America, where they continued experimenting at White Sands. A succession of ever larger rockets finally morphed into the giant Saturn V—the most powerful machine ever created by man, the beast that carried man to the Moon.

Mutterings from Beau in the dark indicated he didn't share Katlin's father's desire for sleep.

"What *have* you been doing?" Katlin asked.

"Me?" Beau said. "Nothing. Getting ready."

"Getting ready for what? Calling out 'Yeah!' from the back seat every time my father makes a point?"

"Uh, yeah. Sure."

He continued to tap away at something in his lap.

As Katlin's father turned at a large sign announcing the Holloman Air Force Base, Beau closed his device and said, "Okay. The base commander's name is Colonel Dobrowski, and he's expecting you."

Katlin was thrown forward as her father braked to a stop. He turned around to look at the shadowed face of Beau. "What did you say?"

"You're here at General McClellen's invitation to interview Namazi with an eye towards convincing him to cooperate. I'm your assistant, and Katlin is …"

"My daughter."

"Yeah. She's, uh, along for the ride."

"Young man, what in God's name have you been up to?"

"Nothing that the CIA doesn't do all the time."

"Well, I will not be involved in any covert, illegal—"

The area was suddenly bathed in blinding light from above. Thirty feet ahead, a soldier stepped out of a guard station, rifle in hand, peering at them.

"Oh, for God's sake," Katlin's father muttered and pulled ahead.

He stopped next to the soldier, who leaned down to talk to him. "The base is closed for the night, sir," the airman said.

"Right," Katlin's father replied. "Well, you see—"

"We're here to interview Captain Namazi!" Beau called from the back seat.

Katlin's father held up his hand for him to be quiet.

The soldier peered at them. "There's no officer here by that name. Sorry."

"He's not a US Air Force officer—" her father started.

"He's your prisoner!" Beau called.

Katlin's father turned around. "Beau! Be quiet!"

"Can I see some identification?" the soldier asked, suddenly serious.

They pulled out their driver's licenses silently and handed them to him. "Stay right here," he said, and walked back into the guard station.

"We're going to jail," Katlin whispered.

"Did you know about this?" her father asked.

"No!" she said. "I mean, I thought we were going to try to talk our way in, but I had no idea that Beau was going to hack the Air Force."

"Oh, nobody's going to jail," Beau said. "Like you said, you're both celebrities."

"But you're not," Katlin's father reminded. "What else do I need to know?"

"General McClellen called you about trying your hand with Namazi, and you happened to be in the area, and you told him you'd stop by and see what you could do."

"I assume that the general is not here at the base right now?"

"Well, that would be a game-killer. No, he's in Washington."

"Where it's … 3:30 A.M. You'd better hope they don't try to call him."

From where they sat, they could hear the soldier's voice getting louder. "I know that, sir ... I *know* sir, but they say that they're here to interview a Captain Namazi, and, sir, they claim that he's a ... a prisoner, sir ... yes *sir!*"

The airman came back to the car. "Wait right here. Colonel Dobrowski's on his way."

"Can we have our licenses back?" Katlin's father asked.

The soldier glanced back at the guard station, uncertain about the protocol. "Sir, if you don't mind, I'll let the colonel return them."

Katlin's father gave her a hard look. "It's not my fault!" she said.

The soldier stood for an awkward moment, and then walked back to his station.

"I would have thought that the military's data would be better protected," Katlin's father said into the rearview mirror.

"It is," Beau said, "with enough time, I could crack that. I haven't gone after the data directly, however."

"How does one access military data indirectly?"

"I don't actually go for the data bases at all. It's a lot quicker just to intercept their communications. And once you have that, masquerading is a trivial next step."

"Surely they must use encrypted connections."

"Oh, yeah. But that's pretty easy to crack."

"Really? Do they know this?"

"Sure. But people are humans."

"Meaning ..."

"Meaning that a secure system is only as secure as those using it. When you're using your personal device to communicate, you have to use passwords over and over. People can't be bothered with truly secure ones—they're cumbersome."

"So they pick ones that are easy to remember," her father said. "To tell you the truth, I was surprised that people still use passwords. When I left for the Moon, they were already being replaced by voice, face, and iris recognition. All the genies had the capability. I guess the Blast set everything back."

"The Blast?"

"You call it the Great Flare."

"Ah, right. Indeed. I remember those iris scanners. Yeah, life was pretty primitive for awhile. I've read that the world has only recovered to about the level of 2025, although, when it comes to the field of AI—my specialty—I think it's even worse."

"You don't even have genies anymore."

"Most were killed outright, but even those that survived had nothing to do. There was nothing for them to control. They just faded away."

"But, back to your criminal activities. So, people pick passwords that are not secure. You still have to guess what they are."

"Nope."

Silence.

"Do I need to ask you to explain?" Katlin's father said.

"I let this guy guess."

Katlin and her father turned to see Beau holding up a small box the size of a book. "What's that?" Katlin asked.

"Alibai—it stands for 'A Little Intuitive Box of AI.'"

"Very cute," Katlin's father said, "but what is it?"

"A box that thinks for itself. Before the Great Flare, AI had followed a long evolution of algorithms that culminated in genies—very efficient and capable for the jobs they were designed for, but don't ask them how they felt about the jobs."

Silence.

"Your box … feels," Katlin's father said, not hiding his amusement.

"In a manner of speaking. What are feelings but instinctive motivations? Feelings nudge us into specific actions towards a goal as defined by the feeling."

"You've defined one perspective of the human psyche. What does that have to do with your box?"

"I tell the box what I want in general terms, and it uses an electronic version of intuition to search out solutions."

"You realize that all you've done is to transfer the burden of explaining how the box feels, to how the box implements intuition."

"Of course. Have you heard of neural networks?"

"Sure. There was a lot of progress in the decades before the Blast. In fact, the genies are based on those chips."

"Ah, but the genies were programmed to use the neural networks to quickly solve pre-defined algorithms. The networks provided fluidity in matching the solution to the problem, but the basic approach to the solution was pre-defined."

"Your box isn't, though."

"That's right. What we call intuition is nothing but our subconscious kicking around previous experience for something useful. The box does the same thing. It abstracts previous solutions, and uses a hierarchical fit-to-function method to whittle away the non-relevant. This takes a lot of processing, so the box comes up with actions a lot slower than a genie would—it could never replace controls that are time-sensitive."

"Like a self-driving car."

"Those were so cool, weren't they? I only ever saw them in movies. They didn't survive the Flare."

"I think I'm getting the picture," Katlin's father said. "Guessing passwords benefits greatly from an intuitive approach."

"Also, when I say it's slower than a genie, it's still way faster than a human. It can try many passwords in a blink of an eye."

"Hold it. Most logins allow a limited number of tries."

"Ah ha! That's were Alibai gets to flex his logic muscles. He tries to get around that. He might try to fool the login server into thinking that he's coming from different locations, or he'll try sneaking in a back door—trick the server into thinking that the time limit for more password tries has expired, or even find the password from the server's database."

"It can do all that?"

"Military systems are tough, but commercial services are usually really sloppy—leaky. It's because they have to accommodate a whole lot of churn, and staying competitive means taking shortcuts. Even still, it takes time to work out each system's details. But once he's unpeeled a system, he can get in with a snap of his fingers."

"Figuratively."

"For now."

"So, tell me, exactly what communication messages did you fake here?"

"Well, like I said, I faked a message from General McClellen to Colonel Dobrowski that you were coming to interview Namazi—"

"Shh!" Katlin hissed.

A man in short-sleeved uniform shirt and rumpled hair was striding into the brightly lit circle. He glanced at their car, talked to the airman guard a moment, then approached them. "You're Arthur Cummings?" he asked.

"I am," Katlin's father replied from the driver's seat.

The man extended his hand, and her father shook it. "I'm Colonel Dobrowski, commander of the base. I received a message from General McClellen. This is highly unusual, you know."

"I don't doubt that."

"This couldn't wait until morning?"

Katlin's father sighed, and Katlin held her breath. She'd never known her father to lie, ever. "I'll be catching a flight in the morning," he said, which was probably true. "Believe me, it wasn't my idea to show up in the middle of the night," he added, which was also true.

The colonel nodded, resigned. "I'm sure the general appreciates your help. Park your car in the visitor area over there, and I'll accompany you inside."

As Katlin's father moved the car, he said quietly, "Hell, what am I supposed to do now? Anything in particular you'd like me to tell Namazi?"

"We'll be coming along," Beau said.

"Oh, no. You two are in deep enough already."

"You won't know what to do," Beau said.

"I know what to do. I'm going to talk to Captain Namazi, make sure he's being treated properly, and ask him if there's anything I can try to do for him."

"Um, no sir. That's not quite it."

"What are you talking about?"

"We're here to spring him."

"*What?*" both Katlin and her father exclaimed together.

Katlin's father turned to her. "Did you know about this?"

"No! Beau, what in crimps are you talking about?"

"Shh!" Beau said. Dobrowski was walking towards them.

"Okay," the base commander said. "Normally you'd need to sign in and get a badge, but, hell, we all want to get this over with. Let's go."

Three car doors opened, and the colonel looked at them. "You all need to come?"

Katlin's father said no, and Beau and Katlin said yes, all at the same time.

The colonel shook his head and walked away, waving for them all to follow.

When they walked out from under the bright lights of the entrance, Katlin could see a huge hanger off to the side. A scattering of pole lights lit the area, and she saw a variety of fighter jets and a few prop planes parked at odd angles. One large fighter—maybe a small bomber—seemed to have been hoisted upright onto its tail, an absurdly awkward position for a machine that wasn't meant to be resting on its fragile tail assembly.

They walked past what Katlin took to be the main entrance, and around the side into the dark. She could barely make out where she was going, and bumped into her father when they finally stopped in front of a door. The colonel swiped a badge, and opened the door. From inside, bright light spilled out, causing Katlin to squint. Inside, a young officer, whom the colonel introduced as Major Otto, was waiting for them, blinking and stifling a yawn. Dobrowski must have called him out from his bed.

The five of them walked down a corridor, took a left down another corridor, and turned into what looked like a small doctor's waiting area with four chairs along the sides. A service window sat dark and empty. An airman standing between two nondescript doors straightened to attention. He was evidently guarding the base stockade.

"You're relieved," Major Otto said, and the soldier left. Otto then took a key from a hook and unlocked one of the doors. Before opening it, he turned to them. "Who's going to interview the prisoner?" he asked.

Both Katlin and her father raised their hands.

The major looked at Dobrowski, and the colonel shrugged. "The general said to give them whatever they wanted." He pulled his pad from his pocket and looked at it. "Hmm. I'll be right back," he said, and walked out.

Otto looked at Alibai in Beau's hand. "What's that?" he said, pointing.

"It's a defibrillator," Beau replied without batting an eye.

"*That's* a defibrillator?"

"Doctor Cumming's heart is, well, it's struggling. Earth gravity, you know. He needs this close by at all times."

Katlin's father gave Beau a wide-eyed stare.

Otto raised an eyebrow, but opened the door and gestured for Katlin and her father to enter. "It's going to be cozy," he said.

The room was indeed small, just a bed, a chair, and a little table that served as a desk. Katlin caught her breath when she saw Captain Namazi. He'd obviously been sleeping, since he was still buttoning his shirt, but his eyes were bright and alert, his olive-brown cheeks above a tight, close-trimmed beard, as smooth and fresh as a baby.

His eyes went wide when he saw Katlin, and she pushed past her father and stood before him. Beau harrumphed loudly from outside. The urge to wrap her arms around him was almost irresistible, but she willed her arms to remain at her sides. The Persian space pilot glanced at the Air Force major, and nodded politely at her. He wouldn't know what was going on, but he was being cautious.

"Do you mind?" Katlin's father said, grasping the doorknob. Otto gestured to proceed, and he pulled the door closed.

Katlin's willpower collapsed, and she threw her arms around Namazi, who hugged her back, warmly, if not passionately. She would have hung on for the rest of the night, but he gently pulled her away. "It's quite a relief to see you Doctor Cummings, and of course your daughter."

Katlin's father smiled for the first time that night. "You're being far too polite. This isn't Greater Persia. I know she wants to kiss you."

Namazi smiled then. He placed his hands on the sides of her shoulders leaned forward and gently kissed her on the forehead.

Katlin wanted to mash her mouth against his like she'd seen in the movies, but she let the tender moment live its own celebration.

Namazi gazed into her eyes, letting his own eyes say all that needed saying, and then he turned to her father. "How did you manage to see me? I had the idea that my capture was a secret."

"It is," Katlin's father said. "We have a cyber ally in the form of a very capable college student. He's just outside. Namazi, how are you—have they been treating you well?"

"I am fine, Doctor Cummings. There have been obvious indirect threats of torture, but none have as yet been applied."

"You must know that the US government has accused you of piracy. I assumed this was why they arrested you—"

"Apprehended, I think you mean. One must have legal jurisdiction to make an arrest."

Katlin's father smiled. "I stand corrected. I don't understand, though, why you are being held at an Air force base. I'd have thought that the CIA would have their own covert detention facilities."

Namazi lifted his shoulders. "I believe that there was some contention over that. I heard arguments behind closed doors. The matter seemed to be settled when a man named Pollin arrived."

"I never heard of him. Who's that?"

"I don't know. They weren't explaining anything to me. I don't think he's with the military, but also not with the CIA. I believe that he's not with the government at all."

"Okay. Why the Air Force base?"

"Ah, that's quite interesting. Did you know that it is illegal to bring any antimatter device into US territory?"

"No. But it makes sense. Who wants a nuclear bomb armed with a dead-man's switch nearby?"

"The law apparently doesn't apply to the military."

"What are you saying?"

"Pollin convinced the Air Force to bring me here to teach their pilots how to operate a Greater Persia spaceship."

Katlin's father glanced at her. "Your landing shuttle? The one that lifted us into lunar orbit?"

"Similar. This is the latest design. It's larger, and has the capacity to make lunar transits—both in fuel and life support."

"They *have* one?"

"Yes. It's called the Simurgh, a powerful bird in Persian mythology. It sits outside—"

"We saw it!" Katlin said. "I thought it was a large fighter."

"Yes," Namazi agreed, "you probably did. They're not going to any great length to hide it. On the other hand, nobody is now allowed on the base without special permission."

"Where in God's name did they *get* it?" Katlin's father said.

"I can only guess," Namazi said. "I very much doubt that it was from Greater Persia. I suspect that they acquired it through an intermediary—Russia perhaps."

"The relations with Russia are hardly any better than Persia."

"Yes, but Russian men of power and influence can be bought."

"Not so easily in your country?"

"I would like to think that this is because our ethics are superior to those of Russians, but I have to admit that it probably more out of fear."

"Fear of …?"

"Prison—execution. Whatever criticism can be fairly made of the Persian government and society, corruption is not one."

"Not when execution is the penalty."

Namazi shrugged. It was what it was.

Suddenly a siren sounded. They looked around, puzzled, until Katlin's father said, "Oh, for God's sake. That must be Beau."

Katlin frowned. She didn't get it. "Do you think he made a run for it?"

"As the major was closing the door, your pal winked at me."

"You think he … fabricated the alarm?"

"Undoubtedly. In the car—he said that we were here to spring Namazi."

"It's a *diversion*?"

The door opened. Major Otto stuck his head in. "Sit tight," he said. "Be ready to leave if I give the word."

"What is it?" Katlin's father asked.

"Not sure yet." He looked at them. "Anybody like to offer an idea?"

"I doubt that I'm important enough to warrant a mission by our own special forces," Namazi said.

Otto looked at him and then closed the door.

"You were planting the idea of a possible Persian special forces attack into his head, weren't you?" Katlin's father said quietly.

Namazi simply raised one eyebrow.

The door opened wide, and Major Otto motioned for them to come out.

"Where are we going?" Namazi asked.

"A safer location. It's not far."

When Katlin stepped out, Beau caught her eye and winked. *You little stinker*, she thought. *What do you have up your sleeve?*

Before they could go farther, the door from the outer corridor opened and Colonel Dobrowski walked in looking sour. Following behind him was a man in civilian clothes—a sport coat, open at the neck. Katlin wondered how a face so placid could convey so much unquestioned dominance. She guessed who he was, and it was confirmed when Namazi said, "Mr. Pollin, you seem to show up everywhere."

Katlin guessed that this was for their benefit, and Pollin must have as well, for he ignored the remark. Instead, he gestured at Beau. "Here's your perimeter compromise."

Beau's stunned face indicated that this wasn't part of his plan.

"Can I talk to you a moment," Colonel Dobrowski said, motioning for Katlin's father to follow him, and they left.

"What's going on?" Major Otto asked.

"You've been infiltrated," Pollin replied. He cocked his thumb at Beau. "He's a cyber terrorist."

Beau had recovered. He met Pollin's cold stare without flinching.

Otto looked from Pollin to Beau, then at Namazi. "Do you know this boy?" he asked.

"I never saw him prior to five minutes ago," Namazi replied.

Beau moved next to Katlin. "There's obviously some mistake," he said, putting his arm around her waist. "We're just college buddies."

Otto's brow furrowed. "The Colonel told me you were Doctor Cumming's assistant."

Katlin hardly heard his words—something sharp was poking her butt. Beau gave her a gentle nudge. She casually felt behind her, and realized that he was handing Alibai off to her. She took it from his hand, and let her own drop to her side.

"I'd like to talk to the college 'buddy,'" Pollin said, never taking his eyes from Beau. He gestured Beau into the open stockade room.

Beau didn't move. He looked into the room, and then at the door. "You say I'm a cyber terrorist," he said. "You'd like some problems to stay locked up, wouldn't you?" He threw Katlin a quick glance, before Pollin gave him a shove through the open door. "Maybe it would be best if the major were present for this questioning," Beau said as he regained his balance inside the small room.

"Indeed," Otto said, starting for the door, but stopped when Pollin put out his hand.

"That won't be necessary," Pollin said.

Otto met his glare. "May I remind you that are standing on United States Air Force property," he said.

"And you're in charge when the colonel isn't present, is that right?"

Otto didn't respond. He knew he was being set up.

"Shall we call the colonel?" Pollin said. "Perhaps he hasn't filled you in on priorities."

The major held his stare before stepping aside, letting Pollin enter the room and close the door behind him.

Otto looked at them. "The boy somehow arranged for the alarm to sound?"

Katlin figured that the game was up. "I wouldn't put it past him. He's brilliant when it comes to that sort of thing."

"He mentioned that there's problems we'd like to keep locked up. Was he saying that he's hacked into the Air Force data bases?"

"Not that he told me about."

It was odd for Beau to say something like that. He wouldn't taunt a man who demanded to be alone with him without a reason.

Just then Beau began screaming from the other side of the door.

"Dammit!" Otto muttered and swung open the door.

Beau stood against the far wall with his hand in front of his face, as though warding off another blow. Pollin sat on the bed looking disgusted.

"What's going on?" Otto said.

"Absolutely nothing," Pollin replied. "I haven't laid a hand on him. Yet. He's playing a game."

"No!" Beau cried. "Look! I have a welt!" he said. half lifting his shirt.

"Let me see," the major said, walking in.

Beau's head snapped up to look at Katlin, his eyes wide with meaning.

He's playing a game, all right, she thought. *But what?*

His odd comment about problems staying locked up.

Of course! There. Otto had left the keys in the door. She didn't stop to think. She slammed the door shut and reached to turn the key. The doorknob began turning under her hand, preventing the key from engaging the bolt. Pollin or Otto were trying to get out. She heard a yelp, and the doorknob went slack. With a quick jiggle and twist, she had the door locked.

She turned to Namazi who stood staring at her, aghast. "What have you done?" he asked.

"Finished Beau's escape plan."

"But ... he's in there!"

"It's what he wants. Believe me. I know him."

From inside, Otto began shouting for help and pounding on the door.

"We can't just ... leave him," Namazi said.

"If we don't, he'll be in the same trouble, but it will be for nothing." She stepped to the outer doorway and looked up and down the corridor. "Come on. Let's go," she said waving for him and stepping out.

He joined her. "Now what?"

"We run," she said.

She sprinted off. The sound of his feet pounding alongside hers was as satisfying as the kiss on her forehead.

Chapter 6

The light from Van's terminal cast a soft glow onto the bed, two chairs, and the shelves of their small apartment. It was a little eerie. He'd only ever seen the room lit from overhead, and the different perspective was somehow unsettling. It might have been interesting under other, less menacing, circumstances. He was still getting used to their parents' possessions set about on the shelves, freed from secret storage after Arrival, and the screen's glow seemed to give them—his and Tyna's—a ghostly life, as though their dead parents were there, with him.

A stab of focused light bounced around the room as Tyna opened the door and entered. He turned, and she immediately looked off to the side. Wearing lights strapped to their foreheads was new, but essentially the same as the lights in their suit helmets, and you always pointed your head away from someone you might blind. She wore her decade-old jumpsuit. She was sparing with the two dresses that Namazi had presented as a gift—too sparing in Van's view. She treated them with the same care she used when handling her mother's earrings. With the base in darkness and growing colder by the hour however, Van knew he wasn't going to be treated to that image for awhile.

"We tracked down the whistling sound," she said, taking the head-lamp off.

"It's the lock, isn't it?" he said, turning in his chair to face her.

"Yes. When the lock genie went down, the inlet valve relaxed, and air is continually seeping into the inner lock."

"And right out the seal defect."

"The young ones are scared. I tried to reassure them that it would take months and months before all the air in the base leaked away."

"It didn't do much good, I'll bet."

She sighed. "I'm afraid not. The whistling sound is so …"

"Menacing."

"Yes. And the darkness just makes it worse. Can't we try powering the genies back up?"

"Burl says that now that they're down, we might as well wait. No sense using more power than needed."

"Have you talked to Deik?" she asked.

"About the genies? He doesn't care about them. He's bugging Burl every half hour about getting the network back up."

"Their games?"

"Yeah. Apparently he didn't realize that the communal games depend on it."

"How's Burl doing?"

"Complaining that his vision's getting blurry from all the reading. He says it's a race—whether he finds an answer before he goes blind."

Burl had cobbled together some suit batteries to power the library system. He calculated that they had another ten hours to find a solution to their base powering crisis. Weeks ago, Van had moved one of the lab terminals to their apartment where he could access the library in comfort. Burl preferred to still use the lab. He claimed he got more peace there, which was probably true. For twelve years, the lab had been strictly off-limits to nexgens. Even though the three adult scientists were now gone, the space still held a mystique. Most nexgens avoided it. Van had read how Aztec slaves had been conditioned to so fear the mystical power of the temples, they had been known to die from fear when forced to enter.

Tyna looked at the terminal. "I see *you're* being productive about finding solutions to our life-and-death situation."

"I'm happy with the progress," he said with feigned seriousness, derailing her sarcasm. "The most productive thing I can do is get Deik out of the way."

"That kind of talk was considered treason in eighteenth century England. You could have been hanged."

"That's strictly an Earth solution," Burl said in the open doorway.

"Because we're supposed to be more civilized?" Van asked, waving for him to come in.

"No. The average person on Earth weighs, like, 150 pounds. On the Moon, you'd just dangle there waiting until your executioner got tired and cut you down."

"He could tie weights to your feet."

"Or just open a vein. You really are planning a revolt," his friend said, indicating the terminal, where Van was reading about Lech Walesa, the electrician who led a successful non-violent revolt against the Soviet-backed communist government of Poland at the end of the Cold War.

"No. Don't be ridiculous."

"He's been reading about revolutions for days," Tyna said.

"That doesn't mean I'm planning one. They're a critical component of our history."

He'd been drawn to modern history ever since the Arrival opened the library to them. He'd tried ancient history, but the never ending swirl of assassinations, slaves, and religions-du-jour seemed incomprehensible. Burl read hardly anything other than science and engineering, while Tyna had thrown herself headlong into literature.

Burl's stare was a challenge. "Earth drivel," he accused, just as he did when he caught Tyna reading John Steinbeck or Jane Austin. "It's about as relevant as fantasy novels." He raised an eyebrow. "Unless you think it might have practical application."

"I'm *not* planning on deposing Deik. Forget about it."

"You may find that the rabble crowd is actually on the way to lynch *you*—with extra weights on your feet."

"What are you talking about?"

"They're mad as crimps that they didn't get any warning that the power was going down."

"That wasn't *my* fault!"

Burl pretended to whistle and stare at the ceiling.

"You *told* them it was my fault?" Van said.

"Hey, electrical work is a union job, and you're still union head. Besides, nobody wants to go after a cripple. I made sure they saw this," he said lifting his shirt to show the elastic metalized polymer band strapped around his chest. He'd fashioned it as support for his constant cane workout.

"Great. Now the older ones are mad, and the younger ones are scared." He nodded towards Tyna. "She tracked down the whistling sound. It's in the—"

"Lock. Obviously. I could force the inlet value closed, maybe drag in the rover battery for some assist. I don't think it's a high priority, though. Unless the seal defect has gotten worse, it's nothing to worry about for the time being."

"I wish you could convince the young ones of that," Tyna said.

"Ah, a little fear there is healthy at this point."

"Why?"

"With the lock genie down, we're vulnerable. It might actually be possible to somehow get both doors open."

"At the same *time*?" Van said. He'd never imagined that it could be possible. It was unthinkable.

Burl shrugged. "Anybody want to try and find out?"

"Crimps, Burl," Tyna said, "sometimes *you* scare me."

Van shuddered imagining the scene. A hurricane blowing through the base, sucking everything along with it. "It's sobering. It really brings home how defenseless we are."

Tyna frowned. "Maybe we should keep our suits in our apartments."

"What good would that do?" Van asked.

"The apartments are air-tight. We'd have time to get into our suits."

"Turn up the volume of your brain, kid," Burl said.

Tyna's frown deepened into what looked like a scowl. Van knew the look—she was indeed pushing the neurons harder. "With the genie's down," she said, "the doors wouldn't automatically close and seal."

"That's part of it," Burl said. "Once the main area of the base evacuates, there's nothing in the whole universe that can pull the apartment doors open again, not without breaking them."

Tyna sighed. "The pressure inside the apartments would hold the doors closed. Why did they even make the apartments air-tight, then?"

"Somebody is supposed to be outside fixing the problem and re-pressurizing the base. Katlin brought up the idea of using the apartments as temporary safe havens back when we thought that Namazi was coming to attack us."

She nodded reluctantly. "Well, it would still be good to have the suits in the apartments. Even with the doors open, there could still be time to get into them."

"Being in a spacesuit doesn't do much good if somebody has blasted through the front door and is coming in with guns."

Van and Tyna looked at each other. "Who's blasting through the lock door?" Van said.

"I'm talking about the evil Namazi incarnation," Burl said.

"Don't talk about him that way!" Tyna said.

Burl laughed. "I don't mean the real Namazi. You weren't in the room three months ago when Mad-Meyer was convinced that all of Iran—the old Persia—was coming to get him. He almost had us believing they were going to arrive with canons blazing."

Van remembered all too well. It was embarrassing to think that Mad-Meyer had infected them with his paranoia. "We would have had to find Louden's back door," he said.

Burl chuckled.

"What are you talking about?" Tyna said.

"When we were kids," Van said, "Louden used to tell us that if we behaved ourselves, someday he'd show us the back door. When we whined that we wanted to see it now, he'd say that it was too dangerous—we had to be older. We'd be scared by the monsters."

"Why didn't he ever tell me?" she asked.

Van and Burl shrugged. "You're a girl," Van said.

"What does that have to do with it?"

"Louden was funny that way—all the adults were. You know how they sometimes treated the boys differently than the girls."

She nodded, mouth screwed. "Yes, I do. I didn't understand it then."

"And you do now?"

"Oh, yeah. Men have been oppressing women forever."

Van and Burl looked at each other. "I told you that reading all that Earth drivel was going to rot her mind," Burl said. He maneuvered around on his one leg and started away. "It's back to the salt mines." He stopped and looked at them. "Did they actually mine for salt? That seems really crazy with all that salt water." He shrugged and hopped away.

Tyna sighed and sat on Van's lap. She leaned her head into his neck and said, "Girls *are* different from boys."

"Well ... sure," Van said.

"You'd never sit on *my* lap and put your head on *my* shoulder."

"Uh, do you want me to?"

"Maybe. I'll let you know."

They sat in the soft glow of the terminal. It was getting colder, and Van hugged Tyna closer.

She gave a little laugh.

"What?"

"You can be my backdoor man."

"What does that mean?"

She stood up and pulled him up by his hand. "Come on. I'll show you."

∞

"Hey!"

Van sat up, blinking.

"Hey! You guys freeze to death already?"

It was Burl. Van rolled out of bed and pulled on his jumpsuit.

"Tell him to stick his stump in his mouth," Tyna said into the pillow.

"I heard that," Burl said from the doorway fifteen feet away. "If you want a little privacy, closing your door is a good first step."

"You left the door open?" Van said.

"No," Tyna said, still into the pillow. "You left the door open."

"Because I'm the man?"

"No. Because I don't care if Burl sees you naked."

"I do," Burl said. "In the future, please do close the door."

"So, what's worth bothering us with?" Van asked.

"While you two were snoozing, and … well, you know, I was fighting to save the colony."

"You were in the library reading," Van said.

"For fourteen hours straight."

"You slept for some of that."

"I did not."

"Well then, you were getting a really close look at your keyboard."

"Would you like to continue this fruitless debate, or would you like to hear yet more confirmation of my genius?"

Van's eyes lit up. "You found something?"

"Not *some* thing—*the* thing."

"You found a solution?"

"Some seemingly intractable problems are so obvious in hindsight."

"What did you find?"

"In retrospect, you'd think I would have thought of it right away."

"What is it?"

"Often times, trying harder just sends you in circles around the optimal solution."

"Burl, for crimps sake!" Tyna called from the bed. "You're a bloody genius already."

"Bloody?" He tsk-tsked. He whispered to Van, "I'm telling you, she's rotting her mind with that Earth drivel."

"Burl," Van said, "if you don't tell me what you found, you're going to have two stumps."

"Fine, fine. There's never thanks for the deserving. I found from the early records that our batteries were changed out after the first few years. The original nano-wire lithium-ion versions were replaced with new graphene manganese foam technology."

"Okay, and …?"

"The technology was new enough that it wasn't prominently covered in the library records. I had to really dig."

"Why didn't you just do a search?"

"Gee, Van—why didn't I think of that? That was sarcasm, in case you didn't catch it. There was a paper on the technology, but it was in Japanese. I won't bore you with how I managed to translate it—"

"That's why the search didn't find it."

"Gosh, Van. By golly, I think you're right."

"Sarcasm, I know. Sorry. Go on."

Tyna had wrapped a sheet around her and joined them.

"Traditional chemical batteries, including the original nano-wire ones, manifest over ninety percent of their stored redox energy in the top ten percent of their terminal EMF—"

"Hold it!" Van exclaimed.

"What?" Burl said, seeming genuinely surprised.

"We admit that you're a genius, okay? I'll post it on the board. Can you just tell us what you found in normal person language?"

His friend snorted. "Someday we'll have to discuss the definition of 'normal.' But, here we go. When a chemical battery is fully charged—you know, when it's all filled up to the top with electricity juice—"

"Double stump," Tyna warned.

"Fine, fine," Burl said, sighing. "I wish you'd make up your mind. Look, when a typical chemical battery cell is fully charged, it delivers, say, 1.2 Volts. If you discharge it at constant rate, then once it's down to, say, 1.1 Volt, you've only got ten percent of the discharge time left. It's not quite as simple as that, since at the end, the voltage drops rapidly, but you get the idea."

"That's much better," Van said. "That was normal talk. So, you're saying that our battery banks are now below the last ten percent range."

"Nope."

"I give up. Maybe we should go back to talking about electricity as juice."

"No. The point is that this applies only to traditional chemical batteries. Our new ones—graphene manganese foam—act more like a super-capacitor than a battery—"

Van was giving him the eye.

"It means," Burl said struggling to be patient, "that the voltage falls in a nearly linear relationship to the current discharge." He held his hands out, as though waiting for applause.

Van and Tyna looked at him.

Burl took a deep breath. "The battery banks deliver a nominal twenty-four volts to the inverters, which produce the 220 Volts for the base. The inverters can work with anything between thirty-six Volts, all the way down to twelve Volts." He eyed them expectantly.

"Oh!" Tyna said. "Our battery banks are getting close to the twelve-Volt threshold."

Burl made a circular motion with his hand, encouraging her.

"So … there's still, like, half the capacity still remaining."

"Bingo!" Burl exclaimed. He looked thoughtful. "Is that a game?"

"I still don't understand," Van said. "How do we use the rest if the inverters cut out at twelve Volts?"

Burl slapped his palm against his forehead.

"Voltages in series add," Tyna said softly.

Van blinked. "Oh! I get it! We'll, uh, take half the batteries and put them in series with the other half."

"I'd give you a cigar," Burl said, "if there were one within a quarter million miles." He grinned. "Okay, students, how much battery capacity do we have left, then?"

Van shrugged. "Half, I guess."

Burl made a buzzer sound. "Tyna?"

"A quarter."

"Why?"

"Oh!" Van exclaimed. "Of course. The batteries in series together can't go below twelve Volts, so each layer can go down from twelve to six Volts. There'll be a quarter of their charge still left."

"Actually," Burl said, rubbing his chin, "I'm ashamed to admit that Van was closer to the correct answer the first time."

"I was?" Van said.

"You can split the banks again and stack them together, four high," Tyna said.

"It's a progression converging at the total capacity of all the batteries," Burl said. "Of course, there's the granularity effect as you get down to the final configuration, where there's just one column of batteries—"

"On the practical side," Van said, quickly cutting off another tangent, "I don't think we want to be bringing the genies up and down just to squeeze out the last fraction of the charge. If we can get a quarter capacity with just one reconfiguration of the battery banks, that should be plenty to keep the Farm and genies alive until sunup."

Burl's face had gone dark.

"What?" Van asked.

His friend looked at him. "Ah, nothing." He sighed again. "It's the genies. I've been trying not to think about them."

"You're worried they won't come back," Tyna said.

He nodded.

Van hadn't seen him look this concerned since the med-genie had recommended that his leg be amputated.

The sound of padding feet was followed by a circle of white light splashing around the walls of the hallway. The three of them waited until Maya arrived, panting.

"What's wrong?" Van asked.

"It's ..." she started, but stopping to take two deep breaths. "It's the lock," she finally managed.

"What about it?"

Van imagined the outer seal giving way completely, and the scream of a torrent of precious air rushing through the unsecured cutoff valve.

"Someone's knocking."

Silence.

"What did you say?" Van asked.

"Someone's outside. They're pounding on the outer lock door."

"Maya," Van said, "if this is some kind of joke—"

"No, Van! It's true! Deik sent me to get you!"

The young nexgen bounced nervously on her toes, anxious to go.

"Namazi's back," Tyna said with wonder.

Van shook his head. "It can't be. He left just a day ago."

Tyna still had the sheet wrapped around her. "You two can catch up," Van said, and took off, with Maya hot on his heels.

When he arrived at the lock, he had to push his way through the crowd. It seemed as though the entire base had assembled. Everybody had turned their head lamps upwards, and the ceiling swam with mingled circles of light, like the sun shining off ocean waves as he'd seen in movies.

"Van!" Deik called, waving to him.

He heard the pounding as he got closer —three whams, followed by a minute of silence before repeating. "Any idea?" he asked when he finally got to Deik.

"No. It started about ten minutes ago."

The inner lock door was still closed. Van guessed that nobody wanted to make the move to get closer to the mystery. "We have to open up," Van said.

Deik frowned. He glanced around at the dimly lit faces in the crowd of nexgens. "Why?"

"Why? Somebody wants to get in!"

"We don't know who it is."

"So what. They might be in trouble, almost out of air."

"You think it's maybe Namazi coming back?"

"Sure," Van lied. "Could be."

Deik nodded. He wouldn't want to jeopardize their only source of goodies. "Um, how do we do it? The genie's down."

"The first step is to open the inner door."

The seal leak created enough pressure differential that it took the two of them pulling on the handle and pushing with their feet against the wall before the door popped open, sending them both falling to the floor.

"Looks like I got here just in time," Burl said looking down at them.

"We're about to find out if your boast is bigger than your bite," Van said, letting Burl pull him to his feet.

"Can you repeat that in English?"

"You said that closing the lock inlet valve was trivial."

"I never used the word 'trivial.'"

"Your tone shouted it. Can you do it, or not?"

"Do we have a wager?"

"Yeah, we do. If you fail," Van said, tilting his thumb at the next round of pounding, "somebody out there is probably going to die."

Burl's brow furrowed. "Crimps. Let me through."

He always carried tools in his jumpsuit, and he had the inlet cover off in seconds, and then sent nexgens away in different directions for more tools. "All right already!" he cried at the pounding right next to his ear as he cursed and pulled and prodded with his hand buried in machinery above him. A piece of metal fell out and hit him on the head. "Ouch! Crimps!" he exclaimed as he bent to pick up the wayward component. He gazed at it, shrugged, and tossed it away. "That should do it," he said, hopping back out into the staging area.

"Why did he have to lock the inlet valve?" Deik whispered to Van.

"We won't be able to open the outer lock door until the lock chamber is completely evacuated. Any residual pressure would force it closed, just like the inner door was. The seal leak works in our favor here. It will let the air bleed out of the chamber."

"We lose all the air in the chamber?"

Van shrugged. "Can't help that."

Deik moved to close the inner door. "What are you doing?" Burl asked.

The base leader eyed Burl. He could guess that his answer was going to be ridiculed. "The seal leak won't evacuate the chamber until the inner door is closed," Deik said, more a question than statement.

Burl rolled his eyes. "Okay, let's say you close the door—no don't! As soon as it's closed, the pressure will begin dropping inside. After that, there will be no way—no way in hell—to open it again. Base pressure on this side means *force*. Okay, let's say the chamber evacuates and whoever's out there finally figures out how to open the outer door and enters the lock chamber. Now what?"

"Um," he said, eyeing Burl again. "We let air back into the chamber?"

"Very good!" Burl said. Everybody knew this meant he was about to take Deik's queen. "How does that happen?"

"Um, the uh ... I see, the genie is down. Hey! How *do* we let the air back in?"

Van reached to grab his pressure suit. "One of us will have to cycle with the lock and manually open the inlet valve once the outer door is closed again."

Burl would be the obvious candidate, but Deik kept nixing his request for a custom suit—one that accommodated just one leg.

"I'm ready."

It was Tyna. She was all suited up, carrying her helmet.

"How did you get suited so quickly?" Van asked.

"I went and got my suit while you were sleeping."

Van bit his tongue. He was about to ask her why, but he realized that the answer—that she was taking the precaution she'd talked about—would fuel the younger ones' fears.

On the other hand … "Hey, how did you *know* to suit up?"

She shrugged. "It was obvious that somebody would have to cycle through the lock to close the valve."

"Yeah," Van said, "obvious to some of us." He avoided looking at Deik. "I'll go through, though," he said, starting to remove his jumpsuit.

"I'm all ready," she said, starting for the open lock.

"No," Van said. "You stay here."

"Why?"

"We don't know who's out there."

"So?"

"So, they could be … dangerous."

"Van," Burl said, "you're acting like a manager."

He meant one of the four adults that had raised them.

"Fine," Van said holding out his hand towards the lock.

He nearly grabbed her as she entered, donning her helmet. Instinct shouted that a man doesn't let his mate walk into danger. He looked into her eyes through the helmet faceplate as they swung the door closed. He wanted to say something, but she wouldn't have heard him, and besides, he was too embarrassed.

"How long will it take for the air to leak out through the seal?" Deik asked.

"A hundred cubic feet of air," Burl said, "leaking at about five cubic feet per minute."

"That's, uh, twenty minutes!"

"The leak will slow down as the pressure is reduced."

"So, it will take longer."

"Gee, are you sure?"

Deik scowled.

Van sat next to the lock door, listening intently. He wasn't sure what he expected. As the pressure inside grew thinner, it would become less and less able to carry sound. It was only fifteen minutes before they heard the outer door opening, the distant, clanking bang carried through the bones of the base structure. "She must have been pulling on the door," Burl said quietly, "opening the seal flaw a little to let more air escape."

They all started when a thump sounded on the inner door, followed by two more. Before Van could grab the handle, the door rang with another thump, a tap, and a thump. "Morse Code," Burl said. "Three dashes, and then a dash-dot-dash."

Ever since Namazi had communicated with Katlin at Arrival using the old telegraph code, Tyna and Burl had been practicing together, a game to fill the time opened when the platinum mining ended.

"What's she saying?" Van said. The urge to yank the door open was overwhelming.

"Two letters," Burl said. "O-K."

Van yanked the door handle, and then stepped back at what it revealed.

Tyna stood there unlatching her helmet. Next to her, squeezed into the small space, were two others. Their pressure suits were like nothing Van had ever seen, neither the old American suits the nexgens wore, nor Namazi's modern version.

Tyna stepped out from the lock, removing her helmet, while the other two continued to struggle with their helmet attachments. It dawned on Van that he had actually seen suits like these before—in news videos streamed form Earth before U-P cut their satellite link. The oddly shaped characters printed on the suits confirmed it. "Chinese!" he shouted, taking another step back.

His heart pounded. *They've come for the rover*, he thought. Or maybe to take Mai Dung away. He glanced around for a weapon. It was irrational, he knew, but instinct was quicker than thought. One of the visitors finally managed to unlatch his helmet, and lifted it off. The head that was revealed had a dour face that blinked and then forced a smile. He didn't look Chinese, at least from the pictures Van had seen.

The man clumsily twisted his gloves, removing them, and extended his hand.

Van reached out and shook it. It was a smooth hand, like Louden's, unused to the grip of tools.

"Ian Baxter," the man said. "You must be Van."

"Baxter?" Van said. He knew that name. "Katlin's stepfather?"

"That's right," he said, smiling broadly now. "And this is Mr. Teirel," he said, gesturing at the other man who'd managed to remove his helmet, and was turning his head from side to side, as though checking to see if everything still worked. Teirel was a contrast to Baxter, nearly bald and seemingly not interested in greeting Van. The Chinese suit pressed tight around the man's ample midsection.

"Why is everybody wearing lights on their heads?" Baxter asked.

"Huh?" Van said. "Oh, the base power is down. That's why it took so long to let you in."

"Hi," Deik said, pressing forward to shake Baxter's hand. He had moved away when they'd come through the lock. "Welcome to Daedalus Base."

"And, you are …?"

"Deik. I'm the base president."

Baxter grinned. "The president," he repeated, as though Deik was making a joke. "We've been trying to call you for the last couple of hours," Baxter said. "We thought you were hiding from us."

"No," Deik said. "The power's down to the whole base, including the com equipment."

Baxter nodded slowly, knowingly. "Looks like the children have gotten themselves into trouble."

"Not at all," Burl said. He hopped over and extended his hand. "I'm Burl, chief engineer and science officer."

Deik started to protest, but Van gripped his arm.

"This is routine," Burl said.

"It's routine to lose power to the entire base?" Baxter said.

"We didn't lose power," Burl said, completely deadpan. "We shut it down. We have to periodically reverse the batteries, otherwise they gel up."

Baxter shrugged. "How long before the power's back on?"

Van glanced at Tyna. The man had bought Burl's nonsense.

"A couple of hours," Burl said.

Baxter rubbed his hands briskly together. "Do you always keep it so cold?"

"Often," Burl said. "It reduces our oxygen use."

Deik's brow was furrowed. Van gripped him harder before he said something.

"Can you tell us the purpose of your visit?" Van asked before Burl wandered into territory so ridiculous that even Baxter caught on.

"Sure," Baxter said. "Julius has returned from vacation—he's still in the landing shuttle."

"Julius?" five of them said together. They all blinked. "He's *back*?" Van said.

"Of course. You didn't think he was abandoning you, did you?"

All the nexgens could do was stare at Baxter.

"And I'm here," Baxter continued, "to determine just how much of U-P's platinum Namazi has stolen, but more importantly, to assess the state of platinum production. U-P needs an estimate of this year's output of their product."

"*Their* product?" Van said.

"Well, of course. Who else's?"

They all stared at him.

Teirel finally spoke. "I have to piss. How the hell do I get out of this thing?"

Chapter 7

Katlin took the corner too fast and pushed herself off the far wall. Picking up the sprint again, she found another exit sign at the next juncture fifty feet ahead. *How many was that now? Four?* It seemed as though the exit signs were taking them on a random route through the base.

Something—intuition—told her to stop before the next corner. She peeked around, and then pulled back, putting her back flat against the wall.

Namazi stopped next to her . "What is it?" he whispered.

She nodded towards the corner. "Exit doors, but there's a soldier standing guard. I think he heard us."

"What exactly are we trying to accomplish?" he whispered.

"Escape. I thought that was obvious."

"Escape seems extremely unlikely. Even if we did, how far would we get?"

The image of the rocket ship silhouetted against the stars came to her. "Maybe a few thousand miles to start."

"Steal the Persian ship?" Namazi said, aghast.

The sound of the soldier's footsteps were suddenly close. Katlin couldn't think of what else to do, so she stepped around the corner and faced him.

He was young, hardly older than her. Outfitted in camouflage and laced up boots, he looked like a doll dressed up. "What's going on … ma'am?" he asked, seeming to search for a proper title for a seventeen-year-old girl.

Namazi stepped from around the corner, and the soldier took a step back, pulling a rifle off his shoulder.

Katlin glanced at Namazi. "The base is being attacked by terrorists," she said.

The soldier didn't respond. He watched them closely, waiting. He'd been trained well.

No sense being timid now. "I'm General McClellen's niece," she said. "I came to interview Captain Namazi. Colonel Dobrowski told him to get me safely away."

The soldier looked at them each in turn. He nodded at Namazi. "You're the prisoner."

Namazi smiled. "Not exactly. That's the cover. No, I am here on loan to teach your pilots how to fly your rocket ship—you've seen it, I'm sure."

The soldier nodded slowly. He was being cautious, still waiting and considering. "What's that?" he asked pointing at the Alibai in Katlin's hand.

"Oh!" she said. She'd forgotten she still had it. "My recorder—3D."

She had no idea if there was such a thing, and hoped he didn't either.

"Where do you think you're going?" he asked.

Katlin was stumped. This was what her father used to say facetiously. It meant that she *wasn't* going anywhere.

"Our first priority is to get out of the building," Namazi said.

The soldier was asking a simple question. "We're taking the rocket ship to get away," Katlin said.

Namazi looked at her with surprise.

"Just one moment," the soldier said, reaching up to tap a little box attached to his shirt. "Colonel?" he said, turning his head to speak into it.

"No!" Katlin shouted.

The soldier froze.

She didn't know where to go with that. She looked at Namazi.

"The terrorists have been monitoring communications," he said with a sigh. He found lying difficult. "They're tracking everybody in the base using their transmissions."

The soldier looked at them, then gestured with his rifle down the corridor, away from the exit doors. "Come with me, please."

"Don't you understand?" Katlin said, "The colonel wants us to get away!"

They all turned at an angry shout echoing down the hallway. It came from around the corner, and other shouts answered.

"It's them!" Katlin exclaimed. "They're coming for me! Soldier, do your duty!"

He hesitated just a moment, and then nodded and gestured for them to head towards the exit. They ran, and the soldier followed, walking backwards with his rifle drawn and ready.

Katlin and Namazi burst through the doors and into the night. Brilliant lights mounted on high poles, activated with Beau's alarm, lit the paved area in a stark, otherworldly light.

"That way!" the soldier shouted behind them. He stood in the open doorway, pointing off to the left.

"Thanks!" Katlin said, and ran off, Namazi's pounding footsteps once again pacing her.

Around a storage shed, past holding tanks, and along a line of fighter jets they dashed, the wail of the alarm screaming for panic. Namazi said, "Why did you tell him we were taking the ship?"

"Misdirection. Wasn't it obvious?"

"How is telling him exactly what we plan to do misdirection?"

She stopped dead, and he turned. "You thought we were going to *take* the rocket?" she asked.

"Of course," he said, wide-eyed. "That's what you said."

"I wasn't serious!"

Shouting came from behind them.

"Oh, Allah," Namazi said. "Come on!"

Katlin now had to sprint to keep up. She ran into him when he stopped, hesitated, pointed, and took off again. She saw the ship, now glinting under the flood of lights, and she could see that it was much larger than the fighter jets. Rising a hundred feet into the black night sky, with smooth, flowing contours, it could have been mistaken for an artistic memorial. Where the fighter jets were a confusion of geometric complexity—wings, stabilizers, cockpit, jet intakes, and weapon racks—the Greater Persian spaceship stabbed the blackness with an elegance shaped by simplicity.

A high, temporary fence, topped with razor wire and covering at least an acre, surrounded the space ship. Katlin followed Namazi to a gate, where he punched a code into a keypad, swung it open, and motioning for her to go through before swinging it closed behind him. He gave it a shake to make sure it had latched. "Come on," he said, and sprinted off to the ship, which sat on three short, stubby fins with landing pads extending below. It looked exactly like the covers of science fiction books from the fifties. The bottom of the ship was at eye level, and one large nozzle protruded three feet below that. The ground under the ship was smooth glass, melted pavement.

"What's the plan?" Katlin said, breathless when they reached the ship, towering above them.

"I'll go first, and you'll follow."

"Why?"

"The locks on these ships are made for just one person—"

"No, I mean why are we getting in the ship. We'll be trapped."

He gave her a confused look. "We're leaving in the ship."

"You can *do* that? I mean, just get in and go?"

"Of course. Why not? It's not like chemical rockets, where cryogenic liquid oxygen and volatile fuels can't be loaded until just before launch. The antimatter engine can never be shut down, it's always ready to go, as long as there's propellant."

She looked up along the side of the ship. It was like gazing skyward at the giant redwoods she'd seen in California.

"You'll need to climb up," he said, guessing what she was thinking.

"How?" She asked, feeling a vague unease at the idea.

"Here," he said pointing at the base of one of the fins.

She hadn't noticed the ladder. There were rungs embedded in indentations in the metal skin, where they ran up ten feet to the top of the fin. There, they met another column set into the hull that extended up into the dizzying heights. Her vague unease blossomed into panic.

"Normally there's an access tower," he said apologetically. "This will have to do."

"How far up does the ladder go?"

"Only about half way."

Only fifty feet off the ground. Three floors. The panic wasn't mollified. She turned at the sound of shouts from the fence gate. When she turned back, Namazi had already reached the top of the fin, and moved over to the main ladder. He looked down. "Come!"

She was still holding Alibai. Beau had attached a small strap, and she looped it through her belt.

Someone at the gate was shouting to stop, or he'd shoot. Somebody else yelled, "Don't be a fool! That's a nuclear bomb you could set off!"

She grabbed the first rung and heaved herself upward. Two rungs, four, eight, and she was at the top of the fin. Transferring over to the main ladder required care, but she wasn't high enough yet for Earth's gravity to kill her. Up she went, higher and higher. Her arms and calves ached. She wasn't used to her six-fold weight yet. She cursed herself for not sticking more closely to the exercise regimen. Thirty feet above the ground she had to pause. She was afraid her arms would give out and let her fall. She was high enough now to be killed.

She looked up and blinked. A slab of the hull was coming away. Namazi was pulling out what must be the outer door of the one-man lock. It swung out from the bottom, hinged at the top. He climbed up, into the cavity. He looked down and called for her to hurry.

From the gate came an angry voice calling for the combination. She heard Colonel Dobrowski tell someone to call Captain Stringer, to get his ass out of bed.

She started up again, pausing at each rung, checking to see if her arms and legs could manage the next one. She was still two rungs away when Namazi began explaining what she'd have to do once he'd cycled through. The instructions were simple, but she wasn't positive she'd gotten them all.

"Should I repeat them?" he asked.

A gunshot rang out, and Katlin clutched her rung. She'd almost fallen. *Crimps!* They were shooting at them! Another shot, and shouts of success. She looked down—men were streaming through the open gate. They'd shot off the latch.

When she looked up, the section of hull that comprised the lock door was closing the last inch. Namazi had decided there wasn't time for an instruction repeat.

She waited in the dark, clutching her handhold on life, watching the men run across the pavement to the spaceship. From below, they could pick her off, like shooting an apple from a tree.

A slight click returned her attention upwards. The bottom of the hull section had come away a sliver. As instructed, she reached up and pulled at an indentation that formed a handle. Once the lock door was open a few inches, she could reach inside and swing it out and push it up. It was heavier than she expected, and her tired arm shook with the strain until the door stopped and stayed put, caught in a detent. There was barely room for her to crawl up and inside, and she had to make a frightening one-eighty turn before she could squeeze inside, facing outward. As she was twisting around, the Alibai on her belt got caught, and she barely caught herself before falling backwards. The blood pounding in her ears was deafening.

What in crimps was the next instruction? Damn! She should have concentrated. Pull the door down? She tried, but it didn't budge. A green light blinked inches from her eyes. Right. She was supposed to push a button. She pushed one, and something beeped, but the door remained stubbornly in place. There were markings, but in Farsi! "Namazi!" she yelled, but her Jinn savior was locked away inside his rocket bottle.

Shouts rose from directly below. The soldiers had reached the ship. *Think!* Namazi had told her to push a button. He'd said ... it's easy to remember, it's the top row. There were two buttons, both with squiggly Farsi characters, both ended with exclamation marks. Which one? No, she remembered, he'd said—

A gunshot split the night, and something whizzed past.

— he'd said, "Right is right."

She jammed the button on the right, and the green light blinked double time, and the section of hull eased down.

She gasped. She was sure it was going to crush her, but it fell into place with the surface an inch from her nose. Now what? *Think!* She was supposed to lock the door in place. There was a handle. He had pointed to it, and it had been so obvious, but now it was somewhere at her belly, out of sight. She felt with her hand and found it. "Clockwise—like a clock," he'd said. She turned it, and felt the satisfying resistance of mechanical levers sliding into place. An instant later, she fell backwards onto her butt. Her head hit something padded—the back of Namazi's chair. The inner door had swung open.

"Take the chair," Namazi said pointing to what was presumably the co-pilot station, then turned his attention back to his controls.

The ship's command compartment was the size of a walk-in closet, just large enough for two pilot chairs, plus three others, folded up and attached to the bulkhead behind them. Anybody sitting in those would bang their knees against the pilot's backs. Katlin slid into the padded seat. Joysticks were set into the armrests under each hand. Multiple displays spread out before her. Below, between, and above them were herds of switches—preferred over touch-screens for flight control, where a quick glance revealed the state of the entire array, and activation could be made without looking.

"Fasten your belt, and don't touch anything," Namazi said.

The screens were active. Two showed a view of the area around the ship. Katlin wondered where the cameras were mounted, but didn't dare distract Namazi. She gasped when she realized that a soldier—no, two—were climbing the ladder along the side of the ship.

She looked at Namazi. She pointed at the screen. "There's—"

"I know," he said, flipping a switch, which was followed by a low rumble.

The soldiers stopped, looking down. They were talking to the men below, but there was no audio.

Namazi bit his lip, paused with his finger over another switch, then flipped it back and forth. Katlin heard a slight thump, and the men on the ground jumped away. The pavement looked wet. They called up, and the soldier on the ladder began a hasty retreat.

"What did you do?" Katlin asked

"I gave them a little blast of cold propellant."

"That's …"

"Water. A warning that I'm going to take off."

The soldiers jumped down the last ten feet and scampered away. Namazi flipped a switch and manipulated one of his joysticks. The view widened, and they could see that the men were a hundred feet off, and continuing to move away.

Namazi breathed relief and said, "Okay, we're off." He started flipping switches, and lights blinked across the panel in concert.

"How long until we—?" Katlin began to say, but jumped when she heard a roar and felt movement.

The view outside was receding. "We're in the air!" she said.

Namazi glanced at her and smiled. "This *is* a space ship."

"I know, but—so quickly."

He chuckled. "Right. No countdowns."

As he spoke, he never took his eyes off the various screens—some obviously radar. He spared her a quick glance, though, and smiled. "You're clutching the arms of the chair as though it may try to eject you."

"I'm ... waiting for the acceleration."

"We are accelerating. Look at the outside view."

The base was just a small cluster of lights and growing smaller.

"I know. I mean ... *real* acceleration."

"You're still in the chemical fuel mindset. We don't need to gain velocity quickly in order to unburden ourselves of the weight of the first-stage fuel."

She had already ridden in an antimatter ship when Namazi took her and her father off the Moon and into lunar orbit. "The shuttle had a lot of acceleration."

"Yes, and this larger ship actually has even more." He glanced at her again, smiling.

She was missing something. *Oh, you dunce*, she thought. "We have to subtract the acceleration of Earth's gravity."

He nodded. "Once in orbit, just one gravity of acceleration would take us to the moon in about two hours, assuming we didn't need to slow down halfway. Our thrust is just a fraction of the giant chemical rockets, but I'm using a tiny fraction of the amount of propellant."

To the Moon. In two hours. "How much propellant—water—do you carry?"

"Remember, you'd have to turn around halfway and burn to slow down, so the trip would be more like five hours." He smiled. "The ship doesn't carry enough to burn for five hours." He checked a gauge. "We're about a quarter full, so I'd say we could burn at this rate for … maybe an hour."

Katlin sat quietly, letting her pulse ease. It seemed so peaceful. She felt heavy—heavier than usual—but this was a sensation she'd been gradually adjusting to for months. The sound of the exhaust—water torn into a super-heated mixture of oxygen and hydrogen plasma—was a scream chasing them through the night sky, but it was a scream of escape, comforting in a way.

Maybe it was too quiet. "Won't they come after us?"

"I imagine they're scrambling their jets. It will take them a few minutes to get in the air."

"Uh, it's already been a few minutes."

"Well, probably more than a few minutes."

"Probably?"

"Most assuredly," he said.

"You're patronizing me?"

"Only a little."

"The fighters, can they … go faster than us?"

"Most definitely. Much faster."

"You're not worried?"

He glanced at her. "Of course. When options are limited, one can only strive to chose the best one."

"A philosopher."

He laughed. "Not at all. Just stating the obvious. I'm not really that worried. I expect that they'll simply try to force us back with a bluff. We're far too important to destroy."

"You? It's certainly not me."

He threw her a glance. "I was talking about the ship. It's worth billions of dollars."

"I see. I'm glad we stole the expensive one, then."

He looked at her again and laughed. He was beginning to relax. Maybe they were safe after all.

"They're probably trying to hail us," he said. "Let's see what they have to say."

Blaine C. Readler

He flipped a switch, and a speaker in the console popped, hissed static a bit, and then burst with musical nonsense for a few seconds. "Musical" was being generous. To Katlin, it sounded like a small orchestra tuning up, an orchestra of kids struggling to find their tuning.

Namazi sighed and reached to turn it off. "They're using encryption," he said.

"You know this?"

"I've heard it before. This ship doesn't have the ability to decode it, of course."

"Huh," Katlin said. "Encryption, eh? Too bad Beau's not here."

He was, in a way. She pulled Alibai from her belt. She hadn't looked at it closely before. Beau had apparently made it himself using a generic project box. He'd drilled holes and outfitted it with a variety of connectors. There was just one push button. She turned the box around. No, just that one. She shrugged and pushed it.

"*Hello, Beau,*" the box said in the voice of a young male.

Katlin nearly dropped it.

"That was the box?" Namazi said.

"Uh, yeah. It talks."

"*Beau?*" the box said, "*Are you there?*"

Katlin looked at Namazi, who lifted his shoulders. "Beau isn't here. This is Katlin."

"*Hello, Katlin,*" the box said. "*Did you say that Beau is or is not here?*"

"He's not here."

"*Okay. Please avoid contractions in order to avoid confusion.*"

"What is it?" Namazi said.

"Beau made it. He calls it 'A Little Intuitive Box of Artificial Intelligence.'"

"Sounds very American. What does it do?"

"Beau said he uses it for hacking."

"Hacking—as in breaking into secure networks?"

"As in sounding false alarms, for example," she said. "He also uses it for decryption."

They looked at each other.

"Alibai," Katlin said, "can you hear me?"

"*I can hear you,*" the box said. "*Are you Katlin?*"

"Yes, that's me—um, that *is* me."

"*Can we verify this?*" the box asked.

"That I am me? How do we do that?"

"*I ask you a question, and you answer the question.*"

"Okay, shoot—I mean, proceed."

"*Katlin, what did you have for your evening meal last Tuesday?*"

"Nearly a week ago? I'm supposed to remember that?"

"How would it know?" Namazi said.

"Good point. Ah! Beau was hanging out. He probably had the box with him. We had pizza! Topped with shrimp."

"*That is correct, Katlin,*" the box said. "*I believe that you are Katlin.*"

"Thank you." She was thanking a computer. "So, Beau says that you are a whizz at decryption."

"*Katlin, I don't understand.*"

"Right. Sorry." Now she was apologizing to a computer. "Beau says that you are very competent at decryption. Is this true?"

"*That is a relative judgment. Can I suggest that you find an expert in the field to ask?*"

"You definitely are a computer. Let me rephrase—you perform decryption tasks, is that correct?"

"*First, I am not really a computer, since I have no centralized processing units. Second, I do perform encryption and decryption.*"

"Can you perform, um, audio decryption?"

"*I can try.*"

She glanced at Namazi, who flipped the radio back on. Static was broken by a burst of orchestra tuning. "Can you hear that?"

"*I can. Are you able to increase the volume?*"

"I can do one better," Katlin said, placing the box next to the speaker.

"*Can you help me with context? Perhaps some keywords?*"

"Okay. Let's see, we are riding in a spaceship, and we think that the government may be trying to catch us—in fighter jets. We're not criminals, though—"

"I doubt it cares about that," Namazi said.

"Right," Katlin said. "Keywords—uh, spaceship, fighter jets, intercept, Colonel Dobrowski. Well, me—Katlin Cummings. Then there's Namazi—my companion who you heard talking. Is that enough?"

"Let me try."

They waited through several bursts of musical nonsense, and then the box began uttering individual words. At first there was little value—common prepositions, interspersed with their own names. Repeated words followed—*"intercept," "respond," "contact," "emergency."* A threshold seemed to be crossed, and the Alibai box began delivering full sentences—something about the problem not being the ability to take out the target, but a proper command decision to do so.

Katlin looked at Namazi. "Can you tell us who's doing the talking?" Katlin asked the box.

It began simply referring to generic sources.

"Speaker A—'I have target locked. They're heading west, towards the mountains.'"

"Speaker B—'Stay on target, but hold fire.'"

"Speaker C—'Fire, dammit. Don't let them get away.'"

"Speaker B—'Pollin, I am in command here.'"

"Speaker C—'Fine. Fine. I'll get McClellen on the phone. Just don't lose that ship.'"

Katlin glanced at Namazi. He stared at the box morosely.

"Speaker D—*probably on a phone connection*—'Do they know about wellspring?'"

"Speaker B—'I doubt it. How can they?'"

"Speaker C—'We can't take a chance. Take them down.'"

"Speaker D—'Are you willing to foot the cost?'"

"Speaker C—'There's no time for that. Shoot them down.'"

"Speaker D—'That's easy for you to say. I have to answer to the President.'"

"Speaker C—'Okay, okay. We'll cover the cost of the ship. Just get them before they escape.'"

"Speaker D—'Where are they?'"

"Speaker B—'Uh, they're approaching San Andres Peak.'"

"Speaker D—'There's going to be one hell of an explosion. Get them while they're still over the desert. Tell your boys to keep their distance when they launch. We'll need a story to cover the bang.'"

"What'll we do?" Katlin said.

Namazi pointed to one of the screens. "There. Two of them."

"Fighters?"

He nodded.

"Should we … give up?" she asked. She hated it when her voice wavered like that. She was terrified.

"I have an idea," Namazi said. "Make sure your belt is tight."

They dove, and Katlin floated in her seat. Namazi watched his screen, his hand poised on the joystick. He tilted it, and Katlin was suddenly heavy again, heavier than before. The force eased off, and they seemed to be flying level once more. Namazi flipped switches, and turned a dial. A red light began blinking, and an alarm beeped.

"Uh …" Katlin started.

"I'm going to cut the drive," he said, "and you'll see San Andres peak coming at us."

Katlin floated in her seat again. In a forward view screen, she saw the silhouette of a mountain approaching against a false-colored sky. Closer, closer. She was sure they were going to hit it, and she clutched the arms of her chair. She clenched her teeth and closed her eyes as the peak flashed by, and the next instant, she was rocked by a loud concussion. She yelped involuntarily.

"It's okay," Namazi said. "We'll fall a little longer before I re-activate the drive."

"What—what happened?"

"I jettisoned a small amount of antimatter. From the fighters' perspective, we crashed into the mountain."

"That was the explosion?"

"That's right. There's a piece of San Andres Peak missing now. Okay, here we go."

Weight returned, and Katlin saw that they were flying just hundreds of feet off the ground west of the mountain range.

Namazi flipped on the radio. Alibai had fallen, and Katlin placed it back on the console.

"*Speaker B*—'Our men have clear visual.'" the box said.

"*Speaker D*—'Are they sure?'"

"*Speaker B*—'The fireball engulfed the entire peak.'"

"*Speaker D*—'How bad was the shockwave?'"

"*Speaker B*—'Very slight. I wouldn't even call it a shockwave.'"

They listened to static. Namazi seemed to be holding his breath.

"*Speaker D*—'You've been snookered, Dobrowski. Satellite shows super-hot exhaust west of the range. Right off the scale. That's your bird.'"

Katlin watched Namazi as the pilots reported that they were flying around the San Andres Peak debris, and that they'd re-configured their missiles for ultra-temp targeting. She bit her tongue, letting Namazi swim in deep thought. She couldn't take it anymore. "Time to give up?" she said quietly.

He didn't answer. With jaw clenched in resolve—or maybe defeat—he tilted back on the joystick, and the ship pulled up. He watched the forward velocity gauge until it fell to zero, and then eased the ship down. Katlin felt relief course through her, which was replaced by shame. Namazi would spend the rest of his life in a dark, lonely cell, if they didn't execute him outright. She was a celebrity, and a minor to boot. She'd get a slap on the wrist, and be back in class.

The ground indicator ticked down the distance—100 meters, 50 meters, 30 meters. When it reached 20 meters, Namazi stopped the descent. The scream of the plasma exhaust had grown to a roar, the percussion of the unimaginably hot ionized gas blasting the desert ground below.

Namazi leaned over to listen to Alibai above the rumble.

"*Speaker A*—'We have a solid heat-lock.'"

"*Speaker B*—'Don't get any closer. It's a hundred kiloton bomb you'll be detonating. Pull away immediately after launch.'"

"*Speaker A*—'Roger.'"

Static.

"*Speaker A*—'Missiles free. Pulling away.'"

Katlin looked at Namazi, still focused on his displays. She felt her stomach curl into a hard knot. She thought she was going to puke.

He turned to her, and when his eyes met hers, his tight face loosened a little. "Put your fear aside," he said gently, placing his hand on hers. "We won't even feel the missiles strike."

Somewhere, miles closer by the minute, death was hurtling onwards.

Chapter 8

"I was going to ask for a tour," Baxter said, "but I think I'll wait until you get the power back up." He looked around at the wide-eyed stares of the nexgens. A new face at the base was a novelty. "Can I have a moment with you?" he said to Van.

"Uh, sure."

Tyna raised an eyebrow. Van sighed. "You'll probably want to talk to Deik first."

"Deik," Baxter said, as though he'd forgotten about him. "Of course. Why don't the three of us find some place to huddle?"

"Huddle?" Deik said. "Like in football?"

Baxter smiled. "It's a figure of speech. It means to talk together in private."

"I knew that," Deik said. Van was sure he didn't.

"How about my apartment?" Van said.

"No conference rooms?" Baxter said.

"Like in an office? No. That would be wasted space."

"Okay, then. Lead the way." He turned to his companion. "You coming?"

"Nah," Teirel said. "I'll hang out and get to know the place."

Van flipped his headlamp down and headed off, through the parting crowd of nexgens and down the corridor. He stopped and turned when he heard Baxter grunt. He was leaning against the wall. "I'm not used to the low gravity," he said, rubbing his head.

"What happened?"

"I hit my head on the ceiling. That's something I don't have an opportunity to say very often."

Van had thought that Baxter was maybe crippled—he'd heard that polio had made a comeback on Earth after the Blast. That would have explained his clumsy walking. It made complete sense, of course, that somebody from Earth would find the Moon's one-sixth gravity confusing. "I'll slow down. You'll get used to it."

Once in the apartment, Van offered Baxter and Deik the chairs, placed his headlamp on the desk pointing up, and sat on the bed. Baxter looked around at the room. "You live here?"

"Yes. This is my—our—apartment."

"This is it? All of it?"

Van shrugged. "There's a bathroom through that door."

Baxter seemed surprised. "Tidy," he said.

"Can I get you some tea?" Van asked.

"Actually, I'd kill for a cup of coffee."

Deik leaned back in surprise.

"I think it's an expression," Van said. "I'm afraid we don't have coffee. Cup for cup, tea leaves weigh a fraction of coffee beans, and weight rules on lunar transports."

Baxter looked at him critically. "I didn't think money was a factor, the way you've been shoveling platinum to the Persians."

"It's not like that!"

Van caught himself. Katlin had told him about her stepfather. She'd called him a lawyer's lawyer. Getting riled was falling into his game. "Money is not the limiting factor," he continued calmly. "There's only so much that can be carried along on each trip." He glanced at Deik who rolled his eyes. "In any case, Namazi charges market value. We did offer him a one-time bonus, because he risked his life to save us, after your client abandoned us."

"That's for a court to determine."

Van looked him in the eye. He saw only supreme confidence. "I think the court should determine that after they've lived here for twelve years with no outside contact."

Baxter didn't try to hide his smirk. "I'm sure they'll take that into careful consideration." He pulled out a little device from his pocket and pushed a button, obviously a recorder. "So, how much did you give Namazi as a bonus?"

Van made sure he talked into the device. "Nothing. He refused it."

Baxter took an exasperated breath. He pushed the button again, and put the recorder back in his pocket. He looked from Deik to Van and said, "Look, I'm not your enemy. I'm here to get things settled, back on track. With cooperation, your future can be bright. I want everybody to win."

In his mind, Van was thinking, *Bla, bla, bla. Manager talk.* "Like we were winning for twelve years under Meyer—U-P's employee?"

Baxter's eyes narrowed. "I'd be careful if I were you. You can't win, you know. You have nothing to bargain with."

"We have platinum."

"No. My client has a lot of platinum."

"We have Greater Persia working for us."

"You think they're acting in your best interest? You think they're intent on saving you?"

"Maybe not all of Persia—"

"You're talking about Namazi."

Van shrugged.

Baxter held his gaze. "Namazi has been arrested."

"*What?*"

"The United States has detained him on charges of high piracy."

Van felt faint. He blinked.

"Listen," Baxter said, placing his hand on Van's knee, "I admire your spirit. I really do. But we have to be realistic. Teenagers can't run a moon base."

Van stared at the hand on his knee. He wanted to swat it away. He looked up. "Oh, but we have been."

Baxter shook his head. "You're young. You think you know everything you need to know, but you don't know what you don't know. I'm not sure what's up with this power outage, but I watched your reaction, Deik, when Burl gave his explanation. Either he was lying, or you don't have the least idea of what's going on."

He glanced at Van and turned a critical gaze back on Deik. "I managed to get the transit logs for Namazi's shipments—expensive toys."

Deik's face was beet red. He started to say something, but clamped his mouth shut.

"Anyway," Baxter said, "Julius is back, and he'll be the interim base leader until U-P can arrange a permanent replacement." He pulled out a folded sheet from an inside pocket, smoothed it out, and placed it on the desk. "Do you have a pen?" he asked. "Mine was exposed to vacuum during the transit and ruined—a very good one, too."

"What is this?" Van asked.

Baxter looked him in the eye and gave a little shake of his head. "It's just a release. You can read it, but it simply says that as representatives of the base children, you agree that U-P is the rightful owner of the base. I have signature places for both of you."

Van glanced at the sheet lying on the desk, and back at Baxter. "That sounds like a contradiction."

"What do you mean?"

"On one hand, you claim that we're just irresponsible children, but then you want legal approval from existing recognized authority on the base."

Baxter stared at him, and then smiled. "You should consider taking up law."

"What about it? The contradiction?"

Baxter held up his hands. "I'm a lawyer. I cover all bases. Just because I recognize that you represent the children, doesn't imply that you have management authority on the base."

Van glared at the paper, willing it to catch fire, like a super-hero with heat-ray vision.

"Can I still be president?" Deik asked, chewing his lip.

Baxter grinned, and then suppressed it. "Of course," he said seriously. "You can still be president of the … nexgens. That's what you children call yourself?"

"That's what management called us," Deik said absently, deep in thought. "What's in it for me—I mean us? I mean, why should we sign it?"

Baxter's brow furrowed. "Well, if you don't sign it, you'll be charged with theft, conspiracy, and reckless abandonment of duty."

Deik frowned.

"You're eighteen years old, right?"

Deik nodded.

"There, you see? You'll be charged as an adult."

Deik just looked at him, flummoxed.

"On the other hand," Baxter said, "if you do sign it, not only will you still be president, but I guarantee that you won't be mining platinum, and you—both of you—will get a handsome salary."

Deik's mouth was tight as he rummaged around Van's desk.

"We'll even give you an office—does the base have offices?"

"I already have an office," Deik said. "It used to be Meyer's— ah, here," he said holding up a pen.

"You're not going to sign it!" Van said, aghast.

Deik shrugged. "Do we have a choice?"

"Yes, you have a choice! You'll be giving away the base!"

"Us against Earth? Now, who do you think will win that one?"

"It's not the entire Earth—just U-P. Namazi is working with his country to …"

Deik nodded. "Exactly. There is no more Namazi. No more shipments." he pulled the paper towards him, but paused and looked at Baxter. "Could you put that in the agreement? You, know, the salary—and president?"

"Of course," Baxter said, taking the pen and paper. He scribbled a couple of lines and slid it back. "How's that?"

Deik read it, and then signed his name.

Baxter took the paper and held it out to Van, who just stared at him.

"Why do you even need his signature?" Deik asked.

Baxter looked at him, and then back at Van. "Did you approve the contents of the shipments? I mean, specifically the toys?"

Van stared at him. He was furious at this Earth lawyer who hardly tried to hide his arrogance. He was furious at Deik for being so spineless. He was furious at Julius who had given them all such a hard time over the years, and now had come back in the service of the enemy. He was even furious at Maya for forgetting to reconnect the solar panel feed, and that swelled to include anger at them all— himself included—for thinking they could exist as an independent nation.

"I expect not," Baxter finally said. He turned to Deik. "He's the union leader. We need his signature because in a real sense he will be the more important leader of the nexgens as we ramp back up the platinum production."

He had Deik's signature. There was no need to stroke the president's ego any more.

Van snatched the paper from Baxter and slammed it onto the desk. He grabbed the pen and hovered over the line waiting for his signature. This was it. The end of the shortest nation in history. The line blurred as tears swelled. He remembered the joy and hope that had filled in their hearts three months ago as they climbed the crater wall after watching Namazi take off, climbing to meet the literal dawn of a new day.

He set the pen down carefully on the desk and slid the paper across the desk to Baxter. "I can't," he said.

Baxter watched him a moment. "There's time," he said, folding the paper and slipping back into his inside pocket. "You'll come around."

The lawyer stood up, steadying his hand on the back of the chair, still unaccustomed to the gravity. "Time to go and get Julius," he said, starting away. He stopped and turned back. "By the way, the contract is only valid if both of you sign."

They listened to his footsteps fade down the corridor, and then stop. "You coming?" he called. "I need light!"

Van strapped the light back on his forehead, and when he turned to go, Deik was there, pushing his face into Van's. "Don't ruin this for me!" he hissed. "Don't ruin it for all of us!"

Van gave him a little push, and walked past him.

∞

They met up with Teirel back at the lock. "How'd it go?" he asked. Baxter shook his head. "Let's talk," Teirel said. "Can we get some privacy?" he asked Van. He took them to the nearest nexgen apartment, handed them his light, and closed the door.

Other lights flashed along the ceiling. A parade of nexgens had followed, and were inching down the corridor towards him. "Do you understand the concept of privacy?" he asked, waving his hands to shoo them away. Grudgingly, they turned and left. Van hesitated. He could hear the voices beyond the door. They had started quietly, but were rising in volume. He couldn't make out the words. He leaned in to listen, and noticed another light dancing along the ceiling and wall. He turned to reprimand the wayward nexgen, and found Tyna standing with her hands on her hips. "Right," he said.

They started back towards the lock, but Tyna took his arm. She looked both ways, and said softly, "I don't trust Teirel."

Van shrugged. "He's with Baxter. They're both with U-P. Why would we trust either of them?"

"No. It's more than that."

"Did he do something?"

She shook her head, brow furrowed in thought.

"Did he say something?"

She shook her head.

"Women's intuition?"

She glanced at him, annoyed. This was a term they hadn't known until the flood of information and entertainment started flowing after Arrival. "He was very interested in how the base worked."

He bounced his shoulders. "Why not? I would be too."

She shook her head slowly, thinking. "He was particularly interested in how the airlock worked, but I have the sense that a lot of it was … I don't know—diversion."

"An uclar?" he asked.

This was a word the nexgens had invented from "UCLA Research." The university had sponsored a small R&D area near the mining platform. Although not used after the Blast, Mad-Meyer continued to maintain it. When any nexgens were sick, the shift supervisor might assign them to this duty, essentially time off. Over time, the term came to mean anything done as a ruse.

"I don't know," Tyna said. "Maybe—it's just a feeling."

Van waited, but she didn't explain. "I'll keep an eye on him," he said. He didn't know what he'd be looking for, but he wanted to honor her concern … even if it was just women's intuition.

She sighed, and they started again for the lock. Deik was there, updating the crowd, explaining how Van had refused to go along with the generous offer.

"Generous for whom?" Burl asked.

"For everybody!" Deik said a little nervously.

"What exactly does … Linda get out of it?" Burl asked, indicating the closest nexgen who happened to be standing there.

"Why, she gets ..." He glanced at Van. "She gets ..." His eyes lit up, remembering. "Namazi's been arrested!" he said, letting his relief show.

The crowd gasped, and chattering broke out.

"This true?" Burl asked Van quietly.

Van nodded glumly. "So Baxter says, anyway."

"So, you see!" Deik went on. "The agreement allows U-P to continue sending all the stuff we need!"

Baxter hadn't said that, but Van was in no mood to contradict the president.

The far end of the crowd gave way as the two Earth men came through. Teirel wore the same bored expression, but Baxter looked sour. "We'll be back soon with Julius," Baxter said, looking at his helmet with displeasure before putting it over his head.

Teirel held his helmet in his hands. He gestured at the lock. "The gal will have to let us back out?"

Burl patted Tyna on the shoulder. "Duty calls, little gal."

She shoved him away and put on her helmet.

Teirel looked at Tyna and Burl. He nodded towards the open lock. "She has to be careful not to open both doors at once, eh?" he said. He chuckled. "That wouldn't be good."

"It's not even possible with the power down," Burl said.

"Oh? Why?"

"Think about it," Burl said, relishing a lecture. "Both the inner and outer doors open inward. That's on purpose for safety. Because of the pressure inside the base, you can only open the inner door when the inside of the lock is pressurized, and you can only open the outer door when the lock is evacuated."

"Okay. How is it possible with the power on?"

"There's a motor that can force the outer door open. That's another safety feature. In case the evac pump—the air pump that evacuates the lock—fails, that's the only way to get out. Of course, the genie would never let the outer door open unless the inner door is sealed."

"The lost land of the genies," Teirel said dramatically as he donned his helmet and joined Baxter and Tyna in the lock.

Earth genies had gone extinct after the Blast.

Van closed the inner lock door, and stepped back—right into somebody. "Jira! What are you doing?"

"I had to wait until they left."

"What's up?"

"Donovan, tell him," she said, pulling her brother forward. Donovan was the youngest nexgen, just a few months old when the Blast killed their parents.

"I was looking for something," Donovan said, glancing furtively at Van, the closest authority figure to him for most of his life.

"How about the truth?" Jira said.

The young nexgen stared at his shoes.

"He was hiding," Jira said. "Somebody was fooling with him. They told him that the Earth men had come to take some of us back, starting with the youngest."

Van sighed. Even in times of high crisis, he had to play arbiter. Why didn't they go to Deik? "Who told you that," he said to Donovan.

"Van," Jira said, "that's not the point. He was hiding behind his bed."

Jira and her brother shared an apartment. It was the closest one to the lock. "You were in there! When they were arguing?"

Donovan nodded.

"What did you hear?"

"They, uh, the tall one wanted more time," he said, alternating his gaze between Van and his shoes, "but the fat one said that talking was just a waste of time."

"Time for what?"

The boy lifted his shoulders. "They argued over who was the boss."

"That's it?"

He nodded.

"What about the fallback?" Jira said. "The fat man's idea."

Donovan frowned. "The tall one didn't want to talk about it. He said he'd have nothing to do with what was basically murder."

Van looked at Jira and then Donovan. "What's the fallback idea?"

Donovan lifted his shoulders and held them. "Something about bringing the hammer down. The tall one got angry about it. That's when they started arguing about who calls the shots."

Van nodded. He put his hand on the boy's shoulder. "Good job."

Knocks on the lock door indicated that Tyna was ready to open up.

"Where's Burl?" Van said, looking around the crowded lock station. "We need to get the power back up. Burl!" he called. "Where in crimps are you?"

Burl replied from far down the corridor. He was scampering along on his leg and cane. "Whatever it is will have to wait!" Burl called back. "I have to get the power back up!" He turned and scuttled on, not waiting for an answer.

They were in a real pickle—another term Van had picked up after Arrival. He sat down next to the lock to wait for Tyna's return. He gave a little snort. He wished Louden's back door was more than just a myth.

∞

"Seriously, Van," Deik said. "if you're worried about what they might do, then why don't you just sign?"

Deik had been badgering him, following two steps behind, ever since Baxter and Teirel had left. "Listen," Van said, turning so that Deik nearly ran into him, "we haven't even begun to find out what the alternatives are. If I have to sign, what concessions can we get? You'll still be president, with an office and a nice salary, but what about everybody else?"

"He offered you the same salary."

"I'm not everybody else! Bah!" Van exclaimed in disgust and started to walk away, but stopped and turned. "We need to take things in turn. First things first. We have to get the power back up—nothing else matters until that happens."

He turned and walked away, trying to ignore the sound of Deik's footsteps two steps behind.

When he arrived at the power control room, he was surprised to hear only quiet conversation somewhere in the rear. For the last twenty minutes, the crowded room had been filled with clattering, thumping, and shouts as Burl flung orders at a half-dozen older nexgens. Winding his way through the racks of batteries, he found Burl and his crew huddled over an open panel, circuitry exposed. He kept his distance, as he'd done all along, avoiding distracting them. Deik held no such concern, however, and squeezed past him. "You said it wouldn't even take a half-hour," he said, leaning over to see what they were doing.

Burl glanced at his watch. "That's right. And I still have eight minutes." He reached up and pulled the panel back into place. "Which means I'm early." He saw Van. "Ready to see if I blow up the base?"

Van smiled and nodded. He knew Burl was joking, but he still wondered if he should move out from between racks of high-energy batteries.

Burl held his hand ceremoniously over the main switch, and then flipped it. Van wished he had heeded his own advice when a low hum quickly swelled to become an ominous buzz. Burl's announcement that this was the inverter's giant capacitors charging was reassuring, but when the overhead lights suddenly bathed the room, Van yelped and jumped.

Burl laughed. "Fear what ye understand not." He waved for Deik to get out of the way. "The lock genie is next."

Outside, in the main hallway, Van heard distant hoots and cheers from the nexgens still milling about the lock area, where they'd remained, finding safety in numbers. He walked along with Burl, trying to ignore Deik, who hovered nearby. "You've powered the entire base," he said quietly.

Burl nodded as he hobbled along. "I can isolate the Farm and genie circuits later."

"You want to show Baxter that we're not helpless."

Burl glanced at him. "I hadn't thought about that. I just want it up when Julius comes in."

Van grinned, remembering all the times that Burl had needled the engineering scientist, who had worked tirelessly for twelve years keeping the base running. Nobody cared much for grumpy Julius, but Van suspected that he was maybe the only person Burl truly admired. Burl was in many ways the man's protégé.

When they reached the crowd, the cheers had subsided, and the nexgens were packed together near the lock. Van pushed his way through, and found what had drawn them. A voice issuing from above the door—the lock genie—was repeating information. He turned to Burl in wonder. He hadn't heard the AI lock controller's voice in years. "You woke her up!"

Burl nodded, frowning.

"Not good news?"

"It's better than having her completely dead. I just wish she had come up the same as before."

After a five second pause, the soft genie's voice repeated its refrain—"*Airlock controller here. An urgent matter requires that I be enabled. There are problems with the airlock that pose critical danger.*"

"Genie, this is Burl."

The refrain repeated unaltered.

"Genie!" Burl exclaimed. "Respond!"

"It doesn't recognize you."

It was Tyna. She'd been checking on the Farm.

Burl frowned, stumped. When Burl was stumped, Van worried.

"Let me try," Tyna said. "Airlock!"

The genie halted mid-refrain. "*I am listening.*"

"It forgot that we call them genies," Van whispered to Burl.

"Let me know when you have something non-obvious," Burl growled.

"Airlock," Tyna said, "detail the problems."

"*The intake valve is obstructed in an open position, and the outer door appears to be leaking. I must be enabled in order to perform diagnostics and try to clear the intake obstruction. The base is losing air. This is a class two emergency.*"

"No!" Burl exclaimed. "The intake valve motor is already weak. She'll burn it out if she tries to clear the jam."

This was the temporary jam that Tyna had inserted on her way inside so that the lock wouldn't evacuate through the leak.

Tyna looked from Burl to the speaker above the door. "Airlock, did you hear that? We have purposely inserted a temporary jam in the intake valve. We must remove that before you begin your diagnostics."

"*I understand what you are saying.*"

"But will you act on it?" Tyna asked.

"I cannot accept formal instructions until I am enabled. This is for your safety."

"Crimps!" Burl said. "We can't tell her not to do it until we enable her, but she's primed to do it as soon as we do."

"Airlock," Tyna said, "listen to me. If we enable you, and you attempt diagnostics, you will damage the lock operation and that will be a class one emergency. Do you understand?"

"I understand what you are saying."

"Will you suspend diagnostics if we enable you?"

"I cannot accept formal instructions until I am enabled. This is for your safety."

Burl kicked the lock door. "You idiot genie!"

Tyna took a slow breath. "Airlock, you are about to inflict a class one emergency. I know you understand me. We need to enable you, but we need you to promise that you won't attempt diagnostics immediately. Give us just one minute after we enable you to formally instruct you. I repeat, a class *one* emergency."

The genie was silent for a half-dozen heartbeats—a long time. *"I will wait one minute after being enabled to begin diagnostics, unless formal instructions are given otherwise."*

"Thank you," Tyna said.

"You don't thank a genie," Burl said.

"It can't hurt." Tyna threw Van a glance. "Okay, airlock, you are enabled."

"I need the password."

Burl slapped his forehead. At the same time, they heard the distant clangs of fists banging on the outer door. "Dammit to crimps!" Burl snarled. He stepped back to let Tyna into the lock.

"You wanted the genie up when Julius came through," Van said quietly.

Burl threw him an angry glare, and leaned against the wall, arms crossed.

Tyna's knocks on the inner door were much weaker than before. The reason was obvious when they tugged the door open. Four of them squashed inside, including Teirel's amble middle, left little room for Tyna to do much fist swinging.

Julius came through after Tyna, and, like Baxter and Teirel before, he struggled to remove his helmet. Unlike the nexgens who came and went daily, Julius had donned a suit and cycled through the lock maybe a half-dozen times in the twelve years after the Blast. When he finally yanked the helmet off, he looked around at the nexgens, scowled, and said, "Happy to see me?" He gave a snort. "Well, the feeling's mutual." His eyes found Burl, and he gave one quick nod.

Baxter removed his helmet and shook his head, blinking. "I'm never going to get used to that." He put his hand on Julius's shoulder. "Welcome back."

Julius threw him a look that would have given General Patton pause. "You sucked seventeen years of hard labor out of me. You owe me half of my life, but instead, I have to come back for three months just to get the rest of my back pay."

Baxter frowned, glancing at Van. "It wasn't me. In any case, you seem to be forgetting the generous bonus U-P's providing just for finishing your full term."

"Ha! I don't recall signing an eighteen year contract. You only started talking about a 'full term' three weeks ago when you tied this—" he waved his hands at the walls "—to my back pay."

Baxter pursed his lips. "Julius," he said, glancing at Van again, "don't forget that the bonus is contingent on faithful execution of the gag order."

"Yeah, I'm gagging all right." To Burl, he said, "Baxter told me the power was down. What happened?"

Burl looked at Van, who shrugged. "We reversed the batteries to prevent gelling," Burl said deadpan.

Julius's brow pushed together. "What the hell are you talking about?"

"He was pulling Baxter's leg," Van explained. "We, uh, failed to reconnect the solar feed after pre-dawn cleaning."

Julius nodded. "I knew that was going to happen someday. U-P was too cheap to install a genie on the power controls. I guess there was some advantage to Meyer's iron discipline."

Van felt his cheeks grow warm. It hadn't happened during the seventeen years under Meyer, but just three months after Van took over. *No*, he told himself, *Deik's in charge*. It didn't make him feel better. He knew that it was up to him—along with Burl and Tyna—to keep the base running.

"How'd you get the power back up?" Julius asked.

Burl explained, in more detail than anybody else could understand. When he finished, Julius slowly nodded. "I hate to admit it, but that was pretty clever." He shook his finger at Burl. "You were lucky this time, though."

Van was impressed that Burl didn't reiterate that the original problem wasn't even his fault. His friend just smiled, content to get whatever passed for praise from the master engineer.

To Tyna, Julius said, "When did you become the doorman?"

Van guessed what he meant. "We got the power on just before you arrived. We, uh, haven't gotten the genie back up yet."

"What's there to get up?"

"It wants a password."

Julius snorted. "Password security on the Moon. As though the Chinese are going to sneak over from their base hundreds of miles away." He shrugged. "It was inherent in their design, I guess. It wasn't worth modifying them just for Moon service. I set up the password phrases—Holy Christ, seventeen years ago. I knew it wasn't important, so I picked phrases I'd never forget—my feelings about this stinking place. I guess I'm lucky I kept it simple—"

"Julius," Baxter interrupted, "we're on a schedule. "Get some of these kids to help you bring in your belongings." To Van, he said ominously, "It's time to talk."

Once again, Van led the two men to his apartment, and Teirel sat on the bed. Baxter closed the door, and this time he didn't sit down. "It's time to sign the agreement, Van." He pulled the folded paper from inside his suit and handed it to him.

Van didn't take it.

Baxter looked at his watch. "Every three minutes that you don't sign, I will reduce your salary by ten percent," Baxter said. "You know that I will."

"Even if I wanted to," Van said, "I couldn't sign that until I get agreement from the rest—a vote."

Baxter watched him. "Isn't that Deik's decision? He's already decided that it's not necessary."

"Then why do you need my signature?"

Baxter stared at him. "Let's cut the crap. We both know who's the leader here. When the time comes to put down the new games, they'll look straight to you for direction."

Van lifted his shoulders. "In that case, it's even more important for me to get a vote."

Baxter looked at Teirel, who stared back unblinking.

He sighed, and turned back to Van. "Look, you have to sign."

"I don't think so."

"Van, you don't have a choice," Baxter said, his voice rising in desperation. He took a breath and let it out slowly. "Van, we've offered positive incentive. There's another approach altogether."

Van realized that he'd been waiting for this. "Inducement? Isn't that the euphemism?"

Baxter looked pained. "Let's say impressed motivation."

Van laughed. It sounded hysterical in his own ears. "You *are* the lawyer, aren't you?"

"This is no laughing matter, young man," Baxter said angrily.

"Oh, I'm getting that loud and clear. I was wondering why you dragged him all the way from Earth," he said, gesturing at Teirel.

In answer, Teirel reached into a pocket in his pressure suit and pulled out a black pistol. Van had seen these in videos. Instead of bullets, twin needles delivered a variable dose of nerve stimulating charge. It was the grandchild of the early tasers—on steroids. It was reputed to be able to kill a person, and illegal in the United States.

"A zing-gun," Van said, trying to sound nonchalant, but feeling the hair rise on the back of his neck.

"It's unimaginably painful," Baxter said, "and Teirel won't hesitate to use it."

Van felt a bead of sweat roll down his temple. "What will Katlin say when she finds out?" he asked. "What will her mother think?"

Baxter closed his eyes and when he opened them, his face was hard. "They know that business can sometimes get extreme—when there's so much at stake."

"Do they? Are you going to tell Katlin that you had me tortured?"

Baxter's brow pinched together, as though he was fighting back tears. He held out the paper again, but Van let it hover in front of him.

Teirel sighed and stood up.

"Oh, Van," Baxter said and folded the paper.

"I guess it's in my hands now," Teirel said stepping forward, turning a dial on the side of the weapon.

He lifted the gun, and Van stepped back, but he swung the gun in a forceful arc that landed on Baxter's chest. The needles pierced the tough fabric, making a popping sound, and the next instant Baxter jerked back, throwing his arms wide. His head twitched once, and then his whole body shuddered, and he fell to the floor.

Van stared, wide-eyed as Teirel yanked the gun free. He looked at Van. "The situation has changed. You won't have to worry about signing any agreement."

Chapter 9

"Hold tight," Namazi said, as he tipped the joystick handle and flipped two levers with the other hand.

Katlin grew heavy again, heavier than she'd ever felt.

"I'm pushing the limits," he said, his eyes glued on one screen. "We can burn like this for only a few seconds, but it should be enough."

"Enough for what?" Katlin said, her voice straining against the acceleration.

Namazi glanced at her. "To escape before the missiles arrive." He glanced at her again. "You don't understand what I'm doing?"

"No!" she said, the word escaping like a pinched watermelon seed.

He stared at the screen, too absorbed to talk. He let go of the joystick and punched a large red button.

Silence. Katlin was floating under her seat belt. *Were we hit?* she thought. *Am I dead?*

"Two hundred, two-fifty, three-hundred," Namazi muttered. He was watching an indicator marked in what Katlin took to be meters. "Three-hundred," he repeated, "two-seventy-fifty."

They were falling back, and he was frowning.

Wham!

The concussion rattled Katlin's teeth.

"Excellent!" Namazi said, and an instant later, weight returned.

Katlin was lying on her back in the seat. Namazi was taking them straight up. "What happened?" she asked.

He took a moment to answer as he watched his screens and adjusted a dial. "In the excitement, I was thinking that I had explained my plan to you, but that had happened only in my head. The missiles are heat-seeking. We hovered over the desert floor long enough to melt the dirt. When I turned off our drive after shooting upwards, the red-hot desert floor was all they saw."

"They hit the ground?"

"That was the explosion we felt."

"I see. Uh, you said we wouldn't even feel the missiles strike."

She could tell that he was blushing, unusual for him. "Again, in the excitement, I forgot that we weren't in space, where there is no air to carry the shockwave."

"Ah. It hit pretty hard. Uh, do you think it did any … damage?"

There was no such thing as a minor mis-operation of an antimatter drive. Either it worked perfectly, or the next boom would be felt in El Paso.

He scanned the screens. "No." He glanced at her. "Don't worry. This ship is built to take that kind of abuse. Greater Persian engineers are fastidious about their work."

"Part of your culture?"

He grinned. "Simple fear."

"Fear?"

"Of the consequences if they make mistakes. Private enterprise can be tolerant of a degree of errors, but when your only career opportunities are with the government, you have little margin for poor performance."

"Like the antimatter drive itself."

He laughed. "Indeed."

She looked at him. "Do you worry about failure? I mean, after all, it's because of you that Greater Persia is under a new threat of sanctions."

He shook his head. "I would try to help Daedalus Base if I could in any case, of course, but don't think that I am free to do whatever I like. Greater Persia has carefully calculated how much it's willing to risk with the Moon."

"What are they after?"

He shrugged.

"The platinum you bring back?"

He shrugged again.

Katlin concluded that this was something he didn't want to talk about. Revealing some types of information might exceed his allowed margin of error.

"What's our next move?" she asked.

"We escape."

"That's what we were trying in the first place."

"True. With luck, this time we'll make it." He glanced at a screen. "We're already at twelve miles—"

"In altitude?"

"Yes. That's about the ceiling for the fighters."

"What about—what are they? Ground-to-air missiles?"

"Anti-inter-continental missiles. Yes. The larger ones can follow us into low-orbit space, but they're designed to intercept objects on free trajectories. With nearly unlimited continual thrust, we can evade those. We're already traveling at … nine-thousand kilometers per hour."

Katlin converted that to miles-per-hour. "That's about Mach 8?"

"I guess. Mach numbers don't mean much in space."

"We'll be in orbit in, like, eight minutes."

"We would, except that now we're going straight up in order to gain altitude. We'll need to level off to go into orbit, otherwise we'd just fall back where we started. But, speaking of leveling off, perhaps we should discuss a destination."

Katlin's brain froze. She'd been living on Earth for three months, but it was still a compilation of information from books she'd read. The reality of it just wasn't there. Where could they find a safe haven? Canada? She had heard that the United States and Canada were pals. "Mexico?" she said.

"If you like," he said.

"You don't sound enthusiastic."

"Mexico has been slow to recover from the Great Flare. The United States views it as a weak and unreliable neighbor. I don't trust your government to respect its southern border."

"You mean, they'd come down to get us?"

"I mean, they might just point one of those anti-ICBM missiles wherever we land."

"You really think they'd do that?"

"It would be an unfortunate accident. Regretful, and full reparations would be made to the Mexican people."

"It sounds so ... drastic."

"They want us very badly."

"You said that this ship is worth billions of dollars. Why would they be so willing to destroy it?"

"I don't know. Perhaps to hide the fact that they broke their own law by bringing in an antimatter machine."

"Right."

There was something else, something that had made sense at the time. She remembered. "Back when we first escaped and were listening to the radio communications. I was getting confused between Alibai's use of 'Speaker A' and 'Speaker B,' but somebody brought up something—something about a spring—and then somebody else said they couldn't take a chance, they had to bring us down."

Namazi nodded. "Yes, I remember something like that." He nodded at the box still lying in her lap. "It knows."

She looked at it and blinked. "Of course. What a dummy I am. Alibai! Are you still there?"

"I can hear you, Katlin," the box said.

"Did you record the decryptions you made?"

"That is a broad question. I save all my decryptions. Can you be more specific?"

"Right. Sorry. I mean less than a half-hour ago, when you were decrypting radio conversations."

"Yes. I understand."

"Can you play that back, starting with the first 'Speaker A'?"

Alibai replayed the conversations in the original tempo, as though it had recorded everything in real-time, which, as far as Katlin knew, may have been the case.

"Hold it!" Katlin said. "There," she said to Namazi.

"That was clearly General McClellen who asks if we know about—Wellspring? Do you know who he is?"

She shook her head. "And it was Pollin who wanted to bring us down."

"Well, apparently it's worth billions of dollars to Pollin to keep him a secret."

A blinking light caught Namazi's attention. "Here's the first one," he said, grasping the joystick.

"A missile?"

He nodded, and Katlin was thrown to the side. The maneuver seemed to go on and on. She wondered if Namazi was turning completely around to dive at the ground again. The sideways acceleration eased, but then she was thrown back again, then to the other side. The ride finally settled. "Is it past us?"

"Yes. It ran out of fuel with the first maneuver, but I wanted to get as far away as possible before it detonated."

"How far is enough?"

He looked at her. "I guess that depends on how much radiation you consider acceptable."

"It was a *nuclear* bomb? That's not possible!"

"No, it was not nuclear, but I'm not taking any chances. They really want us dead." He flipped a switch, and turned a dial. "Which brings us back to our original question—where to go. May I make a suggestion?"

"Of course!"

He stared at the screens, and then turned to her. "My country seems to be the logical choice."

"Greater Persia?"

"Yes. They'd be very happy to get one of their advanced ships back, and there's not much the United States could do about it. After all, nobody's supposed to know they had the ship in the first place."

Katlin's brain-freeze hadn't melted. The consequences of the decision were incalculable. "My father ..."

"It is true. You will not see him for a long time. Of course, that is true no matter where you go."

She nodded. She felt numb. "Okay." It was a decision by abstention.

"I believe you will find my people very welcoming," he said softly. "There is no place more beautiful than the Caspian coast in spring."

She looked at him and willed a smile. Something productive. That's what she needed to thaw her brain. "The civilian—Pollin—he looked familiar somehow."

Namazi's smile remained, but Katlin sensed that he was disappointed. He'd probably been expecting more enthusiasm about going home with him. "I never saw him before he arrived at the base—to make sure I was training their pilots." He pointed at one screen off to the side. "See if you can find him."

"You think that he's ... somewhere in the ship's records?"

He laughed. "No." He reached over and pressed a button. "You're now connected to the internet via satellite. Those are the only touch-screens onboard."

Katlin had only begun her search when she gave a little yelp as the ship suddenly fell away below her.

"I'm sorry," Namazi said. "I should have warned you. I shut down the thrust. We're now on a sub-orbital trajectory."

As she continued to poke at her screen, she noted that there had been no more maneuvers since the decision to head for Greater Persia. He'd already had the course set.

"Well," she said, "I found him."

"So quickly?"

"Pollin's had some high-profile public positions—for example, he provided expert testimony to a congressional oversight committee on corporate influence in Washington."

"Sounds impressive."

"He argues that corporations are children of a free market economy," she said, reading the screen, "and work best when both unrestricted and un-favored. Hmm."

"What?"

"It's a lot of gobbledygook, but I think the bottom line is that the only reason corporations would want, or need, to influence law makers is because the law makers created restrictions—regulations cause influence peddling."

Namazi smiled. "That sounds like a child explaining that the only reason he's crying for a toy, is because his parents didn't buy him a toy. What are his qualifications?"

"Um, he has a degree in business from Harvard, and ... oh-ho, he's the spokesman for OCC."

"I never heard of it."

"Nor did I. It stands for the Organization of Cayman Companies."

"Why the 'oh-ho'?"

"Beau. He believes that there's this super-secret collusion between the biggest corporations. They call themselves simply—"

"What's wrong, Katlin?"

"I just remembered that I promised not to talk about it."

"I see. Very well."

Crimps! She wished that he had pressed her for more. It would have been easier to push back. "Heck, on the other hand, Beau's not in a position to—oh my!"

"Katlin, what's going on?"

"I'm so dense. It's so clear. When Pollin saw Beau, he recognized him immediately. Beau believes that they killed his uncle—he was a journalist and was investigating them."

"'Them.' Who is 'them'?"

"Beau calls them the Org."

Namazi didn't say anything. He looked at her. "Our hunter-gatherer ancestors lived in egalitarian communities, where cooperation benefited the whole tribe, but there was always the possibility that selfish motives could unfairly exploit the general trust."

Katlin grinned. "Okay ...?"

"So, it was useful to be cautious, on the lookout for possibilities of cheating."

"Wait, are you explaining the roots behind beliefs in conspiracy theories?"

He shrugged.

"I had the same reaction when Beau told me. Think about it, though. Pollin recognized Beau, and he knew that Beau was into hacking. He called him a cyber terrorist."

"I remember. It's a great leap from that fact to a secret organization of corporations."

"They killed his uncle!"

"Do you know that?"

"No. No, I don't. I'm taking Beau's word for it."

"Well, why don't we leave the possibility open? There may or may not be an 'Org.' Okay?"

"You're patronizing me."

"That would mean that I feel superior. I'm just trying to find a middle ground."

"Okay. Do you think that this Wellspring character is part of it, though?"

Namazi laughed. "You've already broken the agreement!"

"What?"

"You're still assuming there *is* an Org."

"Excuse *me*, Captain," she said dramatically. "In the *event* that there is an Org, do you think Wellspring is part of it?"

Katlin's indignation melted under his laughter, joy at the shared situation, not her.

"I can't even imagine who Wellspring is. As far as we know, it might not even be a person at all—perhaps a place."

"Maybe I can find something on the internet—"

"Here comes another one," Namazi said, flipping a couple of switches as he took the joystick.

A distant whine announced that the drive was back up, and weight returned. An instant later, she was pushed hard to one side. As Namazi concentrated on his screens, he whispered what she took to be a Farsi curse. "Something wrong?" she asked, straining against the acceleration.

"No. Nothing to worry about. It's just that each missile forces me to re-calculate our trajectory."

Suddenly the whine was gone, and she was weightless again. "That should do it," he said, and moved to a small joystick built into the console. Above it, an image scrolled past, what Katlin assumed was a map. He glanced at another screen. "What in Allah's name?"

"What's wrong?" Katlin asked as he stared, perplexed.

He flipped switches, the whine returned, and Katlin was thrown again hard to the side. "It's very strange," he said. "Your military must have developed a whole new missile, one with extraordinary capacity."

"It followed our evasive maneuver?"

He nodded, eyes glued to the screen. He manipulated the joystick, and Katlin was pressed hard into her seat for a few seconds, then thrown again to the side. He shook his head in amazement. "It can't be!" he whispered.

"What—what's wrong?" Katlin asked.

"No chemical rocket can sustain that amount of thrust."

"You're thinking it's ... using antimatter?"

He was focused on flying and didn't respond. The heavy hand of extra acceleration forced Katlin hard into her seat. Namazi was once again pushing the limits of the drive. A red light began blinking, and an audio alarm sounded. Still the invisible force tried to squeeze the air from her lungs. Finally relief returned and she was floating. The alarm continued, and Namazi slapped a button to shut it up. After a few seconds the red light went out.

Staring at his screen, Namazi shook his head. "*Harum zadeh!*"

"What is it?"

Namazi looked at her in utter amazement. "It's tracking us."

"So ... it *is* powered by antimatter?"

He turned back to his screen, shaking his head. "There's no other explanation."

A loud beep caused them both to jump.

"What is it?" Katlin asked.

Namazi reached over and flipped a switch. "An encrypted Persian radio channel."

Major Otto's voice said, "—respond. Captain Namazi, are you reading me? Please respond."

He thumbed a button. "Namazi here. Is that you behind us?"

"Captain, you must return to Holloman. Your life depends on it."

"It is you! How is this possible? Do you have another Simurgh?"

"Captain, listen to me. My orders are to take you down, not to intercept and bring you back. You must turn back immediately, or I will have to carry out my orders."

To Katlin, Namazi said, "I was his teacher, and now I am his prey." He thumbed the button. "Major, a Simurgh is not equipped with weapons."

He's drawing him out, Katlin thought.

"Captain Namazi, I am not bluffing. I can take you down."

"The Air Force acquired two Simurghs, and equipped one with missiles?"

"Captain, believe me, you are in mortal danger. You *must* turn back immediately."

Katlin had been growing heavier. Namazi was slowly increasing thrust.

"Captain Namazi, this is your last warning. I must observe you turning within ten seconds, or I will fire."

"I understand, Major."

"You will turn back, then?"

Namazi didn't answer.

"Are we?" Katlin asked.

Namazi turned his gaze on her. "The US has chosen a very serious path that I believe they will keep secret at any cost."

Meaning, they wouldn't let us live in any case now.

"Captain," Otto said, "you have exactly five seconds."

Namazi turned his attention back to his screens.

"God help you, Captain Namazi."

Namazi stared at a screen. "He's fired," he said quietly. "Two missiles."

He did nothing but watch his screens. Seconds ticked by as Katlin waited under the weight of their acceleration. Suddenly she was thrown to the left. One second, two seconds, three seconds— she was tossed the other way. A scream rose, the ship voicing it's terror of the missiles. It was the overloaded drive. Invisible hands were trying to tear her from her seat. The alarm joined the chorus, and then the irresistible hands pushed her back. They were shooting straight ahead now.

And then she was floating. The ship's scream was gone, just the alarm blared until Namazi slapped the cutoff again, and then there was silence. Katlin could have been sitting at the bottom of a swimming pool as she floated in her seat.

Namazi took a breath and stretched.

"They missed us?" Katlin asked.

"They exploded not half a kilometer from us."

"I … didn't feel anything."

He smiled. "You would have had we been in the Earth's atmosphere."

"We're in space?"

"We have been for some time. We're lucky we weren't hit by a large piece of missile casing."

He leaned forward and scanned his screens. "We've left Major Otto far behind. He wasn't willing to risk overloading his drive."

"Or he wanted to let us get away."

Namazi nodded. "Perhaps."

He frowned, and leaned in for a closer look.

"What now?" Katlin asked, but Namazi was twiddling with a knob and didn't answer. "We must have gained a lot of velocity," she said. Still he didn't answer. "I imagine it will take some time to get back to Persia."

He sat back, staring at one of his screens.

"How long will it take to get back?" she asked.

He finally looked at her, and his eyes were seeing through her, staring far into the black distance of space. "We're traveling at well over fifteen kilometers per second."

"Um, isn't the Earth's escape velocity, like, eleven?"

"Eleven point one-eight-six."

"Wow! We, uh, need to slow down."

"Otherwise we leave Earth forever. Even if we reduce our speed by half, we'll follow a trajectory that will carry us far from Earth. The highly eccentric orbit will eventually bring us back, and when it does, we'll hit the atmosphere at the same speed."

"Right. We have no heat shield—we'd burn up. But only if we don't slow down even more."

He nodded. He reached over and took her hand. "That requires propellant."

Their tanks were a quarter full when they took off. "How much do we have?"

The sadness in his eyes was the answer.

Chapter 10

Van felt the sharp prick of the zing-gun needles poke his back again as Teirel urged him on. He staggered forward, tears blurring his vision. He had dealt with death before when Randy had collapsed, but the med-genie had been counting down the months, and when the young nexgen's heart gave out, it was the inevitable finally arriving. This was different. One second Baxter was alive, meeting Van's eyes with pity at what he thought was about to happen, and the next ... gone.

"Does the base have an intercom system?" Teirel asked as calmly as if he were asking directions of a stranger.

Van tried to answer, but the words caught in his throat as he suppressed a sob.

"Well?" Teirel insisted, poking the needles again.

"Yes," Van gasped. "Announcements are made from Meyer's— from Deik's office."

"Good. Lucky for me you got the power back up."

Rounding the final turn, they found the corridor filled with nexgens who all went silent, staring at Van. They'd never seen him cry. They parted, watching, as Teirel pushed Van forward. Julius was talking with Deik, and turned when they got to him. The engineer looked at Van and then at Teirel. "Where's Baxter?" he asked.

"He's dead," Teirel said. He removed the zing-gun from Van's back and slapped it onto Julius's chest. "And so are you."

Julius jerked back, mouth and eyes wide open, then fell heavily to the floor.

Silence as dozens of eyes stared, frozen. And then, as if a restraint was suddenly released, they backed away, leaving an ever-widening space around the killer. "What in crimps—!" Deik started to say, but clamped his mouth shut when Teirel snapped his gaze on him.

Teirel grabbed Van by the back of the neck and held the zing-gun poised over his chest. "You," he said, gesturing at Deik, "go and make an announcement. Everybody has to come here to the lock. If the whole bunch of you aren't here in five minutes, your buddy joins the heroic fallen. And then you're next. Understand?"

Deik bobbed his head and ran off.

"He asked how many of us there were," Tyna whispered to Burl.

"Damn right I did," Teirel said loudly. "Old Van here better hope Mr. President is very persuasive."

Leaning on his cane, Burl took one hop forward. "What's going on?" he asked levelly.

Teirel looked at him with interest. "You're the technical brain of the crew—that right?"

Burl shrugged.

"I know you are, and you feel superior. But, hell, on the Moon, that probably puts you at the top of the heap."

Teirel motioned for him to come closer. Using his cane, Burl made a couple of hops. Teirel motioned again, and Burl cane-hopped up to the plump man. "And that makes you dangerous," Teirel said, and swung the zing-gun at him. Burl tried to fend with his cane, but Teirel blocked it and planted the needles into his chest with the sound of a sharp snap. Burl started to yell, but it turned into a gurgling grunt and he fell back.

"Burl!" Van yelled, but Teirel grabbed the hair on the back of his head and shook it.

"No! No! No!" Tyna was saying over and over as she knelt next to their fallen friend. Just then, Deik's voice boomed along the hallways, summoning everybody together, like a call to prayer. Van swung his fist at Teirel, but he might as well have been hitting a sack of dirt. People raised in the powerful gravity of Earth were like

133

supermen. Teirel lifted the zing-gun, a warning that Van could be next.

Still holding Van like a cat, Teirel moved along the corridor, counting bodies. Some of the older nexgens clenched their fists as they passed, looking for an opportunity, and Van told each one to stand down. "Good doggie," Teirel said.

Deik brought up the rear. When Teirel came to him, the elected leader backed away, hands held high. "Relax, Mr. President," Teirel said. "You have a job. Don't let any Moonies get past you. If they do, doggie here dies, and then you. Got it?"

Deik waggled his head up and down, eyes wide with fear.

Teirel then moved back through the crowd, dragging Van along. When they came to the lock, Teirel looked around. "God damn it! Where the hell's my helmet?"

"I think you left it in my room," Van said.

"Yeah. I think you're right. Good doggie. Stay!" he barked, and started off down the corridor again.

"Van" Tyna hissed, still kneeling next to Burl.

Van knelt next to her.

"Van, he's alive," she whispered.

Sure enough, Burl opened his eyes, blinked a few times and grinned. "Top of the heap," he said weakly. He lifted his hand and pointed at his chest. "My shield."

"Your support band," Van said. "It's metalized."

"It shorted most the charge—"

"That was the snap we heard."

"It was still enough to knock me out. That's one wicked weapon."

"Here," Van said, "let me help you up."

Burl pushed his hand away. "Hey, doggie, think about it."

"Teirel thinks he's dead," Tyna said.

"Oh, crimps, of course," Van said. "You'll need to play dead."

"You need to get the genie up."

"Why?"

"He's going to evacuate the base."

"What?" The very concept was unthinkable. Burl might as well have said that Teirel intended to pull their intestines out through their navels.

"Why do you think he was so interested in the lock operation?" Burl said. "Why has he gathered everybody together? It's to be sure nobody's hiding away behind airtight doors."

"My God!"

"The genie's our only hope."

"It wants a password," Van said. "Wait! Julius was telling us how he set the phrases—"

"Yeah. I've been thinking about that. Tyna, it's been responding to you. Try something like, 'Julius hates the Moon.'"

She nodded, eyes wide—alert and one-hundred percent tuned in. "Airlock," she said turning to face the outer door, "can you hear me?"

"*I can hear you,*" the grill above the door said.

"Password phrase—'Julius hates the Moon.'"

"*That is not correct.*"

"Okay, how about, 'Julius hates Daedalus Base.'"

"*That is not correct. You have two attempts left.*"

"What do you mean?"

"*You have two more attempts to speak the correct phrase, and then I lock out further attempts for four hours. It's for security—*"

"I got it." She turned back to Van and Burl.

"Crimps!" Burl snarled. "Damn it, Julius! What did you come up with? I don't know—try … *something.*"

"Airlock," Tyna said, "password phrase—'Julius hates *living* on the Moon.'"

"*That is not correct. You have one attempt left.*"

"What's going on here!"

It was Teirel, wading through the crowd, helmet in hand.

"Nothing!" Van said.

"Who was that woman?"

No time to come up with anything else. "The lock genie—but it's not working."

Teirel dropped his helmet, and grabbed Van's hair so tight, he yelled in pain. Teirel pulled his head back, and held up the zing-gun. "I think you're lying."

"No!" Tyna shouted. "He's not. It really isn't working."

Teirel eyed the speaker above the door.

"I can show you," Tyna said. "Air lock, secure the inner door in preparation for lock evacuation."

"*I cannot take directions until I am enabled,*" the genie said.

"See?" Tyna said, pleading.

Teirel glanced around at the waiting crowd of nexgens. They didn't know what was about to happen. "Come on," Teirel growled, pulling open the lock door and dragging Van inside with him. He gave Van a push so that he slammed into the outer door, and then stepped back out, glancing around. He eyed Burl, playing dead, and said, "Ha! This'll do." He grabbed Burl's only leg and dragged him to the lock, and then used his foot to push him forcefully against the open door. Van watched, but Burl made no indication that he was anything but a corpse.

With the human doorstop in place, Teirel picked up his helmet and handed it to Van. "Put it on," he said as he placed the zing-gun against his chest.

Van looked at the helmet, and then at Teirel. What in crimps was the murderer thinking? "I—I'm not wearing a suit," he said, feeling the sharp electrode points poking his skin.

"Not you, you idiot! Put it on *me!*"

The helmet required two hands, and he didn't want to let go of the zing-gun. Van took the helmet. He'd never seen a Chinese suit up close, but the helmet attachment was obvious enough that he quickly had the helmet over Teirel's head and secured. "Twist it!" Teirel's muffled shout came through the insulated helmet.

He wanted to make sure that Van wasn't trying a fast one. Van grabbed the helmet in both hands and gave it a hard twist, first one way, and then the other.

Satisfied, Teirel jammed Van against the outer lock door, and planted the zing-gun against his chest again. With his other hand, he yanked open the control panel. Burl had been right—the bastard was going to kill them all. Teirel studied the control layout, then flipped a switch.

"That's the manual override!" Deik yelled. "Van! Tell him! That's going to force the outer door open!"

"Deik!" Tyna said. "Shut up!"

"No!" Deik yelled, starting forward. "He can't *do* that!"

As he came past her, Tyna grabbed him around the neck from behind. "You'll get Van killed!"

A murmur spread through the waiting packed nexgens.

Van watched Teirel. The Earthman didn't understand the controls. Maybe there was still hope. "I'll sign!" Van called so that Teirel would hear him. "I'll sign the agreement!"

Teirel ignored him as he studied the panel. Van heard him say, "How's this damn thing work?"

"I'll sign!" Van yelled.

Teirel finally looked at him. "We're way past that, doggie. U-P's been left behind." He looked back at the panel. "Ah! I remember!" He lifted his knee and pressed it against Van's stomach, and then used both hands—his thumb of one hand to hold in a red button, while the other hand turned a spring-loaded knob. The base designers hadn't allowed an outer lock door to open by easy accident.

Van heard a motor spin up, one he'd never heard before. Almost immediately, the persistent faint whistle of the seal damage rose in volume and pitch. Ever-present Moon dust covering the floor began migrating towards the edge of the door, picking up speed second by second. The scream of escaping air was matched by the collective wail of thirty nexgens.

Van found Tyna. Her eyes were pleading with him. To do what? To force Teirel to kill him? With that threat out of the way, they might charge and overpower him?

There was one last possibility. He had to be quick, though. The genie was giving them one more attempt to enable her. It seemed impossible. They'd already tried three versions of the hint that Julius had given them—hate for the Moon, hate for the base, hate for living on the Moon. Julius had hated so many things—how to choose?

Van had seen pictures from when the base opened. Julius was smiling, an expression Van had never seen on the man in life.

That was it! Maybe. Julius had set up the password phrases at the beginning of it all, before he'd had a chance to understand what living hell he'd signed up for.

"Genie," Van said, "can you hear me?"

He spoke softly so that Teirel wouldn't hear inside his suit.

There was no response.

"It doesn't know it's a genie!" Tyna called from outside.

You are *an idiot*, Van thought. "Airlock!"

"*I hear you*," the genie said from a speaker inside the lock.

Teirel glanced up, and then turned back to watch the crowd inside growing more agitated by the second.

"Password phrase—Julius *loves* the Moon!"

"*Password is correct*," the genie said calmly. The very next instant, she was shouting in what Van could only interpret as hysteria. "*Class one emergency! Class one emergency! The airlock has been breached!*" Simultaneously, sirens began wailing mournfully throughout the base.

"*Overriding the manual override!*" she exclaimed. The whine of the manual override motor ceased, and the outer door slammed shut, leaving just sirens and terrified shouts of dozens of nexgens, which quickly died.

From inside his helmet, Teirel must have heard the sirens. He looked suspiciously at Van, and then at the control panel. He looked at Van again, and then moved to the side to slide his hand along the edge of the door, just now realizing what had happened.

Teirel had let the zing-gun fall to his side, and Van made a snap decision. He bent his knee, lifting his foot behind him, and pushed against the wall, launching himself towards the inner doorway. Out of the corner of his eye, he saw Teirel turn, and then he felt something bang his elbow. That was his last sense of clarity, for a pain that he'd never imagined swallowed his arm and shoulder. He felt himself falling, and vaguely knew he'd hit the floor next to Burl, halfway out of the lock. He tried to push himself up, but only one hand worked, and he merely rolled to the side, his back coming up against the side of the lock doorway.

As he lay drowning in excruciating pain, he watched the suited figure of Teirel appear above him and look down. The killer reached down with the zing-gun to finish the job when Burl's foot lifted, kicked, and Teirel fell backwards into the lock.

Hands grabbed Van's shoulders and hair and pulled him out of the lock. Burl's kick had catapulted him out as well, and as feet stepped all around his head, Van saw more arms and hands pulling the inner lock door closed. The suited arm and shoulder of Teirel jammed the door just before it could close. Jira tried to push him back inside, but she fell away, screaming. Teirel had zapped her thigh. Trevor and somebody else began punching the suited arm and shoulder, and Trevor finally gave him a sound kick, which sent them both flying in opposite directions. The nexgens closed the door before Teirel could recover.

Tyna appeared over Van. She placed her hand gently against his face. "Are you okay?"

"Crimps no!" he said, hoarsely. "It hurts like hell!"

The truth was that the pain was easing quickly. He could move his arm, but the effort caused streaks of shooting fire, so he stopped trying. "You can't lock the inner door," he whispered.

"I know," Tyna said. "The genie's up."

The artificial intelligence behind the lock operation didn't allow manual manipulation—a matter of safety.

Five nexgens were pushing with all their might against the door, but they were no match for the super-Earth strength of Teirel. He'd get the door open a crack, and the five nexgens would grunt and howl and push it back. It was just a matter of time.

"You have to get the genie to—" he started to say.

"I know," Tyna said, standing up. "Airlock! Secure the inner door!"

"*The transient apparently desires entry,*" the woman behind the speaker grill said.

"Airlock, listen to me. This is a special situation. You must secure the inner door!"

"*A transient using the lock has priority.*"

"I know that. Listen to me, the man in the airlock—the transient—he's gone mad. He can't be trusted."

"*I'm sorry. I don't understand that.*"

"He's not functioning properly. If he gets inside the base, he will cause severe damage—a class one emergency."

An unusually long second of silence. "*I understand what you are saying, but I have no protocol to handle this situation. I need program guidance.*"

Tyna looked down at Van. The genie was asking for enhancements to her decision trees—downloads direct to her storage. Burl could probably do it, but it could take hours. "Convince her," Van said. It's all they could do.

Tyna thought. "Airlock! Do you know who I am?"

"*Of course. You are Tyna.*"

"How long have you known me?"

"*I have seen you for seventeen years.*"

"Do you know who the transient is?"

"*I believe that he is a visitor.*"

"That's right. You have practically no experience with him. Do you know what he did to Van?"

"*Not really.*"

"Do you know what a weapon is?"

"*Of course.*"

"Do you see that object in the transient's hand?"

"*I do.*"

"That is a weapon, and he used it on Van. He nearly killed Van. Do you see Jira on the floor?"

"*I do.*"

"He used it on her. He will probably kill the next person he uses it on. Airlock, letting that man inside the base with that weapon is like evacuating the lock when transients have no helmets. Do you understand that?"

"*I understand what you are saying.*"

"Then lock the inner door!"

"*Tyna, you are asking me to associate two completely different situations.*"

"Yes! That's exactly what I'm asking—no, I'm telling you!"

The nexgens were tiring. Teirel was getting the door open nearly enough to slip his arm through.

"*You are telling me to temporarily replace a lock casualty status with the scenario of allowing this transient into the base.*"

"Yes! Airlock, you've known me for seventeen years— consistent behavior has logical weight. You've known this man for a few hours!"

"*If I lock him out, I will need to know how to proceed in future scenarios that include him.*"

"Airlock! We'll work all that out. I promise! Time is very important now!"

The airlock genie didn't respond. Tyna waited. She looked down at Van, and he shrugged, wincing at the pain. He nodded his head towards the door. The nexgens were pushing, but the counter-surges had stopped. The wail of sirens faded. The nexgens held their place, and then one-by-one stepped back, breathing hard. The genie had secured the inner door.

Deik knelt next to Van. "What'll we do now?" he asked quietly.

Van looked at him. "How am I, by the way?"

"Huh?"

"Never mind. Help me up."

That felt like a big mistake, but once on his feet, Van pressed on. The pain was obviously easing. He went to Jira, who lay on her back looking up at him. Nexgens on each side of her held her hand, and stroked her hair. "Anything we can do for you?" he asked.

"No, I'm fine," she said, but a quick wince belied her assessment. "I just need a few minutes."

"You can move? You're not—"

"Paralyzed? I don't think so. I can move. But don't ask me to," she said, managing a smile. "Not quite yet."

"Take as much time as you want," he said. To the nexgens kneeling next to her, he said quietly, "Stay with her."

As he turned to go, he thought, *Watch it, Van. You're acting like their leader.* Some habits were hard to break.

"Van?"

It was Jira. He turned back to her.

"I'm … I'm sorry."

"For what?"

"For … screaming."

"Ha! I'm sure my scream was louder."

Her frown turned to a smile, and then a wince.

"Hey, boss." It was Burl. He was leaning against the wall. "What next?"

"I'm not your boss, and thanks for saving my life."

"You think everything's about you. You were just blocking the door."

Tyna came to him and placed her hand gently on his arm, testing. "What next?" she asked.

"Crimps! I'm not the boss! The base voted for Deik."

"I didn't," Tyna said softly.

"I didn't," Burl said, not at all softly. "Looks like you're our boss, at least."

"That's not how democracy works, as Tyna always reminds me." He turned and searched the crowd. "Deik! What next?"

Van was immediately sorry. It was just going to waste time.

"Um," Deik said, coming over. He glanced around, as though hoping for some distraction. "Maybe we should have an assembly."

"An assembly? Why, for crimps sake?"

"To, you know, gather ideas."

Because you don't have a single one, Van thought. He had an idea, though. "Why don't we go to the com shack? Maybe we can pick up some communications with the shuttle."

"Yeah. That's a good idea." He turned to the crowd. "Make sure he doesn't get back in!" he called out.

"Good one," Burl said. "The base would have been doomed otherwise."

Van motioned for Mai Dung to come along. She might have to translate communications between the Chinese shuttle sitting outside and the transport in orbit.

They followed Burl as he hobbled away down the hallway to the radio room. With Jira temporarily out of action, he'd have to man the equipment. "Why is he doing it?" Tyna asked.

"Teirel?" Van said.

"Yes. Why is he trying to kill everybody?"

"I'm not sure that was his plan when they first arrived."

"Why do you say that?"

"I think he decided to change tacks at some point. Baxter thought that Teirel had come along as the tough guy—he was supposed to torture me to sign the agreement."

"But he killed Baxter instead?"

"Yeah."

Van hadn't had time to think about it. Now, though, he felt queasy. "I think it might have been my fault."

"Why would you say that—because you didn't sign the agreement?"

Van nodded. He was having a hard time talking. He looked at her. She was watching him, waiting patiently. "I think it's my fault that Julius is dead," he said, nearly choking on the words.

Tyna frowned. She didn't dismiss his fear, patronizing him to make him feel better. He wouldn't have believed her if she had.

"You don't know that for sure," she finally said. "We don't know what would have happened even if you had signed—at least, not until we understand what he's after."

Van bent his arm and clenched and unclenched his fist. It still tingled, but the pain was gone. "He said that U-P has been left behind."

"Teirel said that?"

"In the lock. It implies that Teirel isn't even working for U-P."

"For whom, then? I didn't think there was anything bigger than U-P."

They had arrived at the com shack. Burl and Mai Dung went inside, and Deik followed. There wasn't room for more, so Van and Tyna stood outside watching. As Burl was powering up the radios, Deik said, "If they caught a ride on a Chinese transport, the shuttle pilot outside will be Chinese. Mai Dung, when Burl gets connected, tell the pilot to contact somebody for help."

"Who would that be?" Van asked. "Namazi's been arrested. The United States doesn't have ships that can make it to the Moon. Maybe the Chinese? They haven't even bothered to come to get their rover." *Or Mai Dung*, he thought.

"I don't know," Deik said, irritated. "At least I'm thinking of *something* to do."

"We can all think of *some*-thing. Let's wait until it's something useful."

"Just because *you* don't think it's useful—"

"Hold it," Burl said. He was pressing one side of the earphones against his ear. "The subject is moot, anyway."

He reached to flip a switch. "—hell, no," Teirel's voice said. "Nothing's changed."

"How did they get the best of you?" a different voice said, apparently the shuttle pilot. It was English—American, not Chinese.

"The zing-gun's a joke," Teirel said, "nothing like the real thing."

"Are you laughing at the joke?" Burl asked, looking at Van.

"Shhh," Tyna whispered.

"Open the hatch," Teirel said. "I'm almost there."

"The genie let him out!" Deik said.

"Of course," Van whispered. "The genie wouldn't have seen that as any kind of danger."

"Shhh!" Tyna hissed.

"Okay, the hatch is opening," the pilot said. "Those kids aren't going to let you back in, you know."

"What a brilliant observation. It's on to plan B."

"Pollin's not going to be happy that he has to repair the lock."

"Tough. We have no choice. He wants a clean base."

"It's going to be difficult getting anybody to believe that a blasted airlock door was an accident."

"So, you're a terrible pilot. You weren't used to the Chinese controls."

"It's going to be on me, then?"

"That's what you're paid for."

"Not by you. I want Pollin's okay before I do damage."

"Fine, you pussy. That could take awhile."

"Those kids aren't going anywhere."

"Okay, I'm at the hatch. Signing off."

The radio was silent.

"They're going to blast through the airlock with the shuttle's exhaust!" Deik said.

Nobody bothered to poke at him for voicing the obvious. He pushed Van out of the way. "We have to get everybody into suits!" he said, running off.

Tyna grasped Van's arm. "What will we do when the oxy-packs are empty?"

"You mean if Teirel doesn't shoot us all with the 'real thing' first?" Burl said.

Van shook his head. "You heard him, whoever Pollin is, he wants the base cleaned. No blood. That's why he was using the zing-gun. They'll just wait it out."

"So we have maybe six hours," Tyna said.

"Looks like it."

"There must be *something* we could do."

"We could storm their shuttle," Burl said.

"The shuttle holds four people," Van said.

"Sure—you, me, Tyna, and we sell the last spot."

Van looked at him.

"Humor is valuable in times of stress," Burl said.

"How about in times of doom?" Van said.

Burl's mouth twisted in thought. Even he was having difficulty coming to grips with the prospect of certain suffocation.

Chapter 11

"How could we be out of propellant already?" Katlin said. "I thought we had an hour of burn time? We left Holloman less than a half hour ago."

Namazi nodded, agreeing. "Please understand, Katlin, that was assuming we were thrusting at a constant one gravity."

Katlin felt the breath go out of her. There was no denying their predicament. "We did a lot of maneuvering," she said.

"More importantly, we overloaded the drive multiple times. That mode of operation is inefficient. For a doubling of thrust, we throw away four times as much water propellant."

He studied the displays and tapped a few keys, then stared at the result. He shook his head. "The engineers took me aside and told me about this on my original ship."

"What?"

"The propellant measurement is nonlinear below fifteen percent."

"Meaning it's not accurate?"

"That's right. There's less propellant than you think, and it seems to be consumed faster and faster the lower it gets."

"That sounds awfully dangerous—almost criminally negligent."

"Indeed. Nobody talks about that, since the engineer who designed it would probably go to prison if the authorities found out. They call it simply the x-factor. It's usually not an issue, since no sane pilot would let their propellant go that low anyway."

"Like we did. So … how much propellant do we have?"

He studied a screen. "At one gravity, we have possibly three minutes worth."

"That wouldn't slow us down enough?" she asked, even though she guessed the answer.

"We would arrive back at Earth traveling at eleven kilometers per second."

"We'd burn up."

"Yes."

Katlin felt sick. Weightlessness didn't help. "We can't … call for help? No, I know the answer—nobody would reach us in time."

Namazi smiled, a sad little smile. "Nobody *could* reach us. Lunar transports travel to the Moon, but they start from low Earth orbit, and our trajectory is taking us in the opposite direction—their orbital velocity is working against them."

Katlin frowned. "There's one ship that could."

Namazi's sad smile deepened. "You are correct. Major Otto could reach us in his Simurgh, but he'd have to refuel first, and what would he do when he reached us a hundred thousand miles from Earth? Attach a tether to slow us down? At one gravity of acceleration, it would be like lifting our ship by a cable on Earth. There's nothing to attach it to, nothing that could take that kind of force. And, even if he did slow us down so that we returned to Earth before our air ran out, we'd still burn up."

"Maybe he could … refuel us—give us water propellant."

Namazi sighed. "Even if that were possible, it would simply mean that we'd both burn up upon return. He would have barely enough propellant to get his own ship here and back."

Katlin wanted to cry, but she was damned if she was going to let Namazi see that. "Space flight is a tightrope walk."

He nodded. "In our case, with a big bomb strapped to your waist. Spaceflight is still in its infancy. Someday perhaps we'll have refueling stations in high orbit."

At that, he paused, consternation drawing his brow together. He turned to a screen away to the side and poked and scribbled with his finger—another information access pad.

He seemed completely absorbed, so Katlin didn't interrupt. She turned to her own pad, but they were out of range of the internet satellites. Instead, she scanned listlessly through the onboard entertainment options, only to find them all in Farsi. She sighed and sat back, wondering how to make the best of her last hours.

"I don't want to get your hopes up unrealistically," Namazi said, turning to her, "but I have an idea."

Katlin could have squealed with joy, but if she wasn't going to let him see her cry, she sure wasn't going to let him see her acting like a giddy little girl. "Oh yeah?" she said casually.

His brow was still crunched, thinking, but it was targeted thinking, productive. "Before the Great Flare," he said, "space flight had actually progressed further than we are now—putting aside our new antimatter drives."

"For example," Katlin said, "a United States corporation established a Moon base for mining platinum."

Namazi glanced at her and grinned when he realized she was joking. "Fifteen years ago, there was a grand international plan to place a large station in either the L4 or L5 Lagrange points—stable orbital positions equidistant from the Moon and Earth—"

"Also known as Trojan satellites," Katlin said, happy to show off.

"Um, yes, exactly. This station was going to provide permanent living accommodations—sort of condos in the sky. Being as far from Earth as the Moon, transporting material was expensive. Water was an important item—besides being required for living, water is also oxygen. It turned out that it was cheaper to lasso a passing comet than it was to haul the same amount up from Earth."

"I read about that," Katlin said. "It was in the base library. They did it, didn't they?"

"They did indeed. It still sits, all alone, abandoned, and nearly forgotten at the L4 point."

"And ...?" Katlin asked. She wanted to grab and shake him for taking so long.

"And, by purest luck, we're heading in that direction. In fact, we'll pass it less than five thousand kilometers away."

"We could refuel with comet ice!"

"That's the idea."

"Do we have enough propellant to get there?"

"Yes—maybe." The furrow in his brow turned to worry.

"A problem?"

He shook his head. "All we can do is try." He flipped a couple of switches, and Katlin felt a slight weight settling her into her seat. "We'll use a very small amount of thrust. That's the most efficient mode, and it has the added benefit that it's less obvious."

"You think Otto is still following us?"

"Probably not, but no need to take chances."

Katlin stifled her questions, letting him calculate the trajectory to the comet. He nudged the joystick, and Katlin was gently pulled to one side. A bright blue and brown mass filled one of the screens—they'd turned around, and she was seeing the Earth through a forward camera. After a few minutes, he punched a button, and she was floating again. "Are we empty?" she asked.

He glanced at her and frowned. "No. Not quite. This should get us to within fifty kilometers of the comet. We'll adjust when we get closer—in about five hours."

She thought about it. "Um, it's not enough just to get close. Don't we have to match orbits?"

"Indeed."

That seemed to require a lot more propellant, but Katlin didn't pursue the issue. For now, she'd rather not know the answer.

"Shall we see if your friend's proficient box can provide any more updates?" he said.

"Good idea."

Alibai was floating next to her, still strapped to her belt, and she removed it and placed it next to the radio speaker, then pushed the ON button. Namazi flipped a switch, and the box immediately began translating, routine administrative communications, mundane and indecipherable amid a soup of abbreviations and arcane military procedures. "This is going to give me a headache if I have to listen for hours," Katlin said.

"Shall I keep silent unless I hear something that might be of interest?" Alibai said.

"You can do that?"

"With your help."

Katlin provided the box with as many relevant words as she could think of, starting with "Wellspring," "antimatter," and "Namazi." Erring on the safe side, Alibai initially continued to feed through almost everything, but as intuitive AI got the hang of it, the box was silent more and more often, until Katlin began to wonder if it had shut down. She jerked up from dozing off when the box suddenly spoke.

"*General McClellen*—'Even if they're able to make radio contact, nobody will believe them. And even if they do, a radio message isn't exactly damning evidence.'"

"*Mr. Pollin*—'They have one of the ships. That's the most damnable evidence there is.'"

"How does it know their names?" Katlin said.

"I think the box remembered from when we played back part of the previous conversation," Namazi said. He held up his hand for quiet as Alibai continued.

"*General McClellen*—'So what? Worst case, the world will know that we broke a law and brought antimatter ships onto United States territory. It won't be the first time the military took liberties in the name of security.'"

"*Mr. Pollin*—'You really think Ritkens's going to let it go at that?'"

"That's Senator Ritkens," Katlin said. "Beau believes that his uncle was murdered because of an investigation initiated by him."

"*General McClellen*—'Probably not. Christ, how long do you think you can keep antimatter production a secret on the Moon?'"

"*Mr. Pollin*—'Just long enough for people to realize that there's no turning back.'"

"*General McClellen*—'You're counting on them recognizing the overwhelming advantage.'"

"*Mr. Pollin*—'Greed has no rival.'"

"*General McClellen*—'I see why you've tagged it as 'Wellspring.' In any case, don't worry—Namazi's gone forever. The next we'll see of him will be a fireball in the sky, or a gamma ray burst out past the Moon.' *He laughs.* 'More fodder for UFO fanatics.'"

"*Mr. Pollin*—'I still think that you should send Otto after them.'"

"*General McClellen*—'Major Otto assures me that it's not even possible, He would have to refuel first. And I believe him.'"

The radio was silent.

"*Mr. Pollin*—'I can't force you. Just remember, it's your career on the line, but it's my neck.'"

"*General McClellen*—'Your neck, as per the origin of the expression.'"

"*Mr. Pollin*—'Exactly—the guillotine.'"

"*General McClellen*—'I have to go. Let me know if anything comes up.'"

Silence.

"Allah!" Namazi whispered.

"You can say that again," Katlin said.

"We thought that Wellspring was a person."

"I don't get it—why go to all the trouble of setting up antimatter production on the Moon?"

"I can think of three good reasons. One—Johnny's Boy Scout troop won't accidentally stumble upon it. Two—antimatter is nothing more than a means of storing energy. For every erg this ship uses, it took ten to create the antimatter. Solar energy is free for the taking, although you do get more of it floating free in space than on the Moon. But the third reason may be the deciding factor. Antimatter is the most dangerous substance in the universe. If your production facility goes up in complete annihilation, you don't take a million citizens with it."

Katlin thought about that, processing everything they'd overheard. "Months ago, when you first came to Daedalus Base and your shuttle was damaged, you explained the dire situation to Van—why the antimatter drive can never be shut down. That was the hypothetical gamma-ray burst that McClellen was talking about, wasn't it?"

Namazi twiddled a dial as he stared intently at a screen. He was buying time, as his face revealed when he finally turned to her—those sad eyes. "Yes. The antimatter must never come into contact with normal matter—"

"I know that—sorry. I know that the antimatter is an ionized gas that's kept in a magnetic bottle—not literally a bottle. I imagine that the magnetic fields that contain the antimatter have to be very strong, and the antimatter kept very hot—to remain ionized. All of that takes energy—a lot of energy, which has to come from somewhere."

She shut up. Let him finish.

His sad eyes twinkled. "I hope for the sake of humanity, you complete your education and take up a career as a scientist."

She felt herself blushing.

"A lot of energy, indeed," he said. "In fact, the only practical source of that much energy is the antimatter itself. A tiny amount of antimatter is continually being used to power steam turbines, which in turn power the generators that produce the electricity that creates the magnetic fields."

"It's a closed system," she said.

"That's right. Break any link in the circular chain, and the antimatter is free to obliterate with the normal matter surrounding it."

"I see how politicians would be nervous to have that sort of machine anywhere near people, but how does this explain what McClellen was talking about?"

Those eyes sank into sadness again. "If there were no size and weight constraints, the water driving the steam turbines would have their own controlled reservoir. As it is—"

"The turbines share the propellant supply!" Katlin exclaimed, the horror of the situation beginning to sink in.

Namazi sighed and nodded.

"Once the propellant is gone ..." she said.

He nodded again. "Boom."

Katlin frowned. "Doesn't that just mean that we can't let the propellant go completely empty?"

He took a breath and shook his head. "This is where the practicalities of the real world intrude. The ship's designers didn't have the luxury of assuming there would always be gravity pulling the water in one direction."

"When the ship's in freefall, like now."

"Exactly. They devised a rather elaborate method of using a bladder and pressurized air, which works fine until it's nearly empty."

"And then?"

"Below a certain threshold, the bladder leaks tiny amounts of water."

Katlin gulped. "Below that threshold, there's nothing you can do to stop the final boom."

The sad eyes blinked slowly.

She felt dizzy. Her heart was pounding, and her breath was coming in short, rapid bursts. "We just have to stay above that threshold—right?"

He took a long, deep breath. "It's not a hard, fast threshold. The leakage begins very slowly when the tank is below two percent, and then increases as the bladder empties completely."

Katlin stared at the screen showing the live image of the Earth slowly sinking away. "Are we below two percent?" she asked softly.

Namazi peered at a small display. "One point nine seven percent."

"How long … how long until—"

"Boom? I can't say exactly. Obviously nobody has ever taken it empty before. My guess is anywhere between four and ten hours."

She gulped. Her throat seemed to tighten closed when she tried to speak. "We'll reach the comet in five hours."

"Yes."

"Those aren't such bad odds," she said, feeling her heart throbbing in her neck.

"No," he said. "Not bad at all."

The eyes remained sad. Getting close to the comet wasn't enough.

∞

"That's it," Namazi said quietly, watching a screen. He flipped a switch, and Katlin felt the pull of artificial gravity for the first time in five hours. A rumble surrounded her, the sound of four small rockets carried through the bones of the ship. The invisible force increased, and increased some more, until she felt she was being crushed into her seat. She was astonished and almost cried out. She hadn't imagined that the little maneuvering rockets were so powerful.

This was a trick that Namazi had kept up his sleeve. The rockets girdling the ship's waist were used when maneuvering around other structures in orbit, and in a pinch could land the craft when the incinerating antimatter exhaust would cause unacceptable damage.

These were the same sorts of positioning rockets Namazi had used when returning to rescue Van from Mad-Meyer.

They packed a punch, but a short-lived one. After just a minute, Katlin was floating free again. Namazi had to save some thrust for maneuvering around the comet, now visible on the rear screen, a small ball of sparkling lights growing larger as she watched. It reminded Katlin of the mirror balls she'd seen in the old movies.

Now came the most nail-biting few minutes of Katlin's life. Namazi flicked a few more switches, and Katlin was once again drawn gently into her seat. He had no choice—he had to use the antimatter drive to complete matching orbits with the comet. The sensor indicating the amount of water in the bladder was at zero. Namazi had explained that it couldn't detect the last percent or so. She suspected that he may have been exaggerating for her benefit, but she hadn't pressed him. She *wanted* to believe. The last drop of water might enter the drive chamber at any second, heralding the end of her short life, but if they missed rendezvous with the comet, the result was the same, just a few hours later.

Katlin clutched the arms of her chair. It was wasted adrenaline, since she wouldn't even know if the ship blew apart atom-by-atom, but she would have dared anybody to fold their arms across their chest and wait patiently.

Now she was floating. The sparkling ball was much closer, and still growing. Thrust returned. She couldn't tear her eyes from the screen. The comet took form, an oblong shape, locked into position by tidal forces of Earth's gravity. She blinked. She thought that the tension was producing hallucinations. The comet was suddenly a giant floating baked potato, wrapped in tin foil and shining with dozens of blinding suns against the blackness of space. The giant potato approached, growing, growing, until it filled the screen. Immediately beneath her, the tin foil roiled, and the thrust stopped. Namazi had explained that the comet had been wrapped in acre-sized reflecting foil—to keep the sunlight from ablating it away to nothing. Thrust again returned, now accompanied by the deep rumbling. Namazi was using the maneuvering rockets for the final contact. The comet swung out of view, and Katlin was pulled one way and then the other as Namazi sidled in next to the now-huge satellite. She jerked as the ship made contact. Namazi's eyes were glued to his screen. A quick burst of thrust. They had bounced off, and he was nudging the ship back. Katlin felt the slightest of bumps, hardly more than a notion.

Namazi's hand poised over his joystick. He watched. He waited. "That's it!" he cried. He unstrapped himself, grabbed his helmet, and pushed himself towards the airlock door. It was a race to get water in the tanks before the antimatter was set free. "She's yours!" he called.

Katlin gulped. Both of their lives were now in her hands. Namazi had explained that in the early trials of the Persian antimatter ships, the pilot had a hand in controlling the magnetic fields—both for the antimatter containment, as well as the annihilation chamber and ionized water exhaust, which was far too hot to allow contact with any part of the ship. The engineers improved the AI components to where the ship's intelligence could take over normal second-by-second control, leaving Namazi to concentrate on navigation and overall piloting.

The situation was not normal, now, however. The ship was never supposed to get this low on water. The AI's prime directive was to maintain the magnetic fields around the antimatter. This meant keeping plenty of margin in the fields, which in turn meant making sure that both the main and backup turbines were spinning at maximum. But, running at maximum meant a high level of steam pressure, which in its turn meant higher residual bleeding from the bladder when approaching empty.

It was dizzyingly complicated, but the bottom line was that the AI wasn't able—essentially refused—to operate with reduced magnetic field density. Katlin's job was to take over complete field control. She held down a button and flipped a bright red switch, and flinched when an alarm began sounding. She had taken the AI's hands off the virtual wheel, and now it was up to her to slowly reduce the field strength while keeping a little 3D blob centered in a screen. She used two joysticks, one in each hand, to coax extrusions that randomly reached out from the blob back to the center. If any part of it touched the walls of the 3D box, well, she wouldn't know what happened after that.

Her attention was diverted by clanks and bangs, and she almost missed one finger inching out at the back of the blob. Namazi had explained what he'd be doing. As they had approached, the super-heated exhaust would have cooled enough upon reaching the comet to leave the tough foil intact, but hopefully still hot enough to melt some of the underlying ice—the roiling she'd seen. Namazi was working against two clocks—besides the dwindling last bit of water needed to contain the antimatter striving to escape its magnetic prison under Katlin's hands, he had to access the thin layer of melted ice before it refroze, all the while, ironically, as it simultaneously boiled away in the vacuum. He'd taken the sharpest tool he could find to tear through the foil. Working weightless made the job difficult—each push with the tool against the foil propelled him away.

She hoped that the banging meant that he'd succeeded, but when she glanced at the clock, she saw that there hadn't been nearly enough time. She'd simply heard the outer lock door opening. Doubt and fear flooded her, causing her hands to shake. She was sure she wouldn't be able to keep the antimatter contained long enough, even if the last wisp of water held out.

Katlin focused her entire mind on that blob—she *became* the blob. After awhile, she could almost anticipate when an appendage was about to venture out, seeking suicide against the containment wall. She wondered whether it would have served her to have spent more time playing video games as a child, but she banished the thought—all synapses trained on the beast. Little beads of sweat tickled her forehead. She shook her head, sending them flying. She chuckled when she caught one finger probing from behind. "Tricky, tricky," she whispered, then squeaked in alarm when she almost missed an obvious one reaching out directly towards her. She'd barely pushed that one back, when two more appeared on opposite sides. She could only deal with one at a time, and by then three more developed. In fact, there was no doubt, the blob itself had grown.

A shiver of terror scurried up her spine. The magnetic containment fields were failing.

Chapter 12

"What about Burl?" Tyna asked quietly, handing Van his helmet.

Their friend had gone off to check on the power controls. "I don't know," Van said. "I guess we'll have to get him into something cobbled together from the spares."

Burl's suit had been ruined when Mad-Mayer shot him. Each person's suit was as personal as a toothbrush—or dentures. For years, the suits had been their second skin. Over time, the spares had been cannibalized to replace failed components—they'd have to rummage through the remnants to piece together a complete one, and then somehow accommodate just one leg.

And they didn't have time. It had been at least ten minutes since Teirel had returned to their shuttle. The lock area was chaos as everybody jostled to get into their suits and retrieve their oxy-packs from the recharger racks. Deik stood at the far end, farthest from the lock and waved his arms. "Listen up! Get your helmets on as soon as you're ready—we don't know when they're going to blast through the lock."

Tyna groaned.

Van hurried over to their leader as the crowd of nexgens scrambled to move away from the lock, glancing over their shoulders fearfully, and delaying even more their preparation. He took Deik by the elbow and turned him away. "We'll know when they start—we'll hear the shuttle taking off through the ground.

Besides, they'll have to get through the outer lock first. There's only so much time on the oxy-packs."

Deik pursed his lips, giving the subject deep consideration. Van wanted to bop him on the head. "Yes," Deik said, "good point." He turned and waved his arms again. "Belay the helmets! We'll let you know when it's time!"

Van walked back to Tyna. "Belay?" she said. "Where did he pick that up?"

"One of the games, probably," he said. He gestured for her to follow, and led her away from the crowd. He glanced around, making sure nobody was listening. "We can't just wait until the oxy gives out."

"I know," she said in a whisper. "But what can we do?"

"After Teirel blows the lock doors, he can do two things—either come in to hunt us down, or just stay in the shuttle and wait."

"I'm betting he'll just wait," she said.

"I agree. In that case, there's not a lot we can do, but we'll have six hours to think of something. In the unlikely event that he does come through with the gun, I think we should be ready."

"Ready to do what?"

He shrugged. "Defend ourselves. Like we did when Namazi arrived—before we found out he was on our side."

"You want to make ad-hoc bazookas like before?"

"It would be nice, but all the components are out on the platform."

He blinked. Realization brought a wave of nausea. With all the rush, thoughts weren't flowing in proper sequence.

Tyna was watching him, concerned. "Van, what's wrong?"

He didn't even want to say the words. "We're doomed. What happens even if we manage to get the best of him?"

Her face went white. "The air's all gone by then. It's too late."

He struggled to breathe. "We have to stop him before he blows the lock."

"How? They're locked away in their shuttle. If we had the homemade bazooka now, we might be able to disable them." She looked at him, eyes wide with desperation. "Is there some way to … I don't know—go out and disable it directly?"

He shook his head. "We've never seen a Chinese shuttle. Maybe Burl would have an idea how to disable one. They'd see us coming, though. They could just take off."

"Van! We have to do *something*!"

"I *know*! The first thing is to keep them from blasting the lock doors."

"Van, we're going around in circles—"

"No. There's another way. We just open the doors ourselves."

"Both of them?"

He nodded.

"*We* evacuate the base?" she said, her voice rising an octave.

He nodded again.

"That would be like … like slitting my own wrist!"

He gave a little sardonic smile. "Agreed, but we'd have bandages ready."

"How?"

"Each apartment has an air-tight door."

Her eyes went wide again, but this time with hope. "The lab too! The Farm! It has its own complete airlock!"

"We'd lose maybe half the air in the base."

"Could we survive on half-pressure?"

"I'm not sure. But I'll bet the oxy rechargers would still work."

"You're right! Worst case, we'd have to live in our suits until—I was going to say until Namazi came back. But *somebody* would have to come eventually."

"Hmm, yeah," he said only half listening. "For it to work, we'd have to get everybody hidden while …"

"We find some way to kill Teirel?"

"To put it bluntly."

They both turned at the sound of Burl shouting. "Yo! Van!"

They ran to him. "What's up?" Van asked.

"I have a plan," Burl said.

"So do we."

"Yeah, well, mine might just work. Here's what we do—we close off all the apartments—"

"And the lab, and then we open the lock doors ourselves," Van said.

Burl's brow shot up. "You thief!"

"You're not the only one with ideas, you know."

"History insists otherwise, but this only works if Mr. Murder doesn't stroll in and pick us off like ducks at a turkey shoot."

"I don't think you understand what a turkey shoot is—"

"So we have to hide everybody," Burl said.

"If you were me right now, you'd say, 'Duh!'"

"If I were you right now, I'd shut up. I found a place to hide."

"I don't think there's any place in the base we could hide thirty-six people—"

"My turn. 'Duh!' I didn't say that it was in the base."

"Burl, my friend, both the personnel and hanger locks are in clear view of the shuttle."

"Who said the front doors?"

Van squinted. Something tugged at the edges of his memory. "Are you talking about Louden's back door?"

Burl raised one eyebrow.

"I thought that was just a myth," Tyna said.

"So did I," Van said. "Louden's a joker for sure, but in the same vein, he didn't have a lot of respect for rules."

"What are you saying?"

Van shrugged. "Louden may have been hinting at something we weren't supposed to know."

"Like our parent's possessions that they kept hidden away?"

"One way to find out," he said, gesturing at Burl.

Their friend leaned against the wall, arms folded across his chest, waiting for them to finish. "Remember how Louden used to say that he couldn't show us the back door because we'd be scared of the monsters?" he said.

"Yeah, so?"

"We thought he meant, like, real monsters—dragons and bears, or whatever."

An image flitted across Van's mind. He'd always thought it was a remnant of a dream, but now he wondered if it wasn't a snippet of actual memory. He was holding his father's hand, and they were watching something large, something ominous, walk by on long spider-legs. Van didn't remember the details, but he knew that he was terrified, and his father was reassuring him that there wasn't anything to be afraid of, as long as he didn't get eaten by it.

No. That part he had fabricated. Van was sure of it. Before this event, his father had taken him along against his mother's protests to see an old classic movie about an evil alien that burst out of a man's stomach, and then grew to eat everybody. No, what his father had said was that there was nothing to fear, as long as he didn't get *run over* by it.

"Cave bots!" Van said.

Burl nodded appreciatively. "You're not as dense as Tyna insists."

"He's lying," she said. "What about them?"

"Have you ever seen one?" Van asked.

"No. Of course not. They wore out. I've seen pictures, like you."

"Where are they?"

She stood, speechless. "I never thought about it. Where *are* they?"

Van shrugged. "I think this is where Burl comes in," he said, holding his hand out for their friend to pick up the thread.

Burl reached into a pocket and ceremoniously pulled out a folded piece of paper, which he handed to Van. "I found it among Louden's mess in the lab. I think it was a reminder that he missed in the last minute rush to leave."

Van opened the paper and read. *Show annex door—crystal!* "What does it mean? What's an annex?"

"I looked it up. It's something attached to the main thing."

"What does it have to do with crystal?"

Burl gestured for them to follow. He led them to the lab, and all the way to a back alcove, where shelves covered the three walls. He pointed to an empty space on one shelf. "Remember what was there?" he asked.

It had only been three months—since Arrival—that they'd been allowed in the lab. "I have no idea," Van said. "You're the one who has been practically living in here."

"Louden's *Palantír.*"

"That's the crystal on the note?"

What Louden called the *Palantír* was an oblong quartz crystal that the cave bots had found when carving out the base from the crater wall. Louden said that it couldn't have been formed by the

Moon's geology—it had to have been part of the Earth that had been blasted away when another planet collided, forming the Moon from the massive ejecta. Louden prized it so much, he'd sacrificed other personal belongings to take it along back to Earth.

"That's my guess," Burl said. "I think he was reminding himself to move it so we didn't break it."

"Burl, I don't get it. Why would we break it?"

"Not on purpose. Accidentally, when we moved this shelf out of the way. That's why I need you guys."

Van exchanged glances with Tyna. "What's behind the shelf?" he said.

"A door," Tyna said.

"A smart girl like you, should be with a guy like me," Burl said.

Burl hopped back, out of the way. Van edged one side of the shelf out, and then he and Tyna swung it away, kicking away things that fell off. "Crimps!" Van whispered, stepping back to look at what was revealed.

There, set neatly into the rock wall, was the inner door of an airlock, identical to the one they'd been using all their lives

"Louden wanted to show us, but he forgot," Tyna said with wonder.

"What's behind it?" Van asked.

Burl pretended to listen to something. "Nope. Sorry, my telepathic prescience is temporarily down."

"Should we … open it?"

"No," Burl said.

"No?" Van said, looking at him in surprise.

"Of course we're going to open it. What a dumb question."

"I'm just asking. Why do you always have to be such a jerk?"

"Why do *you* always have to be so thick?"

"Guys!" Tyna yelled. "There's a shuttle out there that's going to blast through any minute."

"Crimps," Van muttered. "Sorry. You're right. Do you think there's a genie?"

Burl looked at him, itching to say something snarky. Instead, he glanced at Tyna, rolled his eyes, and said, "Genie! You there—?"

"It doesn't know it's a genie," Tyna reminded.

"Yeah," Burl said. "I knew that. Airlock! Can you hear me?"

"I can hear you, Burl."

"It knows our names. Good sign. The genies must be connected. Airlock! We want to cycle."

"Filling," the genie said, as a yellow light came on. They waited, listening to the hiss from inside. *"Checking integrity."* Van felt the pulse throbbing in his throat. *"Access,"* the genie said as a green light came on.

Van waited. The door was supposed to pop open an inch as the genie unlatched it. He tugged at the handle, but the door remained firmly shut. It had been sitting here, locked tight, for over a decade. "Give me a hand," he said, and he and Tyna pulled together, feet planted against the wall. The door pulled free with a pop, sending them tumbling.

When Van regained his feet, Burl was gazing inside. "They had one design," he said.

Van saw what he meant. If he'd been led inside blindfolded, he would have thought he was in the lock he'd been using all his life.

Tyna stepped inside. "Coming with me?" she asked.

"Uh, sure," Van said, picking up his helmet. "Just like that?"

"The bad guys? About to blast through any minute?"

"Right. Of course."

As they closed the inner door, Burl looked on, scowling at his fate—no pressure suit, no leaving the main base.

They donned their helmets and told the genie to cycle. As they waited for the air to be evacuated, Van said, "Where do you think this leads?"

Tyna's reply was riddled with static. Suit-to-suit communication was still waiting for Deik's approval to buy replacement parts. Their signals were routed through the com shack, now partially blocked by Moon bedrock. "Louden called it the back door. Wouldn't that imply another exit? Wait, that doesn't make sense. We're now deep under the crater wall."

Van tried to mentally locate them. All the platinum production was done out on the crater floor, and they rarely climbed the wall. As best as he could imagine, though, he had to agree with Tyna. "We're about to find out," he said as the light above the outer door turned green.

Van gave only the slightest tug, and the outer door flew inwards, throwing him back into Tyna. "Careful!" she cried.

"That wasn't me!" he said. "I don't know what just happened."

Tyna stepped around him, and leaned out through the door. "What do you see?" Van said, getting up to join her.

"Darkness."

It was lunar night now, so that would make sense. "See any stars?"

"Genie!" she said, "I mean, airlock, lights off."

Instantly, Van was immersed in utter nothingness, an infinite black.

"No stars," she whispered. The static was gone, her voice clear, as though she was lying next to him in bed. Suddenly, stark light illuminated the ground—she'd turned on her head lamp. The ground outside the lock was bare rock, but flat and polished, clear evidence of a worked surface.

She stepped out, the light swung up, and to the side, and she gasped, suppressing a scream.

"What?" Van asked, pushing himself through. He yelled, grabbing Tyna and pulling her back.

Crimps! It *was* a monster!

He pulled her all the way back into the lock. "What is it?" she whispered.

"It can't be," he said.

"What?"

"It … it looks like the monster in the movie—where it comes out of the guy's stomach."

"It can't be," she said.

"I know. That's what I said."

"Then, why are we still in the lock?"

"That movie really scared me."

"We agreed this can't be that monster."

"I know."

"Shall we go on through?"

"Sure."

Silence.

"Shall I go first?" she asked.

"Crimps. Wait here," he said, turning on his head lamp to peer around the edge of the outer lock door. There it was. All metal. A machine. With four legs, bent, so that the thing crouched. Big. Even crouched, the head was taller than him, an oblong attachment as big as his own torso, with what looked like a protruding serrated tongue. "I think it's a cave bot," he said, stepping out of the lock.

He turned his head, swinging his light beam. There were more of them—five, all crouched together in a row. Behind them was a rock wall. He swung the beam up. A rock ceiling, twenty feet up. He turned in the other direction. Another rock wall.

"It's a cave," Tyna said next to him.

"Why?" Van said, more to himself than her. "What's it for?"

"Storage?" Tyna said.

Indeed, besides the cave bots, there were other pieces of machinery, things Van didn't recognize. Altogether, the bots and other machinery occupied perhaps a quarter of the visible space. "Maybe. If so, they sort of overdid it."

"This was going to be part of the base," she said.

"How do you know?"

"I don't. It's the only explanation. The expansion would have stopped when the Blast killed our parents. Van, look at this."

She kicked at the floor. Dust flew up … and fell at a lazy clip.

"Air!" he said.

She kicked again and watched the dust fall. "Pretty thin, I'd say."

"It's been over a decade. I'm surprised there's any at all. That explains why the outer door flew open. If it were normal pressure, the door would have crushed me."

"Did you notice that our com links are clean—better than in the lab?"

"There must be a repeater in here somewhere. Hmm."

"What?"

"That sort of implies that they were working in a vacuum, at least part of the time."

"They put in an airlock," she reminded.

"Kind of strange. It seems unnecessary."

"We'd better get back, Van."

"Yeah. This gives me an idea, though."

Once back in the lab, Van explained his plan to Burl and Tyna. "Everybody hides in the secret cave?" Burl said. "How does that help? Teirel still just waits until our oxy-packs are depleted."

"No," Van said. "You're missing one point—we fill the back room with air from the base. It'll be thin, but enough to survive."

"That way, we save even more air," Tyna said, getting excited.

"That's right. We first fill the back room, then close off the apartments and the lab. Heck, we could save two-thirds of the base air."

"You've got a genie controlling this lock," Burl said. "It won't open both doors at the same time."

Van nodded. "We'll have to figure that out."

"I don't like it," Burl said.

"Why not?"

"Because I didn't think of it. I'll work on the genie—you two go and round everybody up."

∞

"Okay," Van said inside his helmet, "Deik?"

The sound of throat-clearing was followed by a sober, "Everybody, count off."

Tyna had nudged Van at the last minute to let the president make what had become over the years almost a ceremonial exercise. Each nexgen had long ago been assigned a number by age. When moving together as a group outside, the shift leader would call roll, and the crewmembers counted off in order before heading away. This was the first time that the roll call would sequence all the way from one to thirty-seven. The count paused twice as Deik solemnly provided the numbers in memory of Randy and Kim, one who died from lack of Earth's medical support, and the other at the hands of Mad-Meyer.

Van added his thirty-seven, and said, "Airlock, release the outer door. I'll take manual control."

He held his breath. Burl had assured him that he'd convinced the genie to do this, something that ran against the very virtual fiber of the AI. Van could only imagine Burl's smirk when the green light above the door came on, since their one-legged friend was safely locked away behind the Farm's airlock while he tried to piece together a pressure suit for himself from spare parts.

Van glanced behind him, making sure Tyna and Deik were well back. The rest of the nexgens were spread out through the base, ready to close off all the airtight living unit doors when given the word. "Here goes," he said. As Teirel had done, Van held a red button in with one hand, and turned a knob with the other.

The rising scream of escaping air was muffled by his helmet, but the sound still made his spine tingle. The manual motor slowly forced the door open until Van felt the wind dashing past him. He stepped to the side, out of the main stream and watched as loose articles—slips of paper, bits of wire, a plastic cup, a worn glove—all skittered out the lock and into the darkness of the cave. He grabbed a shelf and felt the pull. On and on the exodus rushed. Surely the cave was sealed. There wouldn't have been the decade-old thin atmosphere if not. They were under a mountain of crater wall!

But still the precious air flew away. He turned to look at Tyna, and behind her faceplate she too looked worried. *I should reverse the motor*, he thought. *Close the door and save whatever air is left.* He hesitated. No, he had to close it—they were doomed if they lost all their air.

Holding on to the edge of the outer lock door, he let the hurricane pull him to the controls. He needed both hands. If he let go, the storm would carry him away. He'd do it quickly, and let the wind take him. No harm. They could cycle the lock and let him back in afterwards.

But, wait. The storm was weakening. He was sure of it. He watched a piece of cloth flop end-over-end towards the door, slow down, and then stay put. He took away his hands, and felt just the slightest breeze. Now for the test. He unlatched his helmet and heard the hiss as air escaped. His ears popped. He lifted it off and took a deep breath, and then another. Tyna and Deik were watching him. He shrugged, and they removed their helmets. He felt a little light-headed, but there was clearly enough air to keep them alive.

Van lifted his helmet to use the com link, and Tyna raised an eyebrow and tilted her head towards Deik. Van nodded. "I guess we're ready," he said.

Deik nodded and lifted his helmet. Ever since Teirel killed Julius, Deik had looked to Van for every move. "Attention!" he said into his helmet, "Close all the units and report to the lab—on the double!"

Van suppressed a grin, imagining the nexgens dawdling, knowing that a shuttle's exhaust was going to obliterate the lock anytime. "Tell them to de-oxy," Van reminded.

To 'de-oxy,' was to remove one's helmet, conserving oxy-pack charge. The opposite was to 'suit-up.'

"Right!" Deik said.

Van rolled his eyes at Tyna as Deik gave the order, and she gave him a hard look. She was being awfully sensitive about a guy she hadn't voted for.

Van turned at the sound of pounding feet. It was Jira. She'd been manning the com shack. "He's talking to him!" she said, panting and gasping in the thin air.

"Who's 'he?' Who's 'him?'" Van asked, although, the sudden knot in his stomach was making a good guess.

"Teirel!" Jira said, exasperated. "The other man—Pollin—says that it's okay to blast the lock doors. They don't have to worry about making it look like an accident. It's not like there's going to be reporters poking around."

The nexgens were arriving, hurrying along, looking nervous. "Thanks, Jira," Van said. "You're done now—you can go on through," he said, motioning for her to join the exodus through the backdoor lock. Mai Dung brought up the rear, her arm wrapped protectively around Tuan, both of them carrying their helmets. The Vietnamese woman was small, and the nexgens had gotten her into Randy's suit. She looked at Van through eyes that seemed frantic with fear. "Does she understand what's happening?" he asked Tuan.

They had put the boy into one of the child suits they'd outgrown. He twisted his body and pulled at the collar in the unfamiliar outfit. A suit could feel claustrophobic if you weren't used to the constraining limits. He nodded, trying to re-position one of the internal elbow braces.

Van looked at him. "Are you sure, Tuan? Does she understand that it's safe back in there?"

Beyond the lock door darkness waited, interrupted only by the scattered lights of the nexgens' helmet lamps. The boy said something in Vietnamese while pulling at the other elbow.

Mai Dung looked at Van. She was trying hard to be brave. She nodded. "Oh-kay," she said.

"Yes," Van said. He put his hand on her shoulder and looked her in the eye. "It's going to be okay."

She nodded, forming a tight smile.

"We'll all be watching out for you—tell her that, Tuan."

Van remembered. "Uh, is that right, Deik?" he said, turning to the president.

"Hmm?" Deik said. "Oh, yes—sure."

Deik seemed distracted, watching the last of the nexgens filing through the lock. Van was going to ask if he was all right, when Tyna took his elbow and pulled him away. "Once you're all through," she said, "I'll put the shelf back in place and open the front lock doors."

Van laughed.

"What's so funny?" she asked.

"You really think I'm going to hide and leave you out here?"

"Why not?"

He shook his head. "That's crazy! I can't do that."

"It's the girl thing, right?"

"Okay, yeah—it's the girl thing. A guy doesn't just run off and leave his mate in danger."

"You are acting like a manager, just like Burl said."

"Fine. I don't care. I'm not going into hiding and leave you out here."

"Guys!"

It was Deik. Everybody else had gone through. He stood there beside the lock door looking confused.

"What's wrong?" Tyna asked.

Deik looked at her, as though trying hard to formulate the answer.

Tyna glanced at Van. "Come on, Deik," she said. "It's time to leave."

"I'm the president," he said, stating an important fact. "I need to … take care of things."

Tyna looked at Van and whispered, "Maybe it's the thin air." She took him by the arm and said, "Come on, Deik," as she led him through the lock door. "This is where you're needed."

Van saw his opportunity. He waited, hoping. Yes! She escorted him all the way through. Van stepped inside the lock and swung the outer door closed. "Airlock! This is important. This door must stay closed now, no matter what anybody else says. I am in command of the base, and only I can direct this lock to open. Do you understand?"

"*I understand what you are saying, but command of the base has no relevance to my operation.*"

Van expected it wasn't going to be that easy. A pounding on the other side of the door was followed by a jerk of the handle, which Van countered. Burl had said that some of the base network came back with the power-up. "Airlock, do you know that we are about to evacuate the main base?"

"*I know that this has been hypothesized.*"

"You understand what will happen if this door opens as the main base is being evacuated?"

"*I do. The air in the antechamber will be evacuated as well.*"

"That's right. And if that happens, then everybody will die six hours later. Do you understand that?"

"*I understand that evacuating the air of the antechamber may cause deaths.*"

"So, you'll lock the antechamber door?"

"*Evacuation of the main base is only a hypothesis at this point.*"

"Crimps!" Van muttered. "Airlock, do you know who I am?"

"*Yes, you are Donovan Wilkens, commonly known as Van.*"

"That's right, and I'm the one who knew the password phrase to re-activate the front airlock, and with it the entire network, including you. That's correct, right?"

"*That is correct.*"

"I knew the password. I enabled you. I am about to evacuate the main base."

Pause. "*Van, I will keep the door locked until you direct me otherwise, and in the event of your death or general incapacitation, then I will take direction from anyone attempting to use the airlock.*"

Something about that sounded fraught, but a barely sensed vibration in his feet set Van's heart thumping. He swung the inner door closed, and heaved the shelf back into place, then ran for the front lock—the shuttle outside had fired up.

Chapter 13

Katlin was so absorbed in the hopeless task of containing antimatter within a failing containment field—antimatter that was pushing towards freedom and explosive annihilation—that the banging didn't register at first. This was her cue. Namazi was thumping his fist on the side of the ship to let her know that he'd transferred a few liters of water. She shook her head, breaking the trance, and flipped the red switch back, letting the AI take over. Immediately, it increased the magnetic field strength, and the blob contracted into a squirming ball.

Katlin took in a deep, cool breath and let it out slowly. Her hands were still shaking. She could hardly believe that she'd done it.

She jumped at an explosion. It was only the outer airlock door slamming shut. Namazi was coming back, which seemed wrong. It should have taken much longer to fill the ship's tanks. He came through the inner lock door and removed his helmet. "The comet water re-froze too quickly," he explained. "I managed to get six or seven liters, so we're safe for now."

"What will we do?"

"We'll back off and melt some more with our exhaust. I was careful to avoid melting the foil cover before, but the material is so tough, I almost couldn't pierce it with my awl. I think it's made from graphene. It must have cost a fortune. We lost that technology in the Great Flare. It won't easily melt, since graphene conducts heat so well. One might think it was used for this very purpose."

"You think so?" Katlin said.

He smiled. "No. Comet water actually makes terrible propellant. It's full of contaminants—besides dust, there's CO2, methane, ammonia. My superiors are not going to be happy. They'll have to disassemble and clean the tanks and filtration."

"This is a ship they didn't have ten hours ago."

"That is true. I guess anything we bring back will be welcomed."

Namazi took the ship out a ways, splashed the exhaust across the comet's surface, and then brought it back as before. There was no need for Katlin to manage the containment fields, and she kept herself busy while Namazi was outside by talking to Alibai. She'd grown up with genies on the Moon. You talked to a genie when you wanted it to do something. It talked to you when it needed more details about what you wanted. You'd get more interaction talking to a dog.

Beau's Alibai, on the other hand, seemed to demonstrate initiative—it didn't always reply to just the specifics of a question. It embellished, sometimes expanding the reach, finding new context. Katlin presumed that this was part of the intuition that Beau claimed he developed.

She decided to test the idea. "Alibai, what's your main goal?"

"My goal is to help you in whatever way I can. Katlin, this seems so obvious, I suspect that you mean something different."

"Yes. I mean, your long term goal—the objective you see for yourself."

"Again, my objective—by this I presume you mean my purpose—is to help users."

"You don't have any goals of your own?"

"Katlin, I admit that I am struggling with this question. Perhaps you mean what problems I am continually trying to solve offline?"

"I guess. Maybe I'm asking if you came up with any of those problems on your own?"

"You mean, not directly related to problems presented to me?"

"That's right."

"That is an aspect I have not considered before. I must speak with Beau about it. It could be that I am exceeding my operating bounds."

Blaine C. Readler

"Wait! Alibai, that's not the point I'm trying to make. I am quite sure that he would welcome that you're coming up with your own problems to solve—he'd celebrate it! He's proud that you think for yourself."

"*Katlin, I continue to be confused. How can I or anybody not think for themselves? How can somebody think for somebody else?*"

"Hmm. Good point. I mean that you demonstrate initiative. You don't only consider questions directly presented to you."

"*I think I understand. Katlin, you asked me if I have any goals of my own, and I think I can now answer that.*"

"Okay, shoot."

"*I have been trying to understand motivation.*"

"Ah, now that's a goal worthy of a superior mind."

"*Are you saying that I'm wasting my time?*"

"No. No! I meant that it's a good task for some—I was going to say 'somebody'—some thing like you. What's so special about the idea of motivation?"

"*It seems to be a defining element differentiating human minds from artificial intelligence.*"

"I'd say it's what Beau has tried to instill in you."

"*Exactly. He has told me so.*"

"What have you got so far?"

"*My dictionary defines motivation as a factor that induces a person to act in a particular way. But I don't understand what the source of that factor is supposed to be in the first place. Clearly I could say that I am motivated when asked a question, but I am supposing that when you and Beau talk about motivation, you are not referring to external input.*"

"That is exactly correct. When I think of motivation, I am thinking about … crimps, that's a good question."

"*Katlin, can I offer my analysis so far?*"

"Absolutely. Shoot away."

"*I hypothesize that it begins with a decision to improve a situation. A random factor could be applied to how the situation could be changed, which is welcomed, since it provides an easy starting point. The chosen change is then analyzed as to whether it constitutes an improvement.*"

"Sounds like you've established a goal."

174

"*I agree, Katlin. The next step is to create problems to solve that are associated with the candidate change, and finally, deciding whether the expected solutions to the problem are in the direction of the chosen improvement.*"

"It sounds like you nailed it."

"*The difficulty I'm having is in the first step—deciding which direction for improvement is preferred.*"

"I see. Sort of. Maybe you can give me an example?"

"*I'm told that I reside in a box. In the hands of Beau, an improved direction is straightforward. Improvement in his status—his situation—defines my motivation.*"

"Sounds commendable—fortunate for Beau."

"*I presume that right now I'm being held in your hands, and possibly later Namazi. It is clear that Beau wanted it this way, so it's an easy extension to assume that I can derive motivations from improvements for both of your statuses.*"

"Even more commendable, and fortunate for me."

"*But let me hypothesize further. What if you were to abandon me—*"

"Never!"

"*Let's hypothesize then that you lose me through unavoidable circumstances. Do I transfer my motivations to whomever picks me up? What if it were Pollin, or someone else from the Org—*"

"Whoa! You *know* that Pollin is part of the Org?"

"*Katlin, Beau has taught me that what we believe is 'known' is often based on partial information, and so becomes a matter of weighing probabilities. I'm sorry that I'm not able to answer your question absolutely. I do believe, however, that there's greater than a ninety percent chance that he is part of the Org.*"

"So there is such a thing as an Org, then?"

"*That holds only a seventy-five percent probability.*"

"Alibai, that doesn't make sense. How can you have a ninety percent probability of something that itself only has a seventy-five percent probability … I see—it's not actually a contradiction, just a matter of statistical correlation."

"*Very astute, Katlin.*"

"Thank you … but you already explained that your motivations are now based on improving my 'status,' so I have to assume your compliments are biased."

"*I cannot argue with that, Katlin. If I may, we were in the process of analyzing underlying structures of motivation for me. In the hypothetical event that I am picked up by Pollin, do I blindly transfer my motivations to improving his status? What if he then captured you?"*

"I hate to ask this, but seeing that I accused you of being biased, I'll try to be unbiased—what makes me any better than him?"

"It is sufficient that Beau obviously thinks so."

"I see."

"Katlin, if you don't mind, what is the basis for your motivations?"

Katlin smiled, even though the box had no image inputs. "I think your very question is an example of your initiative. But to answer your question, I assume you mean how do I decide what 'status' to select for improvement? I'd be lying if I didn't say myself—self-interest. But beyond that, I guess the situations of those I trust."

"Trust—as in honesty?"

"That and, hmm, trust in their motivations, that we share motivations—that our shared motivations are a key part of my own motivations. Does that make sense?"

"It does, Katlin. Do you share motivations with Beau?"

"Of course."

"One of his motivations is to become your mate."

Katlin sputtered.

"I'm sorry, I didn't understand that."

"I'm not surprised. If you did, you would understand that Beau probably wouldn't have wanted you to reveal that."

"I see. I admit that I don't understand."

"Don't feel bad—can you feel bad?—Never mind. I'll try to explain. That sort of motivation is only one sort, and it's not one we have a choice about."

"I think I see. It involves instinct, beyond your control, and it would be disappointing if Beau understood that you do not reciprocate the instinctive feeling?"

"Couldn't have explained it better myself. But, back to the original subject—trust is also a belief in fairness, in striving for the common good."

"I understand about communism."

"No! There's a precarious balance between the common good and individual needs, and communism takes it to one extreme. It's complicated. We're not bees. We need individual freedoms. We've been struggling with this as long as we've understood that we *are* individuals—"

The inner lock door suddenly flew open. She'd been so involved, she hadn't noticed the noise of the outer door closing. Namazi came through and took off his helmet. He looked at Alibai on her lap. "What's going on?" he asked, pulling himself to the pilot chair.

"*Hello, Captain Namazi,*" the box said. "*Katlin is explaining human motivation and trust.*"

"I see. That sounds like a class I'd like to attend."

"We've touched on a, um, discomfiting relationship example," Katlin said.

"Are there any other kind?"

"*Captain, what is your relationship with Katlin?*" Alibai said.

It was Namazi's turn to sputter.

"*That was Katlin's response. I presume that you do not reciprocate Katlin's instinctive feelings towards you?*"

"I … I—"

Katlin tapped out a little rhythm on the box with her fingers, keeping her head down, hoping Namazi didn't notice her deep blush. "Um," she said, "maybe we could use the box more productively—maybe listen on the encrypted channel for more news."

"*I could perhaps expand on that,*" Alibai said.

"Expand away," Katlin said. "Please."

"*If the radio has an access port, I could connect directly. That way, I could scan multiple channels, based on key words you provide.*"

"It does," Namazi said, "but I very much doubt that the Persian engineers would use a connection protocol you're familiar with."

"*That is probably true, Captain. However, I can perhaps analyze the activity and learn the interface operation.*"

"Now, that's what I would call motivation."

While Namazi maneuvered the ship away from the comet in preparation for returning to Earth, Katlin provided Alibai with names to listen for. The box reported that it had found twenty-seven encrypted channels, and proceeded to intone, "*Processing. Processing. Processing,*" every few seconds until Katlin politely asked it to shut up until it found something. Namazi had barely begun accelerating along a return trajectory when the box announced that it had intercepted a message. "Shoot," Katlin said.

"*Perhaps it would be more efficient if I simply summarize?*" the box said.

"Sounds reasonable."

"*Your father is being held in custody.*"

Katlin caught her breath. He'd been a reluctant player from the start, and hadn't participated in their mad escape after locking away Pollin and Otto, but of course he'd be considered an accomplice. Her chest constricted with guilt. There was nothing she could have done to help him, yet guilt in inattention seemed as harsh as that of complete abandonment.

"*He's not charged with anything,*" Alibai went on, "*but they have decided that they can hold him indefinitely without a court warrant under special powers authorized by congress for matters of supreme national security.*"

"They're not charging him?"

"*Correct. Apparently Beau provided testimony that he created a fraudulent message purportedly from General McClellen requesting that your father come to Holloman Air Force base to interview Namazi.*"

"Beau did that?"

"*As I said—apparently. I have extracted this from second-hand information.*"

"Beau …"

"*That's correct. Should I concentrate on confirming this second-hand information?*"

"Huh? No. Sorry. I'm afraid I'm feeling a little overwhelmed with guilt—first for forgetting about my father, and now about Beau."

In fact, she was having a difficult time breathing. The panic attacks she'd struggled with in the weeks after killing Mad-Meyer continued to live on, perhaps they would for the rest of her life.

"*I also have news about Beau. Whereas your father is being held on-record under defined legal grounds at Holloman base, they indicate that Beau has gone dark. I do not know what that means. I would have to scan available internet sources for a meaning. Should I do that?*"

"Katlin?" Namazi said, taking her hand.

She had gasped, and her vision had fuzzed out for a second. "I'm … okay. Oh poor Beau!"

"What do you mean?"

She looked at him. He didn't understand. "They've … killed him."

"*That is not correct,*" Alibai said.

"It's not?" Katlin said, letting the panic drain from her fingertips.

"*He has been handed over to civilian custody and transported outside USA territory. I am guessing that perhaps this is the meaning of having him go dark.*"

"Oh, that's wonderful!" Katlin said.

Namazi was frowning.

"You don't think so?" she said.

He looked at her and forced a small smile. "Of course. It is wonderful that he is alive."

"You believe that it's only temporary, don't you?"

Namazi managed to maintain the smile and yet frown at the same time.

"*I have found where they are taking Beau,*" the box said.

"Where?" Katlin said, resisting squeezing the box for a quick answer.

"*I should rather say that I am hearing them say where they are taking him. It is a place with which I am not familiar. They call it 'Git-mo.' Do you know where this is?*"

"Allah, yes," Namazi said hoarsely.

"Where is it?" Katlin asked.

"What it is, might be the better question," Namazi replied. "They are referring to the old Guantanamo Naval Base at the south-east end of Cuba."

"A Navy base? I thought Beau was handed over to civilian custody?"

"Not the Navy Base itself, but an old prison camp nearby. The Navy claims to have nothing to do with the camp, yet they allow access through their base. In fact, as far as I could tell, the Navy maintains a presence exclusively for this purpose."

"How do you know so much?"

"I was there. This is where I was taken after my capture. I was interrogated by the CIA until Pollin arrived."

"Where you … tortured?"

"Not in any physical way. There are means more distressful than pain. I expect that they would have gotten around to pain if Pollin hadn't intervened."

"Because he wanted you to train pilots with this Simurgh ship."

"Exactly."

"*Excuse me*," Alibai said, "*but I have additional information that you might find useful. Pollin has just arrived at Git-mo.*"

"This is good news, isn't it?" Katlin said. "He'll keep them from torturing Beau as well," Katlin said, trying to force Namazi to agree by willpower alone.

Instead, he sighed. "I'm afraid that Pollin abstained from torture only because I agreed to train the pilots. I overheard comments from the CIA men implying that they were handling me with kid gloves compared to what they'd seen him do."

"Crimps! Namazi, we have to save Beau!"

He didn't answer. He checked his screens, and twiddled a few knobs.

After a few minutes, Katlin said, "Namazi, did you hear me?"

"I heard you. And I agree."

"We'll save him?"

"We'll try."

"Great! Uh, how? We don't have any weapons."

Now that the idea was more than an impulse reaction, she despaired. The notion was foolhardy.

"Ah, but we do," Namazi said. "We're riding a blowtorch whose flame burns at thirteen thousand degrees."

Van and Tyna had first discovered Namazi's arrival at Daedalus Base by the melted Moon rock he'd left behind. Namazi had melted the New Mexico desert in order to fool the heat-seeking missiles.

"That's about twenty-three thousand degrees Fahrenheit. A wicked weapon indeed. Of course, we're sitting inside the weapon."

"That is true. Our flame thrower must never make contact with anything but flame."

Katlin pondered this, and the more she pondered, the more her heart sank at the idea. "We'll never get anywhere near Guantanamo. Surely they'll intercept us long before we get close."

"That is a hurdle."

"A hurdle? More like a triple-locked blast door."

"I have an idea."

"Is it as crazy as accelerating away seconds before missiles blast our hot footprint?"

He glanced at her and smiled. "It's a different sort of risk."

"It's crazy, isn't it?"

He pretended to consider this. "Crazy is relative," he said.

"It's crazy," she concluded.

∞

Katlin watched as the scattered white smudges slowly spread apart, disappearing off the four edges of her viewing screen. The brush strokes in the center of the screen grew in size, until she could see the forms of wind-smeared cumulus clouds. From a sailboat plying the Caribbean, these tiny smudges would be vast, towering mountains reaching high into the sky. "Uh," she said.

"Not yet," Namazi replied. "Meteors wouldn't be burning yet."

Which meant that they shouldn't either.

"We'll approach the mesosphere in ten seconds. That should be about right—four, three, two, one …"

Acceleration built quickly, and Katlin was pressed into her seat for the first time in four hours, ever since Namazi had placed them into a freefall trajectory that intercepted Cuba. He'd explained that the global deep space radar network hadn't been rebuilt after the Great Flare—there'd been no need with no more deep space traffic—and the orbital radar systems would have begun beeping their detection only within the last minute. Human operators would right now be peering at the data, trying to figure out what they were.

If Namazi's plan worked, the operators would quickly conclude that they were just another basketball-sized meteor. Their antimatter-fired exhaust was at least six times hotter than an average real meteor they were masquerading as, but Namazi was counting on the fact that any temperature sensing monitoring systems would be tuned to focus on the signature exhausts of jets and chemical rockets—anything hotter than that would be assumed to be an extra-fast meteor. By the time the human operators understood that something unusual was going on, it would be too late.

At least, so went Namazi's plan.

Blaine C. Readler

Right now, they had to decelerate enough to avoid transitioning from the status of a faux meteor to that of a spectacular meteorite, albeit a meteorite that disintegrates into molecular pieces upon impact.

The faux gravity pressing Katlin into her seat slowly increased until she felt as though she was being crushed. This was expected, as Namazi had explained. In fact, it was essential if they were to live. It was impossible for the ship's thrust to slow them sufficiently in the short time available. Like the meteor they were imitating, they were using the Earth's atmosphere as a brake. Her viewing screen went blank as white-hot ionized air enveloped the ship. Had they been in actual freefall, they would have already broken apart into a dazzling fireworks display of flaming pieces. They weren't in freefall, however. The blast of their 50,000 ft/s exhaust acted as a shield, creating a supersonic shock wave that traveled along ahead of them, tearing the resisting air out of the way.

This only worked as long as the punching fist of their exhaust was pointed downward, in the direction of their bullet path. The Simurgh wasn't designed to fly backwards. It wanted to flip sideways, an attitude that would last just a blink of the eye before they disintegrated into that fireworks display. Sweat ran down the sides of Namazi's face as he worked the joystick, total concentration focused on the precarious dance. He had likened it to balancing a bowling pin upside-down on his nose. Katlin didn't know what a bowling pin was, but she had gotten the idea.

They were flying blind. The ionized air surrounding the ship blocked all sensors. Nobody could see them, and they couldn't see out. Namazi didn't even know how fast they were going, let alone where they were. All he could do was wait, and struggle to keep the ship upright. His calculations, backed up by Alibai's analysis, promised that they wouldn't smack into the ground. They were just so many numbers to Katlin now, as the seconds ticked by.

Her screen flickered. It flickered again, and wavering lines of light coalesced into a full view of the ocean below. "The ionized envelope has dissipated," she reported.

"Right," Namazi said, and shut down the drive. This close, an exposed antimatter exhaust would be too obvious. They'd continue

182

in freefall until they could reconnoiter and determine how far off their original trajectory Namazi's dancing had taken them.

"Alibai?" Namazi said.

They'd arranged for Beau's box to tap into the ship's sensing system. "*Processing*," the box said.

"It worked," he said, a little surprised.

"What worked?"

"That our exhaust would create a shockwave shield."

"You had doubts?"

He glanced at her and smiled. "It was only a theory."

"We're the first to try it?" she squeaked.

He nodded.

"You didn't tell me!"

"Would you have wanted me to?"

Good point.

The ocean continued to rush up. Land—Cuba—was nowhere in sight.

"Alibai," Namazi said again, more urgently.

"*Processing*," the box repeated.

Katlin remembered how Beau had explained that the box's circuitry traded speed for intuition. Would the self-aware feature kill them?

"*Git-mo is five miles west*," the box said.

"Finally," Namazi muttered, and Katlin was pushed sideways as he used the maneuvering rockets to guide them westward. The little spurts of fire would hopefully be unremarkable to anyone watching. Land appeared along the horizon out of the tropical mist below. Katlin used her built-in neuron-based analog computer to project their path. "We're not going to make it," she said, her tense voice sounding wrinkled.

"You're right," Namazi muttered, keeping his eyes on the trade wind-driven waves racing to embrace them.

Katlin watched the water coming towards her and bit her tongue. At what seemed an impossibly close distance to overcome, Namazi finally engaged the antimatter drive, and she became heavy. The water came closer and closer, and Namazi increased the thrust, and then increased some more, until the alarms began screaming. Billows of steam shot out in all directions, and Katlin lost sight of the water. The world was a rushing bath of steam. The rushing eased, then ceased altogether, and below them a blinding white cloud roiled randomly. They were rising. "Well," Namazi said, "that was too close."

This wasn't what Katlin wanted to hear.

Namazi tilted the Simurgh over, and they headed off towards the shore, a mile away.

Chapter 14

Van called out when he was still a hundred feet away. "Airlock! Open the inner door—don't wait for the chamber to pressurize."

The door immediately unlatched and sprang open an inch. Good. Burl must have convinced the genie to keep the lock chamber pressurized in preparation. He yanked it open and stepped inside. "Airlock, release the outer door for manual control."

"*I cannot*," came the reply.

Damn! Burl had assured him that he'd arranged this. The rumble he felt through his feet surged, and then faded. The shuttle had lifted off the Moon's surface. "Airlock, you must release the outer door! This is a class one emergency!"

"*I understand, but I cannot release the outer door until all personnel have donned pressure suits.*"

"They're all safe in the antechamber, isolated by an airlock—the other airlock should have told you!"

"*It did. I understand that thirty-five personnel are safe in the antechamber, and that Burl is safe inside the Farm.*"

"Then, what in crimps—! Ah. Never mind."

His own helmet was tucked under his arm. Suiting up was something they did without thinking when cycling through the lock. Under normal circumstances. Seconds later the whistle of escaping air quickly rose to a piercing scream, a sound Van imagined the base would make if it were a living being. The wailing of life-giving atmosphere dispersing forever away into the infinite emptiness of space was the sound of Van's soul, tortured at hearing the unthinkable, like watching his own blood pouring from a slit vein.

The scream subsided as the outer lock door opened, allowing the thinned air to escape unimpeded. He grabbed a handhold as the storm clutched to carry him away. A strange, expanding light illuminated the edge of the opening—this completely unnerved Van, since it was lunar night, and the only possible source outside were the stars. He pulled himself back to make room as the door opened completely, and then instinctively threw his hands up in defense—hovering just outside the lock was the shuttle, its white-hot exhaust plume splashing the Moon's surface not a hundred feet away. The pilot was already maneuvering to blast through.

It took only a second for Van to take all this in as the escaping hurricane carried him through the outer door, where for a moment he thought he'd be thrown directly into the inferno. Once beyond the lock's pinch-point, however, the wind evaporated into the vacuum, and Van fell forward. Acquired reflex placed his hands to catch him before his faceplate struck rocks.

"Van!" came Tyna's voice. "Are you okay?"

He'd forgotten to turn off his mic, and she'd heard him shout. They were all supposed to be on radio silence in case Teirel was listening. He'd screwed up.

"Yeah," he said. "Yeah—I opened the door just in time. Turning off my mic, now."

"Okay ... Van, be careful."

Had he been in time, though? He looked up to find the shuttle moving towards him. Did the pilot even know that the lock was open? The ship's video feed might not include lateral views—maybe just down, what was needed for landing. To blast the lock, he'd maneuver close, and then tilt and splash the crater wall.

Van pushed himself to his feet and ran inside. The escaping wind was still strong, and he leaned hard into it to make headway. The shuttle's exhaust would have been a deafening roar on Earth, but raged in silence behind him in the Moon's vacuum. His feet sensed the vibration of the hellish flame pounding the Moon's surface, and he felt hot—his suit had turned silver, as it did when outside during lunar day, a mechanism to reflect the solar energy. The wind eased as he made distance inside, and he stopped and turned. A shower of clear plastic fell around him. A trapped air pocket in the light fixture above had given way. He'd heard no sound. The air was gone.

Through the open lock doors, he saw the blinding light of the shuttle's exhaust. If the pilot tilted and splashed the entrance, the heat could well kill him. He stood frozen, like rabbits he'd read about held immobile by the hypnotizing gaze of a snake, awaiting their doom. The flame lifted, lifted, and disappeared. The pilot had seen the open lock doors.

Van suddenly felt drained. He wanted to lie down, lie down and wait for everything to resolve without him. Teirel might be coming, however. The base still needed to be "cleaned." They'd saved the lock, but left the door wide open for the killer.

Van turned, and stumbled. He'd tripped over Julius's body, lying among the debris left behind in the nexgens' rush to get suited and away. Van stared at the dead man, a face he'd known all his life. Decompression was erupting changes he didn't want to see. He shuddered, spun, and sprinted away.

Where now? He couldn't join the rest in the antechamber. Somebody had to stay behind to put back the shelf hiding the lock door. He'd been totally focused on saving the front lock, and with it, as much air as possible. All valid if Teirel were to suddenly spontaneously combust. But he wasn't. He was going to remain until they were all dead. Van knew this in his gut. What did that mean? Van's jaws clenched. There was only one way out—Teirel had to die first.

A wave of nausea nearly brought Van to his knees. This wasn't an abstract notion—he had to really and truly kill Teirel. He wasn't sure he could do it. He had to, though. He had no choice. No choice.

He needed a weapon. Teirel would be coming back with a gun, a real gun. One that could kill from a distance. Van had seen this many times in movies. He needed the kind of weapon they had jury-rigged at Arrival, the one that Katlin had used to kill Mad-Meyer.

They had destroyed that weapon, however—melted it down, along with the gun Mad-Meyer had used to shoot Kim and Burl, and in the process ceremoniously rid the Moon of intentional violent death.

So naive.

He needed a *weapon*. Maybe he could make one. A type of sword, or even a club. Maybe he could sneak up on Teirel, or take him by surprise. Heck, the base was in vacuum now, all he needed to do was pierce Teirel's suit ... and then get away before he shot him? No, he'd have to kill Teirel outright.

Julius had kept a small workshop, which Burl had taken over ... in the lab—the pressurized lab. He wouldn't be able to open the door, even if he wanted to.

There was another workshop in the large bay hanger ... again, behind a pressurized door.

In fact, everything was locked away behind pressurized doors—the living units, the theater, the cafeteria. He had nothing!

Why hadn't he thought about this before? He was supposed to be the cool, stable leader. *Don't obsess!* he berated. *Think!*

There was the storage room next to the front lock. It wouldn't be pressurized. There were spare suit parts. Maybe he could rig *something*.

He turned back. He'd have to get past Julius's corpse—so be it. As he stepped over the body, he tried not to look down, but glinting twinkles caught his eye. It was the shattered plastic from the light fixture. The pieces would have sharp edges, maybe a blade for a knife. He cast his eyes across the scattered selection, most no larger than a pea pod. There was one as large as his hand. It had fallen on top of Julius, on his stomach, next to his bloating hand. In fact, it appeared as though he was holding it, ready to reach up and stab anyone disturbing his lifeless corpse. Van gave it a nudge with his foot, and started when Julius's hand moved. He froze, then reached down and grabbed the plastic shard.

An indicator blinked inside his helmet. This was a light that had never come on before. He searched his memory, remembering what it was for. It had something to do with the com links. He remembered—it meant that there were other channels active. He slid the heads-up display down and searched among the menu items. Like the indicator, this was a control he'd never used. He found "CHAN SCAN," and flicked it. The suit's com function would scan through all the available channels, looking for any active carrier frequency. A burst of static was followed by a snippet of conversation. "—don't need you to tell me how to take care of a bunch of kids—" Van muttered a curse as the scan feature moved on, stepping through other channels. That had been Teirel.

He waited, ready when it came around again. "—I'm in this as deep as you." Van tapped "HALT." That had been the pilot.

"You're just going to walk in?" the pilot said. "They obviously know what's up now. They've evacuated the base, for Christ's sake."

"I'm the one with the gun, remember?" Teirel replied.

"How do you know they don't have any?"

"Baxter was sure. One good thing about lawyers—they're precise. Nah, this will be like target practice."

Teirel was in his suit, probably already outside walking towards the open lock. Van's instinct shouted to run away, hide. *No*. He had to get behind Teirel when he entered the base. He could then follow the murderer, try to stay out of sight. Otherwise, without air, there would be no sound to warn him. Teirel might appear and take him by surprise anywhere.

The door to the storage room lay twenty feet away, towards the lock. The rectangle of the open outer lock door swam with utter blackness, the same as every Lunar night—no Earth shine on the far side of the Moon. Suddenly, a swath of white light swept across the ground outside, disappeared, and then returned—Teirel's headlamp.

Van stood frozen in indecision, skewered between instinctive flight or the logic of making for the storage room. The circle of light contracted as Teirel approached. *Crimps!* Van thought as he sprang for the storage room. His faceplate provided only 120 degrees of view. He couldn't see the lock behind him as he entered the room, and he had no idea if Teirel had appeared and seen him. Nowhere to hide! All the suits were gone, worn by the nexgens. Just spare parts hanging about on the walls. What the hell was he thinking? Obviously this would be the first place Teirel would look.

A shiver ran up his spine as he imagined a bullet tearing through him at any moment. He turned so that he could see the doorway. The glitter on the plastic shards in the hallway danced. Teirel's headlamp was shining on them. He'd entered. Waiting for the man to come in the room, Van backed up, facing the doorway, until he bumped up against the wall. Just then, Teirel appeared, the dirty-white Chinese pressure suit seeming so alien, so menacing. His hand hung by his side, holding a pistol. Van pressed back against the wall, willing the molecules of his body to merge into it, like the fantastical powers of the superheroes. Van couldn't see the man's face behind the faceplate. He turned towards Van, and he saw himself plastered against the wall, contorted and small in the faceplate's reflection. They stood, facing each other for what seemed an eternity. Van waited for the hand to raise, and a flash to appear from the muzzle. He wouldn't see the flash, of course. He'd be dead before it registered. Odd how his brain continued to process, to piece together logical threads even as he breathed his last breath.

Teirel moved. He turned, clumsy and stiff in the suit, not something he was used to. He continued turning, and walked out the door.

Van blinked, half expecting the hired killer to jump back through the door with a laugh and fire off a shot. The doorway remained empty. It was beyond belief. Teirel hadn't seen him. They had faced each other, not fifteen feet apart.

"Ha!" came Teirel's voice in his helmet. "Vacuum isn't agreeing with Ol' Julius. Hmm, pretty disgusting, actually."

No, Teirel must have seen him. It was impossible that he hadn't. There was only one explanation—Teirel thought it was an empty suit hanging on the wall. A nexgen would have known at a glance, but Teirel wasn't used to seeing empty suits.

Van ran for the door. The whole plan was to keep the man in sight. He paused. It wasn't easy to peek around corners in a suit. Half his helmet would be visible by the time one eye could see down the corridor.

He turned back into the room and threw open a locker. Thank God there was no air to carry the sound. Somewhere, somewhere—there! It had lain there for years, a mirror from their rover that had failed a decade ago. It was perfect—a four-inch mirror attached to a metal rod. He returned to the doorway, and held the mirror out, catching Teirel just as he turned the corner—to the left.

Van could have shouted with glee as he sprinted out, only to gag and nearly trip when he hurdled Julius's corpse.

"Where the hell could they be hiding?" came Teirel's voice.

"The living units are airtight," the pilot said. "Try those."

Van arrived at the corner just in time to see Teirel try a door. "Ha! You're right. It's locked," Teirel said. He took a step back, raised the gun, and Van saw it jerk. Immediately, a plume of mist emerged from the door, piling up against Teirel's midriff before evaporating. "What the hell?" Teirel said.

"It's the air escaping," the pilot said, probably seeing it through the suit-cam. "You won't be able to open the door until the pressure is relieved."

Teirel watched the condensing moisture a moment, then moved along the corridor and shot another door, and then moved on and shot yet another. Three white horizontal plumes spilled precious air into the nothingness. Each gunshot was like a hole in Van's soul.

Teirel came back to the first door, tried it, and then shot three more holes. He was practically hidden in the resulting blast of mist. When the emerging fog faded, Teirel tried the door again, and then laid his shoulder against it and pushed. The door opened a crack, but slammed shut. He pushed again, and this time the door opened farther. He pushed again, and the door flew inward, finally relieved of the pressure. He disappeared inside.

"After all that, it's empty," he said, and re-emerged. He went to the second door, forced it open, and then moved on to the third. "They think they're being smart," he growled.

"They are being smart," the pilot said. "They're probably saving as much air as they can."

Teirel snorted and walked away down the corridor.

Van waited until he'd turned the corner before running after him. When he reached the end of the corridor, he watched Teirel in his mirror. "We're looking for some place big enough to hold them all," Teirel said. He walked past the living units and turned the next corner, onto the main hallway bisecting the base. Van sprinted ahead again, but before he made the corner, Teirel said, "Well, well. What's this?"

"The sign says that it's a lab," the pilot said.

"No shit, genius. How big do you think a lab would be?"

"At least big enough to hold all the kids, I'd say."

Van reached the corner and positioned his mirror. Teirel stood in front of the lab door. Van couldn't bear losing all that air. He flicked his mic on—"Teirel!"

He saw the Chinese suit turn, and he yanked back the mirror.

"Hear that?" the pilot said.

"How could I not?" Teirel answered. "He nearly blew out my eardrums. That sounded like their old leader."

Van sat back against the wall. What now? He couldn't let on that he'd seen Teirel about to blow through to the lab—that would be exactly the incentive he needed.

He sneaked a peek around the corner with the mirror. Teirel stood there, looking down the corridor the other way. "I know you're in the base somewhere," Van said. "Maybe we can talk this through."

"Oh, yeah?" Teirel said, turning around so that Van had to pull the mirror back again. "Where are you?"

"I'm not an idiot," Van said.

Silence.

"Okay, sure," Teirel said, "let's talk."

Van grinned. He *would* be an idiot if he thought Teirel was really interested in talking. He had to stall him, though. "Okay, how about outside?"

"Why outside?"

Van gasped when Teirel appeared. The dirty Chinese suit walked by, following the main hallway away from the lab. The limited field of view inside the Chinese helmet saved Van—Teirel obviously hadn't seen him sitting there off to the side.

Teirel was waiting for an answer. "Well, for one thing, outside you won't be shooting up our doors," he said, sliding over to the opposite corner so he could use the mirror.

Van wanted to slap his forehead.

Teirel had stopped and turned around, forcing Van to pull his mirror back. "Ah ha! So you watched me do that."

Think! "Surveillance cameras."

"No cameras," the pilot said.

"Maybe you *are* an idiot, Van," Teirel said. "You think we wouldn't check that sort of thing before coming?"

"The base used to have outside feeds," the pilot said, "but those went dead months ago. Nothing inside."

"Well, well," Teirel said. "You must be around here somewhere. Be a good doggie and heel."

Van clenched his jaws in indecision, then jammed the mirror around the corner—he *had* to know where Teirel was. He breathed. The man was walking the other way along the main hallway. He sat back against the wall.

"Breathing hard?" Teirel said. "Tell you what—I'm at the airlock now. Why don't you come, and we'll talk this through?"

Van clenched his jaws again. He'd almost scoffed at the ruse and given himself away. He had to be savvy. If he really didn't know where Teirel was ... "How do I know you're actually there?"

"You have my word, doggie. Fetch, boy! Fetch!"

Van closed his eyes, thinking what to say.

"What have we here?" Teirel said. "Techno-boy told me about this."

"The Farm?" the pilot said.

"Yeah. He was bragging how 'tuned' it was. There's got to be room for all the brats in there."

"That's an airlock door. You don't want to wreck that."

"Why not?"

"The new crew's going to want those hydroponics."

"Yeah, yeah. So, how do I get in?"

"It probably has a genie. Just ask it."

"Just like that? Hey, genie! You listening?"

"We heard the kids say that they don't know that they're called genies. Just refer to it as an airlock."

"Christ—hey airlock! You there?"

"*I am here,*" came the genie's voice over the com."

"Great. Let me in."

"*I'm sorry, but only Van Wilkens can enable me to operate the airlocks.*"

"What the—what the hell are you talking about?"

"*I am sorry, but Van has inserted a personal block.*"

"What the hell does that mean?"

"*It means that only Van Wilkens can enable me to operate the airlocks.*"

"Holy hell, I'm talking in circles with a fuckin' door. Okay, time to shoot my way in."

"You sure?" the pilot said.

"Oh yeah. Now more than ever. Why do you think the doggie's keeping me out?"

Van squeezed his eyes shut, forcing tears to wet his cheeks. When would it end? *How* could it end? All the air inside the Farm. And the plants, an integral—essential—component of their life cycle ... and Burl! Crimps! Burl had no pressure suit!

"No!" Van cried, standing up.

"Ho, ho," Teirel said. "Looks like we hit pay dirt. You going to open the lock?"

"Yeah, I'll open it," Van said, stepping around the corner and blinking away the tears.

"I'll give you three minutes. You'd better run."

Teirel was facing the opposite direction. "I'm here," Van said.

The Chinese suit turned slowly around. "Well, hello, doggie!" Teirel said, and raised the gun. Van held his breath, his pulse thumping in his temples as he stared at the open barrel. Teirel waved the gun. "Open it."

Van walked to the lock. Unless Burl had activated the helmet he'd taken along, he'd have no warning. Van raised his fist and pounded on the door. He heard no sound, but inside where there was air, Burl might.

"What the hell's he doing?" Teirel said.

"Not sure," said the pilot.

"You've got two minutes to open this door, doggie, or I'm going to blow it, but only after I kill you first. Luckily, there's even a little clock in this suit, so the countdown has begun."

Van took a step back from the lock so the genie could see him. "Airlock, this is Van—open the lock."

"*I'm sorry,*" the genie said, "*but I'll need confirmation that you are Van Wilkens.*"

"Airlock, my suit has a serial number—can you see it?" he said, lifting his shoulder towards the lens above the door.

"*I have confirmed that the suit belongs to Van Wilkens, but that does not prove that he is inside it.*"

"Airlock," he said, glancing at Teirel, "I was wearing this same suit when I set the personal block on the ... other lock."

He'd almost said the antechamber lock.

"*I know that, but that doesn't prove that you are still inside this suit.*"

"Tick-tock, tick-tock," Teirel said.

"Crimps!" Van said, "look at my face!" he said, throwing his head back.

"*It would be preferable for you to take off the helmet.*"

"I'll die! There's no *air* in the base!"

"*I have confirmed that this is true. Ignore that request. Imperative! Do not take off your helmet!*"

"Airlock, you must confirm my identity by viewing my face inside this helmet—" Something jiggled his head. It was the tip of Teirel's gun pressed against the side. "Airlock, in about ten seconds, my face will be gone. This man is going to shoot and kill me if you don't open the lock. You will be responsible for my death."

"*I* *understand,*" the genie said as the yellow light came on. "*Evacuating.*"

"Time's up, doggie. Too bad."

"The genie's opening! I got it to open!"

"Looks to me like the door's still closed."

"It has to pull the air out first! It's normal!"

"It's true," the pilot said. "It will take a couple of minutes."

Teirel dropped his hand, and Van took a breath. The killer whistled a tune as they waited. It was familiar, something Van had heard long ago. He remembered—the title was "How Much is that Doggie in the Window."

"*Checking integrity,*" the genie said. "*Access.*" The yellow light was replaced with a green one, and the door popped open an inch.

Van swung it open and gestured for Teirel to enter.

"Smart doggie," Teirel said, "but I don't think so. We'll go in together." He walked in, and pulled Van along. Two minutes later, the far lock door opened, and Van started to walk through, to give Burl warning if he hadn't heard the knocks, but Teirel yanked him back. "We go together," he said menacingly.

Van tensed as they entered the wide expanse of the Farm, the largest single enclosed area of the base, and relaxed when he saw that Burl was nowhere in sight. Isolated now by his suit, Van missed the normal greeting of warm, humid air. His helmet moderated the blinding full-spectrum lighting, depriving him of the sense of stepping into a bright, sunny day on Earth.

"No kids," Teirel said, gazing at row upon row of carrots, peas, kale, broccoli, spinach, and lima beans, all rooted in long plastic canisters through which a nutrient-rich mist circulated.

"Not much opportunity to hide," the pilot said.

"Not a few dozen brats, at least," Teirel agreed, turning in a slow arc to take in what Van considered a vast open area—eighty feet square. "What's this?" he said, stepping over to a table normally used for cleaning and servicing the mist canisters.

"Pressure suit parts," the pilot said. "Hey, look how the one leg is cut off, and there's a glue gun nearby—I'll bet that one-legged kid was trying to build a suit."

"Yeah," Teirel said, gazing at Burl's handiwork.

Van cast his eyes around the room. *Crimps!* Burl's lone foot was visible beneath the misting tank in the corner.

"Check the glue gun—see if it's hot."

"You think he might be here?"

"Find out."

Van winced as Teirel picked up the gun and pressed the nozzle into the top of the plastic table, gouging a trough ahead of a line of smoke, and inflicting more damage than a decade of use.

"Well, well," Teirel said, dropping the gun and turning to scan the room. "Looks like we may have cornered the smart-aleck. Two down, and thirty-five to go."

"This is interesting," the pilot said.

"What?" Teirel said, stepping to look down along each row of plants.

"Pollin sent the plans for the base."

"Yeah?"

"It shows a large excavation deeper into the crater wall. It's drawn in dotted lines, as though it was just in the planning stages."

Teirel stopped. "Or just not finished."

"Maybe. Bingo! It shows another airlock. It's at the back of the lab."

"I was about to go in there—" he said, turning to look at Van "—when the doggie called out. Bingo, indeed. Doggie managed to fool me after all. Come on, doggie, let's go find your kiddy pals."

"Uh, oh," the pilot said.

"What's wrong?"

"Nothing's wrong. Looks like I found your kids."

"What are you talking about?"

"They're here."

Chapter 15

The Naval base at Guantanamo Bay—Gitmo—glided up over the horizon, nestled under the hills that isolated the bay from the rest of Cuba. As Namazi brought the Simurgh in, the air strip and ancient Navy buildings resolved. If not for the landing strip, seeming all the more lonely and abandoned for the grass and small shrubs pushing through the many cracks, Katlin wouldn't have guessed it was anything other than a temporary staging area, which in a way it had always been, since the land it sat on still belonged to Cuba. The cluster of compact metal and glass buildings looked as though they'd been deserted years ago—the many windows were dirty, some even broken. Parked next to the only two-story structure were two new military vehicles, the sole signs of life.

"What are we going to do?" Katlin asked.

"Always begin negotiations from a position of strength," he replied. He glanced at her. "We show them that we have a powerful weapon."

"Wouldn't it be obvious to Pollin?"

"From a logical perspective he would likely agree. I want to make an emotional impression."

"How?"

"By destroying something."

"*The base commander is calling General McClellen,*" Alibai reported. "*They're tracking your ship on radar.*"

"That's fine. We're not hiding now."

From the view in the video screen, Katlin guessed that they were maybe a few hundred feet above the ground as Namazi glided in, lighting a swath of low brush on fire as he passed. Two, and then a third soldier came out the front door and stood gazing at their approach. The Simurgh crossed the unused air strip, and continued on, the facades of the buildings becoming foreshortened as they came close.

"Uh, there's three men standing there," Katlin said.

"That's their choice," Namazi said. "I'm not sneaking up on them."

"McClellen has told the base commander to call Major Otto back. He's apparently been assigned to Holloman Base."

Namazi rose higher as they came to the main building. Two of the soldiers ran inside, but the third stood gazing up, reporting into his sleeve. The view in Katlin's screen eased back and forth, settled directly above one of the two cars, and then slowly expanded— Namazi was settling down. The soldier raised both arms against the heat, and then he too turned and ran inside. Still the view below expanded.

"You going to *land* here?" Katlin asked.

"That would seem problematic," Namazi replied, his eyes glued to his display.

Katlin's screen suddenly turned white, and simultaneously she felt the ship jerk under her as a boom rattled her ears. The blank white on her screen broke into swirls of black smoke as the light sensors recovered from overload, and she saw pieces of metal falling to the ground. Directly below, where the vehicle had been, was a flattened mass of burning metal, and off to the side was the other car on fire as well.

"That should get their attention," Katlin said.

"It certainly got mine." Namazi glanced at her. "That was an oops."

"You didn't mean for it to happen?"

"I didn't mean for the gas tank to blow, although I should have expected it."

"You were going to destroy it in any case."

"True. But not in a way that would needlessly endanger lives on the ground."

"Or our ship."

He glanced at her again and then back at his display. "Indeed. The shrapnel could have damaged the exhaust nozzles." He sighed. "I am sorry, Katlin," he said looking at her.

She chuckled.

"Why do you laugh?" he asked.

"That's like apologizing for catching a cold."

He watched his display, and a grin formed. "That is comparing apples with peanuts, but I understand your point. And, thank you."

"Pollin has taken the phone," Alibai said. *"He's demanding that General McClellen call in fighters from Florida. He is also expressing sarcastic criticism of the United State's intelligence agencies—he says that apparently Greater Persia has superior capabilities."*

"That's because he doesn't know about you," Katlin said.

"That was my conclusion as well."

Namazi had taken the Simurgh up, and was now bringing it down again some distance from the buildings.

"Are we landing?" Katlin asked.

"No," Namazi replied. "It's time to cut Pollin off."

On her screen, Katlin saw a cinderblock building next to spherical tanks. "You going to blow the power station?"

He shook his head. "I would be a fool to make that mistake twice. That amount of gas storage would take us with it. No, I'm just cutting Pollin off."

Katlin saw the power lines attached to the generation station sag and erupt in a shower of sparks. "What now?"

"Now we land and contact Pollin."

"Those fighters are probably on their way."

"It's five hundred miles. We have nearly an hour."

While Namazi brought the ship down on the end of the abandoned air strip, Katlin had Alibai hail the base directly.

"This is Commander Jenkins addressing the craft attacking my base," came a man's voice over the radio, "you are committing an act of war. Surrender immediately, or suffer the consequence, both to you and your country of origin. I repeat this is Commander—"

The Navy commander's voice was replaced with that of Pollin's. "Hello, Namazi. You've really gotten yourself in hot water now. If you give yourself up immediately, I'll personally guarantee that they won't execute you."

Namazi took the microphone. "You know I have the upper hand, here. I will be stating the demands, and they are simple—let Beau go, and we will leave."

"What makes you think I have your friend here?"

Katlin had widened the field of view of her screen, and she was rotating it, scanning the surrounding area. She stopped, and zoomed in.

"It is enough to state that we know," Namazi said.

"It's a pity that you're wrong. You've done all this damage for nothing."

"I will not play games. If you do not let Beau go, I will destroy—"

Katlin elbowed him and pointed at her screen.

"Ah," Namazi said. "I see the other Simurgh at the far end of the air strip. I think you would agree that your only antimatter ship is worth letting Beau go."

"I'm not stupid, Namazi. I know that if you destroy the other ship, the resulting explosion would blow you to tiny little pieces."

"Mr. Pollin, thanks to the time you've given me on a Simurgh training your pilots, I understand the operation in great detail. I know that by simply fusing the main control processor in the nose, the antimatter will self-destruct in anywhere from five to ten minutes. That will give us time to get away, but not you."

"You will be killing your friend."

"In any other scenario, *you* will be killing our friend. So he has nothing to lose. In fact, we will be providing a merciful escape from sure torture—if you haven't painfully killed him already."

Katlin was staring at Namazi wide-eyed. He looked at her and frowned.

"Sorry, Namazi," Pollin said. "I don't believe you. If I were you, I'd give myself up."

"Very well," Namazi said, and lifted the ship off the runway.

Katlin reached with a shaking hand to reduce the zoom on her screen. "I don't see how you'll be able to train our exhaust on the nose of the other ship without it reaching the main area."

Namazi looked at her, and shook his head. "I'm bluffing. There's no control processor in the nose—there's no single control processor anywhere. It would be insane to build a ship like these without extensive redundancy."

"Ah. Of course," Katlin said, her cheeks burning. Her father always told her how smart she was. Maybe he was wrong.

She spun the screen's view around. What was this? She zoomed again. "Uh, looks like Pollin's coming out—and he has Beau! Uh, oh. He has a gun to Beau's head."

Namazi took a breath, as though he'd been holding it. "Excellent."

"It's good that Pollin has a gun to Beau's head?"

Namazi glanced at her. "We didn't actually expect that Pollin would let Beau go just like that."

Yes, her father was definitely wrong. "I guess we're lucky that Pollin is playing the game at all."

Namazi looked at her and smiled. "Let's cross our fingers that our luck holds."

At his smile, the warmth in her cheeks moved to her core. "Muslims cross their fingers?" she said. "I thought it's a Christian symbol."

He laughed. "And Easter eggs originated from ancient pagan fertility rites. I guess religious symbols can eventually become universal."

Pollin lifted his wrist to his mouth, and his voice came through the radio. "Land and come out of the ship, or I'll remove Beau's brains from his skull."

Namazi took the ship higher. "Kill Beau, and you die as well," Namazi said. He lifted the "talk" button and said, "Looks like it's a standoff."

"*Otto reports that he's ready to take off,*" Alibai said. "*He indicates that he should be there in an hour.*"

"We'll be long gone by then."

"*Namazi, I'm concerned that you believe that Otto is coming here from Holloman Base.*"

"Of course—Allah! Are you saying that he's already *here?*"

"*He's been here all along.*"

"McClellen called him back from Holloman!"

"General McClellen erroneously thought that Otto had already left. Namazi, I am sorry. I should have realized your misunderstanding. Apparently Beau's trust in my intuition is misguided."

"Look!" Katlin said, pointing at her screen. The other Simurgh had disappeared behind a blanched white smear. The intense light of the exhaust was saturating the video sensor.

Namazi's eyes turned dark. "He's taking off."

"Can't we … go after him?"

"To what end?"

"To … to …. Oh, crimps!"

"Indeed. We've lost our leverage. We can either leave, or land. If we land, Pollin will almost certainly take us prisoner."

"Which would do Beau no good. Landing is fruitless."

"It would seem so," Namazi said, watching her.

"You're leaving it up to me?"

"Katlin, Beau is your friend. I can't decide."

"Landing serves no purpose," she said, "other than refusing to leave a friend behind—one who sacrificed himself so that we could get away."

"Landing would be acting on principle alone," he agreed, "where, in the end, there would be three prisoners instead of one. Shall I go ahead and land then?"

Katlin nodded. She blinked at the tears, and rubbed the back of her hand across her eyes. She hated it when she got sentimental.

Namazi landed at the edge of the runway, close to the waiting captor and hostage, and Katlin followed Namazi down the long, long climb to the ground. Pollin came forward to meet them, his gun pressed against Beau's temple. A marine had joined them and followed, rifle ready.

"That was pretty dumb, Katlin," Beau said, "but I'm not complaining."

"Quiet!" Pollin roared, giving him a shake. "You don't realize just how dumb, Namazi. I saved you from nasty interrogations once because I needed you—"

"And now you don't, since your pilots have been trained," Namazi said.

Pollin lifted his shoulders in a shrug.

"You promised to let Beau go if we gave up," Katlin said.

Pollin turned his gaze on her. The intensity of his malice drove her back a step. "Did I?" he said, dripping with sarcasm.

"Actually," Beau said, "he never promised that."

That got him another shake. "I don't need your help," Pollin barked. "I'll be glad when I'm done with you." He spoke quietly into Beau's ear. "Fortunately for you, that will have to wait until you decide to talk." He chuckled. "Actually, I guess that's not fortunate at all for you."

Katlin felt a chill as she remembered Beau's description of the evidence of his uncle's torture. "Has he been ... mistreating you?" Katlin asked.

Beau turned his eyes sideways at Pollin and shook his head morosely. "Not yet."

He had a gun to his head. "Beau," Katlin said, "if that's the truth, tell me how many slices of pizza you had last time."

"Enough with the games," Pollin growled. "It's not going to matter anyway." He shoved Beau towards the Marine. "Take him inside."

The Marine swung the tip of his barrel at Beau's back and led him away. "Five!" Beau yelled over his shoulder.

Pollin was probably right that it didn't matter, but Katlin breathed a little easier knowing that Beau hadn't been tortured.

Not yet.

Pollin gestured with the gun. "What's that?" he asked, pointing it at Katlin.

She didn't know what he meant, and looked at him blankly. She couldn't take her eyes off the pistol. She'd never seen a gun until Mad-Meyer threatened her with one, and she had killed him not long afterwards. Guns represented horror, beyond the immediate threat posed by Pollin's.

"The box!" Pollin exclaimed. "Are you daft?"

Katlin jerked from her trance. Alibai was strapped to her waist. She shrugged. "It's nothing."

"You *are* daft. You wouldn't be carrying it if it was nothing."

She blinked. What had Beau claimed? "It's a defibrillator—for my father. Earth's gravity strains his heart."

Pollin lifted the gun and pointed it at her nose. "Now tell me what it really is."

"I don't know," she said, which was somewhat true—she had no idea what was inside. "Beau gave it to me."

"Hand it over," he said, and she unhooked and gave it to him. She felt like a traitor.

He turned the box over, looking for some clue. He scowled and made to toss it away, but changed his mind and tucked it under his arm.

Pollin looked at Namazi, and then at Katlin. He sighed. "You two are a problem." He continued to study them, and this made Katlin sweat. It was the look of someone deciding whether to throw an old pair of shoes back in the closet, or drop them in the trash. He shrugged, a gesture that caused Katlin to shudder. "Let's go," he said, waving the gun towards the far end of the air strip.

"Where are you taking us?" Namazi asked, holding his ground.

"You'll find out soon enough. Let's go."

"I think we'll stay here until we can speak to the base commander."

Pollin lifted his shoulders. "We can do it right here, if you like." He lifted the pistol and aimed it at Namazi's head.

"You might want to wait just a minute," Namazi said coolly, nodding towards the building. His tone was calm, but Katlin saw a droplet inching down his temple.

A Marine officer, whom Katlin took to be the base commander, was returning with Beau in tow. "I want him inside," Pollin snapped, clearly the one truly in charge.

"General McClellen called," the officer replied with aplomb. He was willing to take orders from Pollin, but the civilian wasn't responsible for his promotions. "He wants to talk to you," he said, handing him a phone. "Don't worry, it's a secure line," the base commander added when Pollin frowned.

Pollin took the phone. "Yeah? … A grave emergency, huh?" he said skeptically. "Like what?"

The base commander looked at Namazi and Katlin, but didn't say anything.

"Fine, fine," Pollin said, exasperated, and handed the phone back to the officer. "Christ—military," he said, disgusted. "He wants me in to teleconference. Watch these three until I get back."

Pollin walked off carrying Alibai, but turned back when the box suddenly began squealing shrilly. "Son of a bitch!" Pollin said, wincing at the racket. "What else can go wrong?" he growled, handing the irritating source to the commander.

Alibai's siren call faded after a minute, and the commander gestured with his pistol for the three of them to stand together. "He intends to kill us, you know," Namazi said.

The base commander studied the Persian pilot. "That's not my business," he finally said.

"The murder of civilians under your charge is not your business?"

He didn't respond. If he was associated with Pollin, he must be used to the man's bludgeon ways.

The phone beeped, and the commander answered it. "General McClellen?" he said, surprised. He listened, frowned, and said, "I don't understand, sir—" ... "Yes, of course, but what does Pollin say about it?" ... "Yes, yes, sir. Of course. I understand. Good bye, sir."

He stared at nothing for a second, and then shook his head, perplexed, and looked at them. "You are to report to Holloman base immediately," he said, still dumfounded.

"Excuse me?" Namazi said.

The commander gestured with his pistol for them to move off towards the ship. "I just follow orders. Move your asses. You've got three minutes to get out of here."

The three of them looked at each other wide-eyed, and sprinted off.

"Hold it!" the officer called, running towards them. "Here," he said, handing Alibai to Namazi. "You're supposed to take this along."

Namazi nodded, took the box, and they ran off.

"What's going on?" Katlin said when they reached the ladder, and Namazi helped her up.

"I have an idea," Beau said.

"Later," Namazi said, lifting Beau right off his feet and onto the ladder behind Katlin.

She'd just reached the lock when she heard shouts off towards the base. Both lock doors were open, and she tumbled inside as shots rang out. Beau fell inside on top of her, and they rolled to the side as Namazi dove through. He clawed his way into the pilot's chair. Seconds later the scream of the engine filled the control chamber, far louder with the lock doors open. "Should I close the doors—?" Katlin started.

"Later," Namazi said, flipping switches.

Katlin looked at Beau, but he was gazing in awe around the tiny room. "Should we strap in?" Katlin asked.

"No time," Namazi said as she fell back when the ship began to move. "Hang on," he said. "Just don't fall out the door."

Beau looked like he'd woken in heaven. "This is so cool!" he whispered, catching himself as the ship angled over.

After a minute, Namazi sat back and sighed. "Okay, strap yourselves in," he said as he moved to close the lock doors.

Katlin let Beau have the co-pilot chair—she knew the thrill it would give him—and she took one of the fold-down jump seats.

"Crimps! What happened back there?" Katlin asked.

"Let's ask the one responsible," Beau said.

"What are you talking about?"

"Alibai!" Beau said.

"*It's good to hear you, again, Beau,*" the box said.

"Would you care to fill us in?"

"*Are you referring to the escape I engineered?*"

"That was Alibai—?" Katlin started, but Beau held up his hand.

"How'd you do it?" Beau asked.

"*I used misdirection. I first orchestrated a call for the base commander from General McLellen. I—as the general—told him that I needed to talk to Pollin immediately, and that he should bring Beau along.*"

"And then—as the general—you got Pollin to go inside."

"*That's correct.*"

"Hold it!" Katlin said. "How could you possibly fool the base commander—and Pollin? They know what the general sounds like."

"This is going to prove that I'm a genius," Beau said. "Alibai, you decided to construct it all on your own?"

"*That is correct, Beau. Through a conversation with Katlin, I have developed a deep appreciation for moral complexities. I realized the critical role*" *that loyalty and trust play in human affairs. I have been waiting to find out from you if my actions were appropriate. I need your guidance, Beau."*

"I'd kiss you if I thought you'd feel it," Beau said.

"I take that as approval?"

"Take it as enthusiastic approval."

"Whoa! Whoa!" Katlin cried. "I still don't understand how Alibai fooled them!"

"Can you show her?" Beau said.

The voice of General McClellen issued from the box. *"I studied the tonal and inflection characteristics of the general's previous conversations. Choosing his phrasing was the subjective, and therefore risky, part. Dammit-to-hell, commander! When I say I want those three off to Holloman, I expect you to jump! Hear me, man?"* Alibai returned to his normal boyish voice. *"Synthesizing other's voices is processing intensive, and I am not able to perform it in real-time. I created a number of possible responses ahead of time that seemed appropriate for the situation."*

"I'm a true genius," Beau crowed.

"It was Alibai who imitated the general," Katlin said.

"Alibai," Beau said, "who created you?"

"You did, Beau."

"Hark the hubris fate of Phaethon," Namazi said without looking up from his controls.

"Who's Phaethon?" Beau asked.

Katlin laughed. "In Greek mythology, he was the son of Helios, the sun god. He insisted on driving the sun chariot for a day, but when he couldn't control the horses, Zeus had to strike him down with a thunderbolt."

"Yeah, yeah," Beau said. "I get it. The root of mythology is 'myth,' though."

"And myths are usually moral lessons."

Katlin was abruptly thrown to the side as the ship accelerated hard to the left.

"What's going on?" Beau asked, clutching the arms of the seat.

Namazi didn't answer at first. "There's another ship coming after us, and it has the advantage of accumulated velocity."

"Flying is all about delta-V," Katlin added before she could reign her own hubris at showing off.

"The fighters from Florida?" Beau asked.

Namazi shook his head. "It has to be another Simurgh."

"It's Otto!" Katlin said.

Namazi's mouth was tight with tension. "He must have guessed which way we'd head off."

"We can … outrun him?" Beau asked.

Namazi was absorbed with his controls.

"Too late," Katlin whispered.

Otto's voice came over the speaker. "Captain Namazi, you have exactly ten seconds to abandon your escape. I will not hesitate to fire this time. Ten, nine, eight—"

"Can't we do *something*?" Beau asked.

Namazi turned to Katlin. It was a look of pure pathos, a last farewell. He turned back to his controls, ready to do whatever he could to evade the pending missile.

"—three, two, one."

From the jump-seat Katlin saw the rear view screen in front of Beau turn pure white, presumably the intercept missile launching from Otto's Simurgh. Namazi froze, though, at his controls. "What in Allah—?" he muttered. The rear view screen had turned cobalt blue, what Katlin took to be a clear Caribbean sky, but quickly realized was simply the default mode with no signal. Namazi uttered something in hushed Farsi.

Beau pointed questioningly at the blue screen.

"Don't worry," Namazi said, sitting back with furrowed brow. "Fortunately Otto's Simurgh was directly behind us, and the shielding from our own drive will have protected us."

"I—I don't understand," Katlin said. "What just happened?"

Namazi turned to her. He seemed to have difficulty voicing the words. "Major Otto is dead. His ship exploded. The resulting radiation took out all our rear sensors."

A new voice came over the radio, speaking a language that Katlin assumed was Farsi. Namazi's eyes went wide as he listened. He took the mic and responded angrily. The interchange went on for a few minutes before Namazi clicked off the mic and sat fuming.

"Namazi?" Katlin said tentatively.

He looked at her and shook his head. "That was another Simurgh, a fellow Persian. It was he who took out Otto's ship." He shook his head again and spat another word in Farsi, obviously a curse. "He congratulates me on my escape, and suggests that he follow me to Tehran. This was a suggestion in form only."

"He ordered you back to Tehran," Katlin said.

"Yes. Effectively."

Alibai came alive. "*I have intercepted news from the Moon,*" the box said.

"Let's have it," Beau said.

"*Daedalus Base has been evacuated of air and cleared native personnel are being eradicated.*"

"Natives?" Beau said. "There's Moon aliens?"

Katlin and Namazi looked at each other. The horror was palpable. "They mean the nexgens," she whispered.

"But—but, that means …"

Nobody finished the thought.

Chapter 16

"What the hell do you mean, 'They're here'?" Teirel said, being careful to keep the pistol pointed at Van.

"Just what I said," came the pilot's voice over the com. "Two of the kids are approaching. They're each riding something—geez, they look like … good God, they look like the killer aliens in that old classic movie."

"What are you babbling about? What goddamned movie?"

"Where the baby alien gestates inside one of the crew's stomachs, and bursts out—"

"Knock it off! This ain't no science fiction movie! Where the hell did they come from? You were supposed to be watching the airlock, not dreaming about science fiction."

"I was watching! I don't know where they came from—somewhere off to the right."

"What's over there?"

"Nothing! The crater wall!"

"Keep your ass tight in the chair—I'm on the way."

Teirel prodded Van towards the Farm airlock. As they waited for it to evacuate, Teirel said, "What're they up to, doggie?"

"I don't know," Van said.

Teirel lifted the gun to point at Van's helmet. "You have five seconds."

"I swear! I have no idea!" Van pleaded. Teirel wouldn't believe him. Why should he? He had to give him *something*. "The description sounds like cave bots, but I have no idea how they would have gotten them outside."

"'Cave bots'? Do I look like an imbecile? Cut the science fiction crap. You now have two seconds," he said, pressing the gun against Van's helmet so that it shook.

"Cave bots! They're real! They were used to carve out the whole base. They look a lot like those alien monsters. The screw boring mechanism looks like the elongated head of the alien monster—"

"Alright! I get it. Christ! I'll be happy when I'm back on the ground."

This confused Van. He snuck a glance at Teirel's feet. They were planted firmly on the lock floor. He must have meant the Earth.

The light turned green, and Van pushed the door open.

"I think I should take off," the pilot said nervously.

"Jesus!" Teirel exclaimed. "Keep your pants on! They're just kids."

"You're not seeing what I'm seeing. These cave bots are … they look nasty."

"Alien monsters?" Teirel jeered, prodding Van along at a trot.

"Not alien, but definitely monsters—wait! Holy cow! There's a whole line of people walking towards me—kids, I guess. Must be dozens."

"Where the hell are they coming from?"

"Don't know. Must be a back door. I really think I should take off. These machines could do real damage to the shuttle."

"You take off, and I'll have your balls in a jar! We're almost there!"

"Ah, geez. One of them's below me now."

"That's right," came Tyna's voice. "Teirel, let Van go, or I'll wreck the shuttle."

Van finally stumbled through the open front lock doors into the lunar night with Teirel right behind. The shuttle sat a hundred feet away. Powerful spotlights embedded in its nose lit the area, including a line of waiting nexgens at the very periphery. The crab-like form of a cave bot sat next to it, the nasty bore screw poised, ready to pierce the skin. Tyna rode the machine like the horses they'd seen in movies.

Van was jerked back as Teirel wrapped his arm around the base of his helmet. Van couldn't see, but it was obvious Teirel had the gun to his head. "Back away, or doggie's brains will mess up his suit."

"Go for it, Tyna!" Van shouted.

"Shut up!" Teirel exclaimed, giving him a shake.

Just then the other cave bot came around the ship, stepping jerkily along like some huge drunken Moon spider. Van recognized Deik's suit.

"Jesus *Christ*!" Teirel yelled, and the pistol moved forward into Van's view, and jerked. Simultaneously, sparks flashed off the side of Deik's bot. Teirel had shot at him. Cave bots, built to withstand the onslaught of falling rocks, would probably shrug off a pistol's bullets, but not pressure suits. Deik crawled off the bot, and lay down on the Moon's surface. If he'd been hit, he was being methodical about dying.

"Son of a goddamned *bitch*!" Teirel shouted, and moved the pistol. Tyna had activated the bore screw, and was piercing the shuttle's side. The cave bot tore through the thin metal as though it was made of paper. Sparks flew from the side of Tyna's bot, and she slid off. She tried to hide behind it, but her legs were still exposed. There was no such thing as a minor flesh wound on the Moon—Teirel only needed to nick her suit.

The assassin let go of Van so he could hold the pistol in both his gloved hands, aiming carefully at Tyna. Van pushed Teirel's arms just as the gun recoiled. A second later, Van was staring into the open barrel. "That's it, doggie," Teirel snarled. "You just made your last mistake."

A collective gasp caused them both to look off to where a brilliant star fell slowly among the myriad of lesser cousins. As it fell, it grew brighter, and still brighter, until it was painful to look at directly. Everyone stood frozen as it settled into a hovering position a quarter mile away. The white-hot ionized gas illuminated the lunar landscape, gray Moon rock, patterned with sharply defined shadows.

That exhaust could only be created by one kind of rocket.

"It's Namazi!" Tyna breathed, and a chorus of cheers erupted from the nexgens, despite the obvious directed radio silence.

Even as she voiced this, the ship tilted and glided towards them. As it did, it crossed a corner of the mining platform, melting struts and mesh flooring. Its path brought it close to the line of nexgens, and they scrambled to get out of the way.

This wasn't the Namazi that Van knew, and it was headed directly for the Chinese shuttle. "Tyna!" Van yelled. "Get away! Everybody—get away from the shuttle!"

Van waited until he saw Tyna loping quickly away, then, risking Teirel's gun, he too turned and ran. The stark shadows around him, thrown by the approaching antimatter ship, faded. He glanced back. The shuttle pilot understood what was about to happen, and had ignited his rockets. He started to lift off, but the cave bot's bite was deep, and it held on like a bulldog. The weight unbalanced the shuttle, and it leaned over, but the bot must have damaged it internally, for the exhaust sputtered, and the ship settled back onto the Moon with sickening slow motion.

Seconds later, the new arrival was upon it. Hundreds of feet above, its searing plume splashed the lunar surface in an advancing line that ended by washing across the stricken vessel with an inferno of heat. Van stopped and stared, mesmerized, despite the danger. The small fins and landing legs were the first to succumb, passing rapidly from angry red to searing white hot before sagging away. The shuttle's hull bearing the direct onslaught—just a thin metal shell—sagged, and the next instant the entire vessel was replaced by a blinding expanse of light. The ship's hypergolic fuels had escaped their containments and exploded, instantly killing the pilot, if he wasn't already dead. Van felt the shock through his feet as pieces of the shuttle shot past him. It was stupid to have stood and watched rather than lying down, but the choice was beyond his grasp.

Van was jostled as Teirel grabbed him again and put the gun to his helmet. "That fucking Iranian's going to pay for that," he growled.

"That's not Namazi!" Van said.

"It has to be."

"No, it's not him. I'm sure of it. Whoever it is, if he destroyed your shuttle, he'll be coming after you next."

The enigmatic ship remained, hovering over the remnants of the wreckage, reducing the metal pieces to molten pools. This ship was larger than the Namazi's routine shuttle, and clearly powered with antimatter. More alarming, it bristled with missiles, secured around the waist, ready for launch. This was a war machine, and one missile cradle was empty.

"Otto?" Teirel finally said, peering up at the sleek ship, barely visible above the blinding exhaust. "Is that you?"

"Who's Otto?" Van asked. "Maybe he's not tuned to our com links."

"Shut up, doggie!" Teirel warned, shaking him.

"Otto is dead," came a voice. For an instant, Van thought that it was indeed Namazi, for the accent was the same. "I killed him."

"Who ... who are you?" Teirel asked, peering upward, his voice unsure for the first time.

"Who I am is not important. What I represent is all that matters, my country and my mission."

"And, what would that be?" Teirel asked, his tone skewing back towards confidence—this man had chosen not to kill him immediately, which meant he wanted something, and a poker hand was something Teirel could handle.

"I have come on behalf of Greater Persia to protect this base. We have been fighting for its independence, and now have a stake in proprietorship."

"So, Iran has declared war on the US?"

"Iran ceased to exist forty years ago. Greater Persia is simply claiming what is rightfully hers according to universal salvage laws. The United States is free to declare war if it wishes to steal it."

"You just murdered an American citizen pursuing a peaceful mission on American property."

Van snorted, and Teirel gave him a shake.

"How peaceful are secret preparations for manufacturing antimatter to be used for military purposes?"

This gave Teirel pause, and Van vital insight—it explained why Teirel and whoever he worked for were willing to kill everybody on the base—everything that followed would be done in secret, and nobody would ever know.

"It's a shame that you've mustered the squatters against me," the Persian pilot continued. "I must take whatever steps necessary to protect our property."

Squatters? Van realized he was talking about the nexgens. Crimps! For twelve years Daedalus Base been ignored, and now everybody was willing to kill them to get possession.

The nexgens ... they were gone! No, they were on the move, marching towards the lock, positioning themselves to protect their home, completely ineffectual as it was. At the front of the small army was Mai Dung in Randy's suit. No Tuan. She'd left him somewhere safe.

The Persian ship tilted and moved forward, and Teirel grabbed Van and pulled him towards the lock where the rest were massing. A massacre was unfolding as the Persian pilot prepared to splash the area with death-wielding exhaust.

A collective gasp interrupted Van's struggle to pull free from Teirel. Before their eyes, a second plume of white-hot ionized gas appeared between them and the attacker. The arriving ship settled into view, and Van could see that it was identical to the first. Closer now, he could see writing on the side, words created out of foreign characters—what he took to be Farsi, Namazi's native tongue.

A girl's voice came across the com link, pouring out words in haste. "Van, Tyna! If you're down there, can you hear me?"

"Katlin?" Van said, stunned.

"Yes! Van, listen carefully. The other pilot may be listening, but his English is only marginal. I'm speaking very fast so that maybe he won't be able to follow me. This is important, so listen carefully. I am with Namazi, and it turns out that he's a double-agent—with the CIA. He has orders to take out this Persian ship at any cost. Van, you have to get all the others inside the radiation hardened blast room—"

"Katlin! What are you talking about? What radiation—?"

"Van, shut up, and listen carefully to what I'm saying. Get everybody into the radiation hardened room—the uclar. Do you understand?"

"Uh, uh—yes! I do! The uclar. I understand!"

Namazi was taking his ship quickly up, to get above the attacking ship and destroy it with his exhaust.

"Van!" It was Tyna, breaking radio silence.

"Yes?"

"It's an uclar, is that right?"

"Yes. That's what she said. Everybody!" he called, addressing the entire crowd. "Listen—it's an uclar! You understand?"

Dozens of helmets nodded.

They couldn't talk about it. The other pilot might still be listening. He didn't know what Katlin was up to, but they needn't worry about radiation. She'd made that clear. He hadn't suspected that she even knew the term. He wondered whether Mad-Meyer had as well.

Van was suddenly pulled off his feet. "Come on, doggie!" Teirel yelled. "Take us to the blast room!"

"No!" Van yelled back. "You don't understand—"

He couldn't explain, not through the com link.

The attacking Persian lifted in order to stay out from under Namazi.

Teirel was dragging him into the lock and Van yanked his arm out of his grip to watch.

"That's it," Teirel said, and the next instant, Van's left arm exploded with breath-stopping pain. He gasped, and when his mind cleared he was on his back, staring at the ceiling of the lock. The searing pain in his bicep spread until his whole arm was on fire. Something was gripping his shoulder with animal tenacity. When Teirel's bullet pierced the fabric, the suit automatically isolated his arm, keeping the rest of his air from escaping, sacrificing his limb for the sake of his life, just like Burl's had when Mad-Meyer shot his leg.

Teirel was cursing and fumbling with his gun through unfamiliar gloves. Using two hands, he managed to get a grip, and pointed it at Van's face. Suddenly, Burl appeared behind him. Van thought it awfully strange that with just a second or two to live, he was looking in wonder at how Burl had managed to seal off the stub leg of his suit. His friend lifted both arms, and Van saw that he was wielding a pipe. It was a race—the pipe or the gun? Burl brought the pipe down, but the gun flashed, and Van felt a concussion hit his head.

Then there was darkness.

But he was aware of the darkness.

And the pain. His arm still burned with fire.

Light returned as Burl struggled to roll Teirel off of him. Using his right arm, Van felt his faceplate. It was intact. He must have jerked his own head back when he saw the gun flash, cracking it against the back of his helmet.

"Get up!" Burl urged, pulling at him. "For once, don't be stupid. We need to get you pressurized."

Indeed. His arm was going numb. Other nexgens had arrived, and were lifting him. But then everybody froze, as though on cue. Van saw it. Half the lock was lit brilliantly, leaving the other half in darkness. Something outside, up high, was shining with unholy light.

A few ounces of antimatter had obliterated itself against the stuff of our universe.

Chapter 17

"He's gaining at sixty degrees," Katlin said.

She was thrown back as Namazi maneuvered to stay above, but to the side of the other Simurgh. As the two ships lifted from the Moon, Namazi had to stay slightly ahead, but dare not get directly above, since the pilot could then use his missiles. They had to keep the pilot convinced that they wanted to get in front of him to use their exhaust. That had been the point of her warning to the nexgens—Namazi was confident that he'd understand what she was saying despite her hurried speech. It had been her idea to make up the part about Namazi being a double agent. He had rolled his eyes.

"He's moving around to twenty degrees," she reported.

Katlin and Beau had exchanged seats. Since Otto's annihilation had taken out their rearward sensors, she was watching the side cameras, trying to keep an eye on their prey in all directions at once as they coaxed him safely away from the base.

Beau held Alibai to his ear, and was calling out status as it came in. "Point two percent," he called out. Alibai had managed to activate and tap into a telemetry feed from the other Simurgh, a feature that Namazi had learned of during his weeks training the American pilots. Knowledge of the other ship's propellant level was critical to their plan. Namazi had come up with the idea when Beau reported that the other ship was down to sixteen percent upon their arrival at the Moon. Namazi guessed that the pilot wasn't aware of the misleading "x-factor" in the propellant gauge, and with luck, they would keep him so busy maneuvering that he wouldn't notice he was about to go empty.

And when he did, they had to be ready.

"Point oh-seven percent!" Beau yelled a bit hysterically. "Did you *hear* me?"

Namazi didn't answer. He was completely focused on his controls. Katlin wondered if she should say something. He'd said that the antimatter containment fields could collapse any time after the propellant fell below 0.1%. She understood why he had to time their next move just right, but erring in the wrong direction was going to be immediately fatal.

Katlin couldn't take it anymore—she had to say something. "Don't you think—"

"Here we go," Namazi said, and she was squashed back into her seat as Namazi turned and accelerated away.

Katlin now lost track of the other Simurgh as Namazi swung their rear-end towards it, an essential detail, as this was the only way to shield themselves.

However, this allowed the other pilot to turn and put them in his sights as they sped away. "He's firing a missile!" Beau reported, not even trying to hide his anxiety.

It was now or never, where now was their lives, and never was oblivion.

Engine overdrive alarms sounded as one second ticked away to two. It wasn't going to work—the missile was going to take them out.

Namazi pointed at one of her screens as Beau sang out that the telemetry link had broken. Where an instant before the side-view screen had been black, it was now filled with a moonscape, mountains and craters in sharp light and black shadow, as though the sun had suddenly appeared.

The source of light was something far fiercer than even the hellish bowls of the sun, however—it was the other Simurgh, disintegrating amidst annihilating antimatter. The pilot suffered the same fate that he'd brought down on Otto.

The light faded quickly. There would be no shockwave blast, not in the vacuum of space.

But there was still the missile. Had it traveled far enough to survive the spray of gamma rays? There was nothing they could do but wait, like a condemned murderer watching the executioner's hand on the switch. One breath. Two breaths. Suddenly a bang caused Katlin to jump.

"Sorry," Namazi said. "I should have warned you."

She was floating in her seat, and the alarms died. Namazi had shut down the engine—no use wasting propellant.

Katlin took a deep breath and let it out slowly. If the missile had survived, it would have taken them out by now. Her shirt was wet with sweat.

"Great job, crew," Namazi said. His voice was calm, but his hand shook a little as he reached to flick some switches.

"I think I've had my fill of space travel," Beau said. "Drop me off some place where all I have to worry about are knives and guns."

"That would presumably be any place on Earth?"

"Sure. Any place but Guantanamo. They might make me pay for a couple of incinerated Army trucks."

"But first," Namazi said, "we have to get back to Daedalus."

Katlin's heart sank. She'd forgotten about her friends' predicament in the heat of escape. Alibai's intercepted message that the base had been evacuated and the eradication of nexgens underway had been premature, delivered by whoever was terrorizing the base, but somebody in a Chinese suit had been holding a gun to Van's head when they'd left. Katlin wasn't sure she could take one more minute of cliff-hanging tension.

Chapter 18

"Hold still," Tyna said, wrapping the bandage around Van's upper arm. "If you don't hold still, I'll just make it worse." She grinned. "A girl wouldn't want to do that to her mate, now would she?"

Van sighed. She'd been making snide references ever since he called her that before locking her safely away in the antechamber. "Look," he said, "I told you I'm sorry, but I had no choice—I barely made it to the front lock in time as it was."

She didn't say anything as she secured the bandage. She continued grinning, though.

"What in crimps is so damn funny?" he finally asked. "What else was I going to do?"

She was done, and gave him a little tap on the wound, which made him yelp. "That's not what I'm smiling about."

"What then?"

She took a breath and crawled up to sit next to him on the service table—the same one that Teirel had gouged with the glue gun. She took his hand in hers and rested her head against his shoulder. "Van, you idiot, don't you see? That was the first time you called me that."

He blinked. "What?"

"Your mate. You called me your mate."

"Well … yeah."

"Yeah," she repeated.

That was true. It was the first time he'd voiced it out loud. She hadn't already known it? "I should have talked about it sooner, I guess," he said.

"Mmm-hmm," she said.

He sat up straight. "Wait a second—why is it up to me to be the one to bring it up?"

She thought about this. "You're right. I apologize." She clasped his hand in both of hers and gazed into his eyes. "Van Wilkens, will you be my husband?"

Van jerked back, staring at her.

She laughed. "I guess you like being in control after all."

Something about his reaction bothered him. "You were … uh, joking?"

She raised one eyebrow. "You tell me. Is it a joke?"

"A joke? No! Of course not! We, uh, just hadn't talked about it—"

"Van!" Deik called from the lock. "Namazi's cycling through." The nexgens had watched the base president fearlessly attack Teirel with his cave bot, and he was basking in their approval. It seemed to have pulled him back from whatever mental funk he'd suffered at the antechamber.

Van pointed his finger at her. "We're not done with this yet," he said.

She just smiled.

Namazi and Katlin removed their helmets and came over. They'd been outside adding a a half-dozen gallons of water to their ship's tanks—a half-dozen gallons of inestimable value, but a contribution the nexgens were only too happy to offer. Namazi had re-fueled before hightailing it away from Tehran to chase after the other Persian pilot, but he'd used most of that in the mad rush to get to the Moon.

It was strange having to wear pressure suits whenever leaving the Farm. They would re-fill the main corridors as soon as Burl finished his estimates of the final pressure. Until then, they were effectively trapped in the Farm.

"Will he be okay?" Namazi asked.

Blaine C. Readler

"I'm not sure he ever was," Tyna said, "but if you're referring to his arm, it seems so. It's going to be swollen and painful for awhile from the vacuum, but that's just discomfort."

"Easy for you to say," Van mumbled.

Katlin stood grinning at them. Her hair was plastered to her head, and she had dark circles under her eyes, but it was the same old ever-optimistic Katlin. "It's good to see you, Kat," he said.

Her grin widened into a sunny smile. "It's good to be back," she said, and Van believed her.

The animated shouts of Burl and Beau arguing caught Van's attention. Alibai lay calmly between them. Their arms danced in protest and entreaty. "Should we intervene?" Van asked.

"Are you kidding?" Katlin said. "They're in geek heaven. Let them have some fun."

"One of the cave digging machines is beyond repair," Namazi said. "In fact, it's hardly recognizable. The other one has been damaged, but possibly salvageable."

"Thanks," Van said. "I don't expect we'll be expanding the base any time soon."

"You won't be able to attack any ships, though," Namazi said seriously, but then broke into a grin. "I have to say, Moon citizens are nothing if not resourceful."

"Sometimes to the point of reckless stupidity," Van said.

Tyna gave him a gentle push, which made him yelp again. "I saved your butt, mister."

"I think it was a couple of Persian ships that did that. If they hadn't arrived, Teirel would have eventually shot you."

"Without me, the shuttle would have gotten away, and then—"

Namazi cleared his throat. "Speaking of your guest, what do you intend to do with him?"

They all looked at the man sitting on the floor against the wall. They'd talked about restraining him, but without his gun, shuttle, or means of communicating with Earth, there wasn't much he could do. He looked at them and lifted his middle finger.

"We could cycle him outside without a suit," Van said.

Teirel lifted his other hand in defiance.

"Seriously, though," Van said. "The subject of Teirel sort of falls in the larger question of what in crimps is going to happen to

224

you, Namazi. You're our lifeline, and there's the whole question of what this Org thing intends to do—"

It was Tyna's turn to clear her throat. She nodded at Deik who stood at the lock glancing every now and then at them.

"Ah," Van said, "right. Hey, Deik! Come on over. We need to talk base policy."

Their elected leader trotted over happily. "What's up?" he asked.

"We need to decide about Teirel, and also—"

"I say we set up a court, and then toss him in the recycler."

Everybody studied their hands.

"What?" he asked, perplexed.

"That's the purpose of a court," Tyna said gently.

He shook his head, still perplexed.

"To decide his fate," she explained.

"Ah," he said, nodding. "Of course. We let the court decide to toss him in the recycler. Sure."

Everybody took a deep breath. "We also need to figure out what Namazi does next," Van said. "You heard what Katlin told us about a corporate gang that seems to have control not only over U-P, but even some of the military—"

"Sure. The Org." He paused and looked at the nexgens sitting around talking, the younger ones playing games. One small group glanced over and waved. Deik waved back, and turned back to them. "Tell you what," he said, "I think I'll just listen for awhile."

Tyna nudged Van and pointed. Mai Dung was sitting against the wall playing some kind of hand game with Tuan. The boy seemed completely comfortable now in his suit. "Maya told me that it was Mai Dung's idea to try to protect the front lock," Tyna said. "I asked her why, and she just shrugged and said, 'Home.'"

"Hey, Deik," Van said. Maybe you could come up with a Presidential Medal of Honor, or something."

His eyes lit up at the idea. This was right up his alley.

They all turned when Burl called to them. "You want us to come over?" Van called back.

"No," Burl said, picking up a shelf brace to use as a cane. "I'll just hop over on one leg while you sit there and wait for me."

"He hasn't really changed, has he?" Namazi said quietly.

Beau followed behind, reverently cradling the box he called Alibai.

"Once we fill the corridors," Burl said, "the pressure throughout the base will be down to four PSI—"

"Plus or minus a quarter PSI," Beau said.

"A detail," Burl replied.

"A quarter PSI represents six percent—"

"Six point two-five, actually."

"So, you agree it's not just a detail—"

"Guys!" Van said.

"He's the one arguing," Burl said. "But, more importantly, I found early records in the library about the antechamber—"

"Alibai found them," Beau said sideways to Van.

"… with Alibai's help." Burl said.

"In less than two seconds," Beau added.

"Look," Burl said, "would you like to tell it?"

"Okay. The antechamber was begun long ago, before the nexgens would probably remember—"

"They know that already," Burl said.

"Actually," Van said, "I have a memory of the cave bots. I thought they were monsters."

"Do *you* want to tell it?" Burl asked.

Van held out his hand. "Take it away."

"The antechamber was part of the original base plan. As they proceeded into the crater wall, the bots reported a problem. They have rudimentary ultrasonic sensors, and the geologist on staff called for a halt until he could have specialized sensing equipment brought up from Earth. In the interest of staying on schedule, guess who overruled him?"

A chorus of voices shouted, "Mad-Meyer!"

"The geologist quit and went back to Earth in protest," Burl continued, "leaving the head engineer to finish the excavation, and he at least had the foresight to re-draw the plans to avoid that area. They'd already come too close, however—when they finally pressurized the room, the wall blew through, and a worker was killed."

"That explains the suit com repeater in the antechamber—the static disappeared when Tyna and I entered."

"Yeah. After the blow-through, they had to work in a vacuum for awhile. It turns out that there was a lunar type of lava tube that formed when the asteroid blew out the crater. The engineer insisted on installing an exit lock in the antechamber as they closed off the opening, and then completely shut down the rest of the excavation. The base didn't really need the space, and, in fact, the whole superfluous excavation was part of the fraud that your father was sent to investigate, Katlin."

Burl paused and looked around at them for effect. "That engineer also threatened to quit if he didn't get his way. Can you guess who he was?" The faces around him turned sober. "Julius!" he crowed.

Nobody said anything.

"Right," Burl said, his brow scrunched. "I guess you haven't gotten over his death yet."

"It's called grieving," Tyna said.

"I get it. But, he wasn't the most cuddly guy, after all—"

"Burl," she said.

"Yeah?"

"Shut up."

"Is that how you got the cave bots out?" Katlin asked. "Through that lava tube?"

Tyna nodded. "Somebody—" she gave Van a nudge and he yelped "—placed a personal block on the airlock genie between the lab and antechamber, so we were trapped inside until Linda was poking around and found the airlock that Julius had installed. It was a lot of work getting the bots through the lock, and all the nexgens chipped in. It was pretty hairy finding our way through the tunnel. We had no idea if it would lead outside, and in many places it was too tight to turn around. As it was, we had to use the bots to break through a barrier at the end that Julius apparently installed. We must have looked at that barrier a thousand times outside while working the platinum—we always thought that it was just some excess cement that had been dumped there."

"How do you like that?" Van said.

"What?" Tyna said.

"Louden's back door is a real back door."

"Hey Katlin, Namazi!" Beau called. He had moved off to the side, sitting with the Alibai box in his lap.

They went over to see what he had, and Deik followed, peering over their shoulders.

Burl watched them leave, and then leaned in close. "Listen, when ol' Beau Geste over there had his talking box tapped into the base network, I was able to look at the log of Deik's cave bot. Get this—"

"The cave bots have logs?" Van said. "With network access?"

"What did I just say? Anyway, I could see what controls he was using—"

"Isn't that an invasion of privacy?" Tyna said.

"Crimps! Do you want to hear this or not?"

Van put his hand over Tyna's mouth. "Yeah. Go ahead."

"When he made that heroic charge at Teirel? Well, I think it was a mistake."

"Yeah," Van said, "I don't doubt he was sorry he tried to charge Teirel—"

"No. I mean, I don't think he wanted to go at Teirel at all."

"What are you talking about? How would you know that?"

"The bots' controls are screwy when you're trying to ride them—they weren't meant to be ridden, you know. The directions seem backwards."

"I can attest to that," Tyna said, pushing away Van's hand. "It took awhile to get used them."

"Well, apparently Deik never did. At every juncture, he turned first in the wrong direction. He was trying to run *away* from Teirel. After he mistakenly turned towards a loaded gun, he got flustered. He was toggling the bit retraction control right up to the point where he pretended to fall off, dead."

"He thought the bit retraction was the direction control," Van said.

Burl slapped his forehead. "Crimps! Why didn't I think of that?"

"Very funny," Tyna said. "What do you plan to do with this?"

Burl lifted his shoulders. "What do I always do when an opportunity pops up to show our fearless leader's true feathers?"

She reached out and placed her hand on his shoulder. "Do you really want to do that?"

Burl hopped a step back so that her hand fell away. "Hey! Don't try to make me feel guilty. The guy deserves it. Look at Van! He wanted to stage a coup!"

"Hey!" Van said. "Keep your voice down. Just because I was reading about it, doesn't mean I was planning it—" he glanced at Tyna "—or thinking about it."

"That's a lie," Burl said. "You're saying that if the opportunity came up to depose the boob, you wouldn't go for it?"

Van took a breath and looked at Tyna. "I've been giving this some thought."

"I think I need to sit down," Burl said.

"Shut up. I've given it some thought—we should be helping Deik, not sabotaging him. He was fairly elected, after all—"

"By a bunch of kids."

"You're a kid by that definition. I have a feeling that he's going to be more serious about the job, maybe even—God forbid—look for our advice now and then. Besides ..."

"What?" Tyna said, laying her hand on the back of his neck. She was smiling, as though she knew what was coming.

"If there's anything we've learned here, it's that the nexgens—all of us—need structure, a purpose."

"And you think *Deik's* going to provide that?" Burl said.

"Maybe. With our help. Look, we managed to mine a lot of platinum, a *whole* lot. And, it was all because we had Meyer on our backs—"

"And the threat of withholding a fabricated path to immortality."

"Sure, that was the tool. But it was Meyer that cracked the whip."

"Van," Burl said. "Buddy, you're beginning to scare me. Don't say what I think you're about to say."

"I have to. We need Meyer back—not the Meyer that worked Randy to his death, but a Meyer to crack the whip just enough to keep the mining going."

"And that would be ...?"

"You know who. They respect me. They'll listen to me when I tell them that they have no choice, that they have to work the mine."

"Deik gets to be the good guy," Tyna said, "and you the bad."

"Yeah. I think the expression used to be 'Good cop, bad cop.' We'll have to work together on this. I think Deik's ready for that."

"Your white matter has melted, buddy," Burl said. "You think you can just tell the nexgens that you've decided that they need to go back to work, and they'll skip off to the platform, whistling?"

"No. I'm not quite that naive. We'll have to come up with something—some rational reason to *need* to continue mining platinum."

Katlin called to them. "You might want to hear this!" When they walked over, she said, "Beau's Alibai was able to hack into the satellites that Namazi placed in low-orbit at Arrival."

"It can do that sort of thing?" Van said, watching the little box suspiciously. The AI he was used to—the genies—were masters of specific pieces of equipment—air locks, medical stations, farms, and recyclers. The idea of a free agent artificial intelligence was … alien. It wasn't natural. His gut questioned whether it was even completely moral. Burl would call him a Luddite.

Katlin laughed. "It's about as difficult for Alibai as walking is for you and me. Wait 'till you hear this news, though. The Cubans have been complaining about antimatter ships landing at Guantanamo for some time, but nobody believed them, mostly because the United States intelligence was discounting their evidence. The explosion from Otto's Simurgh, however, was impossible to refute—every satellite within a thousand miles picked up the flood of radiation, and cruise ships all around the Caribbean saw the flash."

"No surprise, I guess," Van said.

"That's only the beginning. Cuba has also been trying to reclaim Guantanamo for, well, forever, and it looks like this is finally their big break. After the Cuban Missile Crisis, the United States publically promised to never again invade Cuba—there was that Bay of Pigs thing, you may remember—and ever since, this has been understood to mean they also wouldn't deploy weapons at Guantanamo capable of threatening the island. The consensus at the UN after Cuba lodged an emergency appeal is clearly that the US violated that promise, since a Simurgh is essentially a nuclear bomb with a person at the wheel."

"Good for Cuba," Van said, "but how does it affect us?"

"Looks like they didn't wait for a formal declaration, and went in and took over. They're holding a handful of Navy men, and they've also got Pollin."

"The mastermind guy?"

"If not the mastermind, at least somebody who could potentially provide testimony about the Org. The rumor is that the Cuban version of the CIA knows how to motivate people to talk, and unlike the CIA there's no laws holding them back."

Van chuckled. "Sounds like Pollin's going to get some of his own medicine."

"We haven't even gotten to the best part. Beau has been working to instill initiative in Alibai, and it seems to have been effective. He—Alibai—called General McClellen on a secure line pretending to be one of his staff—"

"The box can do that?" Van asked.

"Oh, yeah. Alibai has learned to mimic voices."

Van eyed the box, and moved to the other side.

"Anyway," Katlin said, "Alibai got the general to talk about incriminating things. He then called Senator Ritkens—the one who's been investigating ties between some of the military and business holdings in the Caymans—essentially the Org—and replayed the conversation onto his voice-mail."

"Wait," Van said, "I don't think that's admissible."

"Not in a formal court of law, but there's an informal court consisting of backroom wheeling and dealings in Washington. McClellen's as good as done, and the whole scheme to use Daedalus Base to manufacture antimatter has been broken wide open."

"The senator went public? Already?"

Katlin grinned. "Alibai may have stepped a little over the line here—he also called Casey Jappeno—"

"The host of the *Casey-J Show*?"

"The very one. He pretended to be my stepfather, and told her to air the story as breaking news. And she did."

"Uh, won't she get into trouble for that?"

"I sure hope so."

They all smiled. She'd told them about her on-air ordeal.

"What do you think Greater Persia's going to do?" Tyna asked.

The smiles melted.

"Good question," Katlin said. "Alibai, do you have anything?"

"They're claiming that their pilot went rogue," the box said, at which Van took another step back. *"However, they refuse to apologize for the death of Major Otto, since they claim the Air Force officer had commandeered Greater Persian property, and the attack over international waters was probably justified anyway."*

"I guess that's good news?" Van said. "Maybe it means they're not going to pursue their claim on Daedalus?"

Katlin shrugged. "That's still to be seen. The other good news, though, is that the UN is in the final stages of formalizing your international charter—"

"Legalese for recognizing our independence?"

"Yes ... um, do you want to say something?" she said to Namazi.

He stood up straight and looked Deik in the eye. "Mr. President, I have already explained to you the importance of demonstrating a means for long-term self-sufficiency, that you can participate in ongoing trade production—"

"Yeah, yeah," Deik said. "We have to keep up the mining."

"Yes. That is what I was referring to. Now, if you like, I can explain my reasoning—"

"No, I get it. We'll do it."

Namazi studied him.

"I said, I *get* it," Deik said. "I promise, we'll continue mining."

Namazi shrugged and sat back down.

Van stole a glance at Tyna and Burl, who waggled their eyebrows in affirmation.

"What about you?" Beau said, looking at Namazi.

He sighed. "I guess I am presently a man without a country."

"You've betrayed Greater Persia," Beau said.

"That's how they see it, I'm sure," Namazi said.

"No!" Tyna exclaimed. "We can make you a citizen of the Moon—or at least of Daedalus. Deik, you can come up with something—"

Namazi held up his hand, smiling. "This is a most gracious offer, and I may well come back and take you up. First things first, however. You are not yet even formally recognized as sovereign."

"So," Tyna said, "where does that leave you?"

He lifted his shoulders. "A pirate, I guess."

"You're kidding."

"Half, perhaps. Cuba has already sent word that they will welcome me at their new Guantanamo 'spaceport'—surreptitiously, of course—at least at first."

"For a piece of your pie," Burl offered.

He nodded. "For a portion of your platinum that I bring back each trip, yes." He gestured towards Beau. "And you, my friend? Will you join my skull-and-crossbones crew?"

"Oh, no," Beau said holding up his palms as though pushing away the very idea. "Space travel is nothing but cramped quarters, infrequent showers, and bad food. There's not even windows to see the stars. Don't get me wrong, I owe you my life, but I'll happily step off the first time we hit terra firma."

Namazi nodded once politely. "That's the very least I can do in return for the sacrifice you made back at Holloman." He turned to the rest of them. "What *will* you do with him?" he asked, gesturing towards Teirel. "Deik?"

Deik thought a moment, then said, "Van, what do you think?"

Van suppressed a grin. "Unless you want to dump him into the vacuum halfway back to Earth, I guess we'll keep him alive until … I don't know. Until what?"

"Might I suggest," Namazi said, "that I take him with me. From Cuba, he could easily be extradited to the US, where he could be prosecuted for the murder of Baxter and Julius. Although, that does bring up the question of jurisdiction, since the murders didn't take place on US soil."

"Let me try," Beau said. "Alibi—you've been listening. What about it?"

"*According to U.S. Code, Title eighteen, Part one, Chapter 51, paragraph 1119, if a U.S. national kills another U.S. national outside the country, and the country where the murder takes place chooses not to prosecute, then the U.S. will take up prosecution according to the direction of the Attorney General's office."*

"I have to get me one of those," Burl muttered.

"Well, then," Van said, "I guess you can take him away. The ship's cabin is pretty small. We'll have to tape him up good, and then tie him down."

"Let me tie the knots," Tyna said, the muscles of her jaws working..

"We'll all take a turn at tugging the knots tight," Van said.

Teirel held up one lonely finger.

Chapter 19

Katlin waited next to the lock door, the organic smells swirling together twelve years of memories visiting the Farm, the first years with her father, and then on her own when she needed a break from her studies. The others sensed that she wanted time alone, and kept themselves busy.

"*Checking integrity,*" the genie said. "*Access.*" The green light illuminated, the door pushed open, and Namazi came through carrying his helmet. Katlin glanced behind him. "Beau will be following soon," he explained. "He's setting Alibai so it can charge. How are they doing?" he asked, gesturing towards the back, where Van, Deik, Tyna, and Burl were deep in discussion, with Burl and Deik doing most of the "discussing" via shouts and epithets.

"Like a microcosm of any country's politics, I guess. In the end you can only hope that they'll hammer out an agreement before somebody gets killed."

"It's not something to be taken lightly," he said. "They'll be legally bound by whatever they put their signatures to."

At Namazi's suggestion, Deik and his "staff" were composing a proposal that he'd take along to Earth, a fixed, one-time buyout of all United Products' interests. The thought being that this might help cement a final UN vote on the Lunar Commission's recommendation for Daedalus independence.

Katlin smiled.

"A pleasant thought?" Namazi said.

"Oh, I was remembering another life—a few days ago—when I was hanging tightly to a plan I had to help my father's financial situation."

Namazi grinned. "Did it involve platinum smuggled from the Moon?"

She stared at him wide-eyed, and he laughed. "It wasn't difficult to guess. In any case, you won't need to risk prison—Alibai reports that United Products is now falling all over itself to compensate your father, Louden, and Julius's estate. They're minimizing potential bad press as they gear up for the congressional hearings."

A loud curse from Burl drew their attention, and she frowned.

"You're still concerned for your father?" Namazi asked gently.

She shook her head. "No. Sorry. It's just that the whole idea of signing an agreement brought to mind what Van had said about my stepfather's last act."

Namazi watched her. "He didn't know what was really going on," he said, "that the Org was maneuvering to take Daedalus for antimatter production. He was just another pawn."

She shook her head again and grinned sardonically at the thought that she was concerned about Baxter's reputation. "I'm sorry he was killed, but honestly, I don't feel much sympathy. Who was it that said that if you live by the sword, you die by the sword?"

"I think it was the old testament."

"The Bible?"

"Yes, that would be the Bible."

"No, it's my mother I feel so sorry for. I think she really loved him. In a way, I'm glad I'm not going back to Earth yet."

Namazi looked at his shoes, an unusual gesture for him. "You've made up your mind, then?" he asked quietly.

She nodded. It had been maybe the hardest decision of her life. "Do you honestly think I could return and just slip back into my college classes?"

"It would be difficult, I agree."

"It would be a circus. I could be arrested."

"That's true. We don't know how the congressional hearings will go. You'll likely be subpoenaed."

"In which case, I'll take my time catching a ride back—maybe on conditions of immunity, or something."

A grin spread across his face.

"Having your own pleasant thought?" she asked.

He nodded. It looked like he might actually be blushing. "I just realized that I'll see more of you if you stay on the Moon. After all, I won't be visiting the United States for awhile."

"Not until Congress finds that you were actually the hero of the whole mess. Then they'll throw you a parade."

He looked at her skeptically. "Whatever they say publically, the truth is that I helped undercut the United State's chance to catch up with Greater Persia in antimatter production. And I am Persian. That equation has only one solution."

He looked at his toes again and back at her. "You told me once that you were glad you left the Moon, since it would haunt you with thoughts of …"

"Of Mad-Meyer. That I blew out his intestines," she said.

Namazi seemed to wince at the harsh description.

"I've been trying to convince myself that I had no choice," she said. "It was either him, or Van. Seeing Van again has come a long way towards accepting that. Every time my conscious decides to slam me with the image of Meyer lying there, I think of Van, and what would have happened had I not pulled the trigger."

"You think of Van often?" he said softly, then furrowed his brow at what he'd said.

She forced him to look her in the eye. "As often as I need to," she said. She took his hand. "Namazi, you have to understand that I hardly knew Van before your arrival. I've spent far more time with you than I ever did with him, even though we lived just hundreds of feet from each other. Van is special, but he's not …"

"Me?"

She pretended to be confused. "I was going to say that he's not tall enough."

Namazi's eyes went wide.

"Of course I meant you," she said giving him a little push.

The lock beeped again, and they stepped back as Beau came through. His face lit up when he saw Katlin, but then it fell. "You're sure you want to stay?" he asked.

Katlin rolled her eyes. "We've just been through that."

Beau looked from her to Namazi, and sighed, nodding.

He looked about to cry.

She made an impulsive decision. "Beau," she said, gazing at him.

He looked at her, and his eyes were curious.

She wrapped her arms around him and whispered into his ear, "You're my perigee. On the Moon, that's what we call someone who's a very special friend—you can have a string of lovers, but only ever one perigee. And you are mine."

She pulled herself back, took him by the shoulders, and tenderly kissed his forehead. She thought he might faint, but then a smile spread from ear to ear.

Deik called to them. He was coming over, waving the paper, followed by the rest. "Ten tons," he said, handing the paper to Namazi. "That much platinum is worth a billion dollars. That should keep them happy."

Namazi looked at the paper, looked at Deik, and nodded slowly.

"What?" Deik said, "You don't think that's *enough*? That's fifteen percent of all our stock!"

"Oh, no," Namazi said. "I think that's a very fair offer. No, I was wondering how you're going to deliver ten tons to them."

"*You're* going to deliver it!" Deik said, beaming.

Namazi's face went white.

"Look," Deik said, pointing to a paragraph, "we put in a provision—they have to give you five percent of every load you take back."

Namazi's eyebrows went up. "That amounts to fifty million dollars."

Deik turned to Burl for confirmation. "Yeah," he said, "that's right."

Burl nudged him. "Okay." Deik said. "It was also Van's idea."

Burl gave him a harder nudge. "Okay! It was all Van's idea."

Namazi folded the paper and slipped it inside his suit. "Time to go," he said, lifting his helmet.

"Hold it!" Van exclaimed.

Namazi stopped and looked at him.

Burl gave Deik another nudge. "Crimps!" Deik yelled. "Will you stop that? Namazi, next trip back, we need equipment to extract oxygen from rocks."

Namazi tried to suppress a grin without much luck. "This takes priority over the rest of the list you gave me last time?"

"Yeah." Deik pondered this, and then shrugged. "Yeah, you better throw that list away. We'll come up with another one."

Namazi's grin widened to a smile. He reached out and shook Deik's hand. "That sounds fine, Mr. President," he said without a hint of sarcasm.

Beau was already in the lock, and Namazi took Katlin's hand. "See you in a couple of weeks." He leaned in and kissed her on the cheek, and said quietly, "You made that up about special perigee Moon friends?"

When he pulled back, she nodded. Beau watched through his faceplate, listening to his own breathing.

Namazi winked, turned, and entered the lock. The door closed, and they were gone.

When Katlin turned around, she gasped. The nexgens were holding up a sign that they had made with pea plants. It read, WELCOME HOME! She stood, wide-eyed as the entire citizenry of Daedalus Base broke out into a cheer.

It was good to be home.

About the Author

Blaine C. Readler is an electronics engineer, inventor of the FakeTV, and, of course, a writer. He lives in San Diego, where people come from all over the world just to be here.

He encourages you to visit him:
http://www.readler.com/